FALLING FROM GRACE

BOOK 3 OF THE GIFT OF GRACE SERIES

FROG JONES

ESTHER JONES

Impulsive
Walrus

EXCERPT FROM FALLING FROM GRACE

Thaddeus had just threatened to kill Andrea.

Over the line.

I brought my Sense back up and stripped Thaddeus of anything on him containing a rune or the ability to make one. It wouldn't neutralize him, but it would kneecap him. I placed his gear in a neat little pile outside the cabin. He brought his Sense to life immediately, trying to grasp for his gear back.

Nielsen was a very skilled, precise, and lightning-fast summoner. Without his runes, though, it was a Sense-on-Sense fight. Skill and precision went out the window at that point; Sense-on-Sense had all the finesse of an arm-wrestling match, and I had the bigger biceps.

"Nielsen, *enough*. You are the Grove Director of Spokane, but you have abused my hospitality far too long. You will not come to *my* house—"

"Your house? This is the headquarters of the Grove, and I am its director."

"Get a new headquarters, then. This cabin and the land around it are in *my* name. You are in *my* home. And you have just threatened the life of *my* guest. Leave. Now."

To Crystal Bolster - Without you these books would not exist

Our pursuit reminded me of nothing so much as the running scene from any action movie that involves a tornado. Except, we were headed toward rather than away. We pursued the shadow ahead of us, never getting a clear look at it. A pickup fell directly to my right, missing me by inches. A sedan dropped just behind Jeremy; he ducked and rolled to get out from under it. I offered him a quick hand to pull him to his feet, then continued our chase.

We kept up the race at a dead sprint until a forty-foot deep crevice opened in the ground before us, cutting off our pursuit. There was simply no clearing the massive cleft in the earth.

"The cops will have to handle it from here," I said, putting my hands on my knees and gasping for breath after our prolonged sprint.

"We made him run, though!" said Jeremy. He peered down, shining his flashlight into the depths of the fissure. "This thing is wicked. The doubters will have to take SARTWAP seriously now."

"Yeah, I guess."

"Dude, we totally chased off an RT!" He held his hand up in the classic gesture for demanding five. I slapped it obligingly.

"Didn't get him, though," I said, shrugging.

"Next time, man. We'll totally get him next time."

I gave Jeremy a nod, though the chances of the two of us successfully wielding our flashlights against the kind of magic I'd seen summoners use seemed remote.

Campus Police began to arrive, documenting the brave SARTWAP members who had valiantly chased off a reality terrorist. They sternly cautioned us against heroics, and pointed out at *great* length how close we'd both come to being killed.

I took the tongue-lashing in stride, but kept quiet. Jeremy came out looking better; I had no doubt that by the end of the night he'd be the grand hero of this story, protecting me from the reality terrorist. Still, the story would stick; I'd been part of a chase against an RT. I'd been nearly killed by an RT. Again.

As I was the only summoner within twenty miles of here, that sort of rumor could be useful. Which was, after all, why I'd created it.

FROG JONES & ESTHER JONES

~

As PUBLIC RELATIONS STRATEGIES GO, I do *not* recommend the use of nuclear weaponry inside a metropolitan area. It leads to, among many other things, meetings of self-important bigots in college cafeterias.

"Gentlemen, we had our first encounter with an RT last night, and I am proud to announce that our patrol successfully forced the bastard to retreat." Clem, an overweight, goateed student, sat at the "head" of a conglomeration of small, round cafeteria tables in the student union building, aka the PUB. The flab sagging under his upper arm undulated as he gestured to Jeremy and me.

"Well done, the both of you. This is the reason that SARTWAP exists, and our fellow students can feel the safer because of it." Clem smiled at his own pompous pronouncement. The eighteen members of SARTWAP all nodded. Clem launched into a speech, and from his self-aggrandizing fervor, I didn't think it'd be a short one. The general tone differed little from his previous rants. All the students at the University could be a target, anyone could be a suspect, constant vigilance, blah, blah, blah. We'd heard it all before.

Around the meeting of our little band of brothers, the student populace of Eastern Washington University hummed and buzzed. No doubt the tale of Jeremy's grand battle to protect me from the reality terrorist made up a significant part of that buzz. Students throughout the PUB shot glances at our gathering.

"Robert? You listening, man?" Shit—I'd drifted off again. "You patrolling again this weekend?"

"Uh, sorry. And no, I took the week's shift. I've gotta catch up on schoolwork now that I burned my nights down." My brethren all nodded their heads thoughtfully as I pointed out my sacrifice. Other volunteers quickly stepped forward, anxious to get a piece of the attention being lavished upon Jeremy and me.

Clem took a moment to gesture toward the big-screen television. The massive TV screen was displaying some cable news show. As one, the members of SARTWAP turned their heads toward it. The rest of the cafeteria followed suit.

4

The picture showed a group of people on gurneys, all wearing bright orange prisoners' pajamas. Each prisoner had an IV needle stuck in his arm, hooked to a bag above. They were restrained, but that seemed an afterthought given that their eyes were closed, unconscious from whatever fluid dripped from that clear plastic bag. Their custodians wheeled them into a stark, gray building with an ominous smoke curling up from a stack in the roof.

As Clem grabbed at the remote and turned up the volume, the whole room heard a young, pleasant, female voice:

"...first-priority inmates were processed today. The Federal Department of Corrections reports that the elimination of reality terrorists will continue through the next month, in compliance with the recently-passed Higgins Amendment."

Another piece of footage flashed to the screen, this one of the charred interior of my former high school's gymnasium. The lady on the TV continued: "Aggressive anti-terrorist measures have been implemented since the nuclear attack on *this* high school gymnasium."

I shook my head, disgusted. This part of the story had been aired thousands of times before. Reality terrorist Grace Moore suicide-detonated herself with a dirty bomb in the middle of a high school gymnasium.

"You see?" said Clem. "This is what we face. We stand between the students of this campus and this very fate. Robert, you faced the summoner Moore yourself, didn't you?"

"Uh, yeah. If by *faced* you mean *got abducted by*. It wasn't my finest hour." SARTWAP members rarely displayed modesty, but I'd found that they liked me more when *I* did. It let them feel even better about themselves.

"But still, you faced her and lived. You may be the most experienced veteran we have in this group, having faced two of these demons by now," said Clem.

I shrugged. "Not sure why. I'm the master of wrong place, wrong time. Jeremy here's the one should get most of the credit for last night."

Jeremy flashed me a smile, and I nodded to him. Clem turned to

Jeremy and began to expound upon his bravery as well, a speech that Jeremy took far more comfortably than I had my own.

America is, politically, usually a polarized place. No matter what your opinion, generally the internet will hand you someone who is vitriolically opposed to it. There's always someone willing to rant and rave and accuse you of being a traitor to your country for your views.

Summoners united the country. The Left, usually quick to support human rights, saw summoning ability as a bigger, nastier version of firearms, a thing to be stamped out and controlled at all costs. The Right saw us as anarchists and devil-worshippers. At long last, there was an issue on which everyone in this country could agree.

Summoners needed to be eradicated. Grace and I had already stacked political tinder before the nuke. In the space of a year, we'd done battle with a Cornuprocyon (or, to hear the news tell it, summoned a raccoon demon to murder people) in the Valley Mall. We'd engaged that same Cornuprocyon in a running battle from the Post Falls Dam along the freeway, eventually banishing it at the cost of a significant fraction of the Spokane County Sheriff's Office. (News version: attacked a power plant, then set the Cornuprocyon loose on law enforcement officers).

After that, Grace actually *had* engaged law enforcement in a running battle, though she'd staged it to give credibility to a couple of our friends on the force. (News version: No Casualties as Spokane Cops Confront Evil).

Then the word "radioactive" hit the public consciousness, and we may as well have poured gas on the tinder prior to hitting it with a flamethrower.

We'd been re-branded from "summoners" to "reality terrorists" overnight in order to give the politicians a bigger gavel. The constitutional amendment defining us as not human, and therefore affording us no human rights, had passed at a record speed over the summer, while the hysteria ran hot.

Now the executions had begun. Summoners were already held in federal prison, kept sedated past the ability to call on their Sense, that innate ability used to work their magic. Now the government "processed" them, a word borrowed from, of all places, Nazi Europe. My stomach turned at the thought, the guilt and the rage beating against my need to Anne Frank my way through this mess.

I'm sure that an occasional voice in the wilderness cried out against this wanton destruction of liberty and life. I'm just as certain that any such voice wound up on one of those gurneys the news had shown us. The overwhelming tide of public opinion against us had drowned them out, turned them from human-rights activists to terrorism accomplices in the blink of an eye.

Summoners have been illegal since the Depression. Don't get me wrong, they've never been well-liked. But when the government needed a scapegoat for the financial crash, summoners took the fall. There's a big difference, though, between being felons and being on the wrong side of a genocide. The cafeteria dining room buzzed with students toasting the better, safer world. I tried to join them, to act like one of them, raising my cheap plastic cup filled with ice and soda to the deaths of my comrades. Under the surface, I seethed with impotent rage.

I was a summoner. I wasn't a particularly skilled one, but I could access the Sense. I could, given enough time, direct my Sense through blood-soaked runes. If discovered, I would be in no better position than those sorry souls being wheeled to their doom in front of me.

Hence my ruse. Having been attacked by a summoner, and being a member of SARTWAP, all served to keep me firmly in the person-of-interest category and off one of those gurneys.

My fellow SARTWAPs were cracking macho jokes about the people on the screen. One of them made a face, his head cocked to the side and his tongue lolling out the side of his mouth. Our companions laughed uproariously, pointing at the screen.

I did my best to join in, to mock the victims on display. SARTWAP claimed to be on the frontlines of a war. More than that, it claimed to be *winning*. I was in the proverbial Rome, and the best way to stay alive was to do as the Romans about me did. So I joined in the macho back-slapping. I joined in the dehumanizing mockery of my own people.

Once the meeting broke, I got the hell away before my nausea betrayed me.

~

I'D KNOWN all summer about the federal crackdown on summoners. I'd been lectured by Thaddeus Nielsen, the stuffy and arrogant Director of the Spokane Grove, about the necessity of keeping a low profile. Thaddeus had ordered me *not* to attend college this year. He'd pointed out that I was almost *certainly* the focus of, if not an investigation, at least surveillance. I'd been too close to too many reality terrorism incidents for the cops to *not* be watching me, he'd said. Going to a state college was the equivalent of walking into the lion's den.

Thad was a prick, but he wasn't wrong about that. I rather carefully walked a tightrope here, and did all in my power to show myself as fiercely anti-summoner as anyone else. After all, I'd been abducted by Grace Moore herself, saved only through the valiant efforts of the Sheriff's Department. Now I'd been targeted again. "Victim" remained a far better option for me than "suspect."

Thad had ordered me to simply disappear, to not attend college. He'd ordered me to remove myself from public view entirely. On that, I'd ignored him in favor of trying to build some sort of life for myself.

Besides, Thad's authority over me had significant limitations.

Any move against me, and he'd find himself face-to-face with my new pet, Rick. "Sic him!" became a really potent phrase when spoken to an overfed Cornuprocyon. Rick sat twenty feet long, with another ten feet of chitin-plated tail. A thick forest of red-orange spines grew from his body like a hedgehog, and he could regenerate the damage suffered in, say, a nuclear blast, within minutes. His favorite game consisted of generating the kinetic equivalent of a freight-train's worth of force and then hurling it at me to see if I would hurl it back.

Some boys pick up stray dogs. I had just gotten a little more exotic.

Rick had destroyed most of the Spokane Grove of Summoners a year ago. A demonic intelligence called Cythymau had controlled him through a summoned bond. I'd stolen a chunk of that bond in a rather reckless move that freed him. In return, I got the undying love of a giant raccoon-spirit, and the absolute assurance that, when I died, he would wreak havoc on any summoner within a hundred-mile radius.

Nielsen couldn't risk it. He couldn't attack me for fear of Rick, but I had no desire to seize control of the Grove from him. He forbade me from attending college, ostensibly for security reasons, though secretly I was pretty sure he just didn't like me. I really didn't care. He ran our Grove Headquarters on land I inherited from my uncle, and he did it in near proximity to a demon that would eat him gladly if I didn't keep restraining him. Nielsen no longer frightened me, and I ignored his order to neglect my education.

I did not, however, ignore his pleas for caution. I didn't want to admit it, but he was right. The anti-summoner fervor whipped up by Grace's decision to end Cythymau and his army with *extreme* prejudice had hit the point of a witch-hunt. Which of these students took a bit of money from the Feds to report on my activities? I didn't know. I certainly didn't trust any smiling face; instead, I spent most of my time in my room or in class, avoiding people and keeping my head down.

The fact that this time the witches were both *real* and *me* simply served to make the whole thing more terrifying.

Just outside the PUB, conveniently located next to the center of campus activity, were two massive, circular dormitory towers. I looked up at them for a moment, wishing my own dorm to be so convenient. Sighing, I turned up the hill towards Streeter Hall instead.

Streeter was not one of the flashier dorms. It's more of a giant brick of a building, itself composed of smaller red bricks. There was a full block's worth of walking until you get to the parking area, and even then it was an uphill climb to get to the entrance. It, and its sister dorm, were possibly the highest buildings on the campus if one judges by entrance level, but such a prominent position was hardly worth the hill climb anytime one needs to grab lunch.

I kicked myself about my performance in the dining hall all the way back to Streeter Hall, but the damage had been done; all I could do now was retire to my dorm room, lay low for a couple of days, and try to do better tomorrow.

A Streeter Hall dorm room is a simple affair. There are two beds; one on either side of the door. The back half of the room is partitioned by yet another brick wall, this one running directly through the middle of the room. This wall formed the closet, with a wooden door facing the front of the room.

The little niche formed by the closet's protrusion into the right side of the room had a desk protruding from both the back wall and the left side of the room, and a cheap chair sitting in front of the desk. Shelves lined the left side of the room, presumably for books, but I had only my textbooks and a box full of summoning notes made first by my uncle, then later my mentor, shoved under my bed.

The one, sole extravagance I had stretched my financial aid check for was a single room. That was the reason I spent so little on food; hardly any money remained for anything else. I was hoping for a corner room, but my lack of seniority stuck me with this side room.

I lay down on my bed, turning on the TV I had placed on the desk at the foot of it. The dorms had full cable, but I only had a small black-and-white cathode ray TV I'd picked up from a thrift store. It had a bright, lime-green case, presumably an attempt to compensate for the lack of color on the screen. I'm not sure when it was made, but I'd spent more money on the maze of adapters protruding from the back of the television than I had on the television itself. I turned the big, clunky knob on the right side to the in-house movie channel. Some cheeseball action flick from the '80s was on, but I didn't really care. I leaned back in the bed and tried to tune out the rest of the world.

That lasted for two, maybe two and a half minutes.

The phone shattered my attempt at reverie. It was a tinny thing, with no caller ID, view screen, or other accoutrements. It was programmed with a high-pitched, beeping ring designed to irritate someone into answering simply in order to avoid listening. I curled my pillow about my ears, but to no avail. Sighing, I stood and answered the phone.

"'Lo?"

"Robert! Are you OK?" An older, feminine voice was on the other end of the line. I smiled in spite of myself.

Francine was my former foster mother. Having turned eighteen, I no longer had foster parents, but this did not matter to Francine. She still considered herself my mother, regardless of legal status.

I'd been cold to most of my foster parents, but Francine had earned the right to act *in loco parentis*; she was still in physical therapy from the effort.

"Hi, Mom," I said, lazily. There was a short silence on the other end of the phone; in my head, I saw the quiet smile that surely crept its way across Francine's face. She was still getting used to the parental title.

"Robert, I saw the news. I wanted to make sure you were OK." Crap; this was a bad call. Francine knew about my other profession; she hadn't done the math on how low I needed to lay. I was on a school phone line; there was no telling who was listening in. I may have blown off Thad's prohibition on college, but he wasn't wrong about the surveillance.

I began scribbling on my notepad as I talked. "OK? Oh, the accident. No, that wasn't my Volvo. I'm perfectly fine." I looked at my note: UNIVERSITY PHONE SYSTEM. CONVERSATION MAY NOT BE PRIVATE. Good enough.

"No, not that, silly. You were attacked! And by--"

Damn it! She was going to press the issue. I appreciated her concern, but if anyone was listening into the university phone system, she could get me killed. I hastily began scribing runes on the back of the note paper. I was never good with runes, and trying to talk my quasi-mother into a different subject while forming the right phrases was causing me no end of distraction.

"Oh, the news is blowing that out of proportion. Hey, I have a story for you; a couple of guys from the floor and I set up a Twister mat in the elevator, and..." I didn't keep blood in my room; that was the sort of thing that could get a guy busted. Above the desk on the left wall was a bulletin board, and I snagged a thumb tack and jammed it into the tip of my pinky finger. That finger then coated the runes with blood. I brought up my Sense.

Instantly I became aware of everything within forty feet of me, simultaneously. The Sense is an intense *becoming* of the world around me. In a college dorm, activating my Sense was a barrage of information about my packed-in neighbors. Two doors to the south and one floor down, a pair of female roommates were experimenting with their sexuality, and that brought me up short. I almost let the Sense slip, but I tried to focus on the runes.

The trick to sending an item is to send your Sense through a rune phrase to the target location, then have it pull the rune phrase to it. For people with a smaller Sense, this is a simple trick. My Sense is, however, a bulky, awkward, hindering sort of thing. Oh, it had been a huge advantage in some situations, but it made tasks like this one insanely difficult.

I struggled to get my Sense to fit through my rune phrase. On the phone, Francine continued to speak in my ear.

"Twister? In an elevator? Where did you put the spinner? I remember this one time when I was in college we played Monopoly in the middle of the union building for, like, hours. But no, I was worried about you, because..."

I had to cut her off.

"Mom," I said, buying myself a little breathing room, "I'm fine. College is great; you don't have to worry about me getting the freshman yips. After high school, it's nice to be getting a fresh start."

"A fresh start? Oh, sweetie, I never worried about you doing well in college. Now, when I was a freshman, there was this girl Vicki Hedridge, she..."

Now that she was on a story, I let her voice become simply one more piece of my Sense. I bore down, trying fiercely to concentrate solely on the runes despite the flood of information coming at me. My foster mother's voice, the hetero-flexible roommates on the next floor down, the people playing Risk out in the lobby; I felt all of them, and I had to force myself to ignore them. I'd been practicing this with Grace all last year, but I'd let it slip over the summer. My mentor wasn't around to chastise me anymore.

I exerted all my control, all my effort, bringing the runes on the page to life through the blood smeared on top. There! I felt my Sense finally give, and then I Sensed the countertop next to Francine. I quickly hooked the note through with my Sense. I leaned back against the closet wall, panting with the effort it had taken, letting my Sense fade before the cacophony of the dorm drove me insane.

"And then she found them in the drier! She was soooo embarrassed, she almost went home. We all had to talk to her for, like, an hour to keep her in school. Anyway, that's not the problem; the news today! Did one of your—" Francine fell silent after the note piffed its way into existence next to her.

"Mom, I told you, the RT didn't get me. I'm fine, you can stop worrying. Hey, did you get the letter I sent?"

"I—yes, of course. Sorry. You know me, such a worrywart. I got your letter. Last week. It was very nice, thank you." There was a tremble to Francine's voice; she knew how close she'd come to potentially outing me.

"No problem. You know I love you. Talk to you later?"

"Mmm-hmm."

"Goodbye, then."

"Bye."

With that, I returned the phone to its resting place, then started back to my bed. On second thought, I walked back to the phone and turned the ringer off. Then I went back to my bed and lay down.

I sat alone in my room. Outside, I could hear the college life happening. Someone was laughing in the common area. The game of Risk had produced another moment of hilarity. I thought about joining them, but thought again; best to let it go. My job was to keep my head down and not form connections.

Now that we were being hunted, connections would either turn on me, or go down with me. Neither was worth being close to anyone. I turned my head back to my lime-green black-and-white television and worked to lose myself.

ANDREA

THE WOODS EMBRACED ME. The Indian summer heat warmed my bones and cocooned me in the aroma of sunbaked grass and fallen pine needles. Closing my eyes, my Sense absorbed all the simple, ordinary activities surrounding me. The roots of the old tamarack stretched deep into the earth as they searched for water; small worms and insects worked in the cool soil, feasting on the rich nutrients they found. In an overhanging branch, a spider repaired its web, many of the strands still damp with dew from the night before. The wind gently played through the tamarack, and droplets fell shimmering into the long grasses at its foot. A ladybug dodged around the drops, narrowly missing their splash, then flew lazily into a small clump of clover. On the way to a nearby stream, a fawn and doe paused to watch.

Experiencing the animals and insects going about their busy lives, I could almost believe in a peaceful existence. I enjoyed the pressing wind, the ants scurrying underfoot, the squirrels taking home their harvest of nuts, the bees rushing to their hives, and even the tall grasses or the granules of the dirt beneath me. In the flow of life past me, nothing demanded my action; nothing threatened to take anything from me.

Here, I could forget that I had lived like an insect trapped in amber for far longer than my unlined blue eyes, fiery-red hair, and fair, freckled face could speak to at first glance.

Adrenaline had carried me through the initial fight with Cythymau; I'd hurled myself forward on nothing more than rage and hate, ignoring the limits of my flesh. But a thousand years strapped down to a stone slab caught up to me fast once my battle rage wore off. I'd felt like a tortoise trapped on my back, unable to move, still trapped inside bonds I couldn't remove.

It had taken months once I arrived in this Weave for my badly atrophied limbs to actually hold my weight for any longer than a few shaky minutes. I cherished my new ability to walk the forest paths around the cabin, enjoying the freedom and space long denied me. The cabin seemed even smaller, more claustrophobic, now that I could finally be out under the sky.

"Andrea!"

I started at the sound of the voice, my heart pounding, and fought not to flee immediately. Warily I looked over my shoulder. The tall, strawberry-blonde girl called Amy was jogging down the path toward me. I didn't want to talk with her. I walked farther down the path, trying to look unconcerned. I didn't have to use my eyes to know she got closer, her feet displacing dirt on the path, the air rushing through her lungs, and the blood pumping through her muscles as she struggled to reach me.

"Wait up! I want to walk with you. Uh, it's too hot for running. Isn't it supposed to be getting cooler as we go into fall? It still feels like July."

"Uhmm." I'd found this vocalization very useful since coming back to this Weave. Whoever spoke at me could interpret it to their liking with minimum inconvenience to me. I kept walking, hoping she would take the hint and leave me alone.

Her voice chased me, strident, attempting to change my mind through persistence alone. It triggered a memory somewhere in the back of my brain. Once, I had known a word to describe her behavior. It hovered on the edge of my memory.

"You should tell people before you go out, you know," she continued. "The woods can be dangerous, and you're still not really used to being on your own."

That was false. I glanced at her as she attempted to match her pace to mine, wondering what her angle was. "Many things are dangerous. These trees and small animals aren't," I told her.

"Well, something could happen to you, and no one would know. What if you fall down a cliff or something?"

Still a trick question. I cleared my throat and tried to speak more strongly. "There aren't any cliffs on this trail."

Amy's lungs heaved as she blew her breath out through her mouth noisily. "That's not—you don't have to take it so literally," she grumped.

"How else would I take it?"

"I'm just concerned for your wellbeing," Amy answered. "This Weave has changed a lot since before you—"

I flinched, willing away the memories of what came before.

"Well, before," Amy finished lamely. She smoothed her hair back from her sweaty forehead before putting out a hand like she expected to stop me. I side-stepped and kept walking.

She still followed. "You could run into authorities, or locals, or something, and don't take this the wrong way but I don't know how they'd react to you." She paused before muttering in a low voice, "Or you to them, for that matter." Not that I had any chance of missing the exhaled words or the vibrations of her voice in the air when she was standing next to me. "Anyway, try to tell people before you take off, okay? It's just better."

Again, better for who? Her presence next to me was making me nervous, but she just wouldn't leave.

Nag. Nagging. That was the word I'd been searching for. Someone who endlessly talked in an effort to get someone else to do her bidding. It suited my interactions with her well. "I'd rather be alone."

Amy, aka *Naggy's*, lips pulled downward, her arms crossing over her chest. "Haven't you already been alone long enough? I mean, you have people around you now. Let us help you."

"No."

"Why not!? We're happy to," she protested hotly. Danger bells went off in my mind, and my heartbeat ratcheted up a notch.

"Don't want it. Don't need it." I tried picking up my pace. She kept right up with me, her skin slick with sweat and her breath coming and going in short bursts. My heart hammered. She needed to go away now. She was too close, too persistent, too demanding.

"You *do* need help," she insisted. "But we can't do much for you if you don't cooperate with us." Her breath huffed out in little puffs, but she didn't show any sign of stopping anytime soon. A thread of panic started curling itself around the base of my neck. Ahead of me, a particularly tall stand of pines offered temporary haven.

"No. Never. You can't make me."

"I'm not trying to *make* you. I'm asking you to just work with me, us, a little here."

I broke into a run.

"Andrea!"

I reached the trees' shady refuge, the forest floor covered in pine needles and crumbled fallen leaves. I immediately started climbing my way up into the nearest one.

Naggy kept up better than expected. I'd only levered myself up onto the third branch before she arrived at the base of the tree. Her face creased in pain, and she put one hand on her hip, doubling over and panting. After catching her breath, she glanced upward and winced.

"Don't climb up there! Please."

I quickly pulled myself farther up into the tree.

Trying to calm myself, I concentrated on the feel of the bark under my hands, the sap running through the tree, the bugs burrowing in its cracks and crevices, the squirrels and sparrows sheltering high in its branches. I moved my left foot to another branch, crabbing my way upward. The wind rustled gently through the pine's branches. I found myself a wide perch with its trunk at my back, and let my legs hang down from about eight or nine feet up.

I was still aware of Naggy at the base of the tree, but she was far enough away for me to concentrate on something else. The wind ruffled my clothes and my hair, carrying with it the scent of the trees and the nearby creek. A hawk circled high in the sky overhead. The activities of the forest crowded my mind, pushing Amy out to the periphery. I leaned into the tree and took a deep breath.

Naggy put her hands on the base of the tree, looking up for several minutes. Finally, she moved her hand to the first low-hanging branch and started to scrabble up, her sneakers scraping across the bark. The far end of the branch swayed with her awkwardness.

"You and I are going to have a conversation," she panted, "even if I have to come up there and join you."

My heart immediately sped back up as I looked down at her clumsy attempt to get to me. She managed to pull herself up enough to hook her foot over the first branch. Reaching for the next branch, her muscles bunched and trembled with her efforts to get to me. I couldn't stay here, couldn't stay still.

In one motion, I swung my body over the edge of the branch, letting gravity take hold. Catching the branch in my hands, I arrested my fall as my feet found the limb below. I moved swiftly, avoiding the branch she occupied, and finally swinging down to the ground.

Naggy muttered a swear word and attempted to disentangle herself from the branch she'd claimed.

I reversed directions, walking back the way we'd just come without looking back.

Naggy dropped to the ground at the base of the tree with a grunted exhalation, landing hard on her right ankle. Warily, I braced myself to see what she would do now. She jogged after me, this time with a slight hobble. Of course, she still couldn't take the hint and leave me be. I let out a nervous sigh of my own.

She reached me, stopping to grab for my arm. Flinching away, I danced out of her grasp, continuing to walk down the path the way we'd come.

"Fine. You win. We won't talk about this right now. But someday you're going to actually think about what you want to do. I'll be waiting for you to be ready."

She dropped into step beside me, way too close. I lengthened my stride to give myself a bit more space. She tried to match my momentum for a few minutes, but she lagged behind by a foot, and then two, and then three.

Her presence stuck in my head like a sliver, causing constant irritation and worry. She stuck to me like an obnoxious burr, digging in a little farther each time. Finally, I spun around, planting my feet in the middle of the road. I took a deep breath and glared in what I hoped was a threatening manner. I really wanted to just bolt farther into the woods.

"Why are you following me?" I demanded. She stopped and threw me a startled look.

"Aren't you headed back to the cabin?" she asked, pointing up the path the way we were headed. "I was just going back."

"No." I veered completely off the trail into the brush beside it. She took a step toward me but I cut her off. "Don't follow me."

"But Andrea..."

"Don't follow me!" I yelled it at the top of my lungs, my heart trying to break through my ribcage, my ears ringing. I headed quickly into the brush, ducking behind the first convenient tree, blocking myself from her sight. I briefly paused there, trying to get my own breathing under control. Then I just started walking. Naggy stood on the road until she was out of my Sense range, but she didn't come after me. The simple forest creatures and greenery closed in around me, and I hugged their simplicity to my battered psyche, using them to calm my still jangling nerves.

The sun slanted downward through the branches above me, letting me know that some time during my wanderings, time had progressed from afternoon toward evening. It didn't concern me. I could use my Sense to navigate these woods, even in pitch black. No doubt, though, staying out past the sun's expiration would earn me another scolding *if* I did choose to return. *If.*

I followed a well-worn deer track down a gentle slope toward the creek. In this area, lacy ferns and shaded mosses grew over old fallen trees and the green canopy grew impossibly high above my head. As I got closer to the creek bed, the trees gave way to an inclined bank. I walked closer, anticipating the meandering stream at its bottom.

Instead, the Cornuprocyon bounded out of the woods from the opposite bank. It landed in the creek and rolled around, splashing water in a giant arc around its hulking, thirty-foot frame. The sight of its sharp claws, pointed teeth, and barbed coat with its red and orange striped quills sent a shudder of dread through me. This kind of demon was thirty feet of armored killing machine. Its chitinous club tail hit the surface of the water, sending up a gout of spray. The other humans called it "Rick" in some strange parody of a cartoon raccoon, but a cute name couldn't hide its true nature.

The beast finished rolling and dragged itself upright, bits of mud, fern, algae, and the occasional small fish stuck to its quills. My foot dragged itself backwards as I wondered if I'd managed to escape his notice. Its tongue lolled out over its teeth in a sharky grin, and it shook itself, sending wet and gooey bits of detritus everywhere. I barely dodged being hit by a speeding glob of murky green fish bits. Spurred into movement anyway, I started backing slowly toward the woods. Its head swung around and it stared straight at me. I stared back, wide-eyed.

Robert had tried to tell me this Cornuprocyon wouldn't hurt anyone. Ha. I'd met far more of these creatures than he had, and they all thought summoners were a tasty treat.

I didn't feel like becoming demon food today. Carefully, I stepped backward again, trying not to break into a flat-out run. "I'm not easy pickings."

It snorted, gathering itself for a kinetic leap. My stomach jumped up into my throat. Frantic, I launched one of the wide, fallen tree trunks at it on instinct. Almost casually, the Cornuprocyon aborted its leap, using the generated force to blast the tree into a multitude of splinters instead. A thick, prickly deluge of pulverized wood pelted down. I diverted the flying splinters that came within range of my Sense into a big mound of debris behind me as the Cornuprocyon released another burst of kinetic energy, shielding itself. Tensely, I waited to see what the beast's next move would be.

I moved a step backward. It didn't budge. Steeling my nerves, I took another step, then another. I waited. The Cornuprocyon's eyes watched intently, but his muscles didn't even twitch. Each step was painfully slow. My heart hammered in my ears, but I finally reached the trees edging the creek. I backed up one final step into them and spun, running for my life. Behind me, the Cornuprocyon released a huffing breath of its own and settled into the creek.

The forest around me no longer felt friendly or peaceful. I fled up the path, trying to reach the cabin and its protection before the Cornuprocyon could change its mind. I reached the cabin door, dashed through it and slammed it behind me.

When I'd first arrived, the cabin had been a simple one-room building with a fireplace. A deathtrap, with all the summoners crowded inside like sardines. I'd refused to enter.

Sleeping outside under the canopy of trees and stars was much more soothing. Yet these humans always herded me back toward it. Naggy would preach about how it was important to stay hidden, and on and on.

Soon after my arrival, more rooms had started appearing every time I gave in to someone's incessant bothering and returned to its vicinity. The extra space had been welcome, had even made standing in the cabin's confines more tolerable—until I realized it meant they expected me to share the space with them. To live here, with them. While they watched me, prodding at me.

Today though, the strong need to hide outweighed all my usual refusals.

In the main room, one of the apprentice summoners looked up from the laptop he had propped up on the coffee table. It wasn't the skinny, cocky one who had gone into Cythymau's Weave and brought me back here with more luck than sense. This one's face showed signs of acne, and his thick, short body looked like someone had accidentally compacted down his normal growth spurt. He wasn't fat, just… solidly built. Of everyone I'd met since I'd come here, he was the only one who spoke as infrequently as me. But I hadn't bothered to learn what the others called him. Something like

Hat or Mat. If I needed to think about him, Stocky was good enough.

He took in my bedraggled appearance and raised an eyebrow but didn't comment. Naggy came out from the kitchen with a cup of coffee and pointedly looked me over but didn't offer any remarks either.

"I'm gonna go wash and change," I mumbled. I fled up the hallway to the room reserved for me and showered, changing into a fresh tee shirt and jeans not covered with tree pitch and pine needles.

I came back out to get food after drying my hair. Outside, I could Sense the Grove director's purposeful walk to the cabin's front door. Director Stuffy ostensibly controlled all the summoners here, this place where I'd been brought after the demise of my demon captor. The summoner who'd killed him died; I'd lived, and I wasn't about to put myself under anyone's control again. That said, at least Stuffy was very straightforward about what he wanted from me. He desired my knowledge of my previous master's secrets. His single-minded pursuit of gaining that knowledge for himself was in some ways much easier to handle than Naggy's unpredictable clinginess.

I stood in the hallway debating whether to just go back and shut the door to my room until Stuffy went away, but I didn't want to be trapped in the small room I'd just vacated.

Screw it. I'd take my chances outside with the Cornuprocyon.

I crossed the living room, intending to exit through the front door and head back into the woods. Just not as far this time. I'd stick to where I could possibly still return for backup.

"Andrea." Stuffy put out a hand as I tried to pass him, trying to grasp my arm. I sidestepped and regarded him with a sinking feeling in the pit of my stomach.

"I'm glad I caught you inside today." He pulled a note from his coat pocket and sat down, deliberately blocking the door. We'd done this dance before, and he'd already predicted that my next move would be to get as far away from him and his questions as possible. I could force him out of the way, but since I wasn't going to answer his inquiries anyway, it seemed like wasted effort. Plus I wasn't actually that eager for a rematch with the Cornuprocyon.

Naggy glowered over her coffee and walked back into the kitchen. Stocky sat typing, apparently oblivious. Stuffy smiled at me, but I didn't trust it. He only showed up to talk to me for one reason.

"I have some questions for you about Cythymau and his Weave."

Yup. Here we went again.

ROBERT

FRIDAY.

In the mouths of students, whether college or high school, that word is holy. Friday is a day of freedom. Friday night is the night of celebration, the night of passion. On a Friday, you are more likely to get drunk, stoned, laid, chased by a goat, or find yourself in a Denny's at 3 a.m. debating retail philosophy with a complete stranger.

Friday is, in other words, pure potential. It begins when the last class lets out, and it ends in the blurry haze between night and morning. Properly done, a Friday passes like a thunderstorm, powerful but short, and leaves nothing but the feeling that you've just experienced a primal force of immense power.

I lamented all of this as I drove my Volvo east and contemplated the reality of my particular Friday.

This Friday, there would be no parties, no booze, no goats, no Denny's. That allure was for normal students, not for me. No, this Friday, as with all my Fridays, I would drive to a small cabin in the Idaho Panhandle. It was actually my cabin, deeded to me on my eighteenth birthday from the estate of my late uncle, Herman Lorents. Unofficially, though, it served as headquarters for the Spokane Grove, a group of summoners responsible for the health of the Weave in

Eastern Washington and North Idaho. That sounds like a large area, and it is, but given that Rick had *eaten* most of the summoners in Eastern Washington and North Idaho last year, a small cabin in northern Idaho sufficed quite well for headquarters.

Once there, I would report in to Nielsen. We'd bristle at each other. He'd give me an assignment for the weekend. This assignment would invariably involve the minor little tears in the Weave that had cropped up over the week, which was sheer drudge work. Nielsen could have handled those tears easily, or sent Amy. Even Matt, whose Sense was barely strong enough to move around paper or beams of light, could probably have mended most of them. Certainly, a combined effort from all of us could've salvaged a large portion of my weekend.

Nielsen wanted to hurt *me*, though, and since he couldn't do it directly, he piled me up with drudgery, driving from tear to tear and knitting the Weave back together.

It had to be done. The Weave is the fabric of reality itself. The politicians brand us summoners as "reality terrorists," but that is the exact opposite of the truth. Reality as we know it constantly frays. It's under pressure from the outside and the inside, and it's the task of summoners to keep our world more or less intact. If the government ever succeeds in wiping us out, it's going to have a *much* bigger problem on its hands.

Regardless, my weekend was to be filled with drudgery. Repairing the Weave is actually a very good description; the process is roughly as exciting as knitting together socks. Every week, Nielsen saved a list of small tears, and every weekend I drove about in my overheated Volvo, sweating my ass off and stopping at some alleyway or old parking lot, fixing the Weave, then moving on. It would have taken Nielsen perhaps an extra thirty seconds to a minute per tear to fix them while he was detecting them, and he could have done it from the comfort of home.

Instead, he collected the information while lounging about, then handed it to me. For me, it was faster to drive to the location; my half-baked rune work simply could not handle fixing that many tears over long distances. No, Thaddeus Nielsen had managed to effectively rob me of my weekends in petty revenge for... well, for my still being alive, really.

So Fridays bore none of the holy power for me that they did for my college cohorts. Free time, for me, lay in the interstices between Freshman English and Psych 101. It's hard to work up a good drunk in those couple of hours, though I suspected my psych professor pulled it off on occasion.

Friday, in short, did not end the workweek for me. It marked the beginning.

My Volvo was without air conditioning. This turned out to be a blessing, as it forced me to keep my windows rolled down. Which, in turn, allowed me to hear the familiar *whoomph* sound *before* my car was completely demolished.

That gave me time to call up my Sense and redirect the massive ball of kinetic force away from my little car. I opened the door and rolled out as Rick the Cornuprocyon bounded into the gravel road in front of the Volvo, bouncing back and forth on his front paws. His layers of red quills shook with his excitement, and his ten-foot chitinous club of a tail twitched right and left, wagging like a dog's, and with about as much caution. It crashed through a tree trunk, sending the confier tumbling down toward—where else—my car. I used my Sense to fling the tree back and away from the car.

"*Rick!*" I projected my anger through the link between the two of us so he would know I was not happy. "Not the car, and not in the road!"

Rick stopped bouncing; his tail stopped wagging.

One of the nice things about not being very good with runes is the fact that most of the summoning I *can* do requires no overt accoutrement. I don't carry blood with me; I don't have pre-scribed rune tags. I do have a pair of bracers with runes etched into them, but they're more for historical value than any practical use. Once part and parcel with the notes in my dorm room, the bracers now occupied a small crevice in the ground thirty feet below my room at the now-expanded cabin, out of Thad's Sense range. He and I'd had something of a dispute about those bracers, one that came very close to turning lethal.

In short, I slipped under the radar as a summoner because I never had evidence of summoning on me. I'd have to summon in front of a cop to get caught.

The exception to this, the Persian flaw in my otherwise perfect disguise, is Rick. A thirty-foot long raccoon/hedgehog/anklyosaur spirit with an exuberance for force-ball catch is *exactly* the sort of thing that could shout to the world that I was a summoner. The world would have one *hell* of a time taking Rick down, but in the end he and I would run out of juice before the army ran out of bullets.

He sat there, trying to look contrite and non-threatening. He lowered his head between his front paws, his swirling orange eyes looking up at me, wide and innocent-like. It was comical, from Rick. A year ago, he'd been trying to kill me. Now he simply wanted my approval. He was powerful, but also as loyal and klutzy as an untrained puppy.

I gave in and let my Sense drop. He'd been chastised, and I was weak to anything that showed me that level of affection. I walked up to Rick and began scratching him behind the ears, careful to avoid being pricked by his spines. Rick rubbed his gigantic muzzle against my chest, sending me staggering backward.

Seeing me off-balance, Rick decided it was play time now. He leaped back with a *whoomph,* using his kinetic blast to drive himself up and away from me. That gave me time to bring my Sense back up; it took Rick a couple of seconds in between his force blasts.

Only a couple of seconds. The next *whoomph* shook the air, and the force drove at me. I was ready for it this time, though. I took hold of the force with my Sense and guided it around my body, wrapping it into a half-orbit. That let me send it back at Rick.

The Cornuprocyon had jumped back for a reason; in the time it took the force ball to get to him, he'd generated a second one and sent it into the heart of the first. The forces met in a blast of air pressure before dissipating. Rick came bounding back up to me in a gleeful zig-zag. He nuzzled in to cadge more petting, which I delivered as requested.

When I was a young child, before my parents died, a family who had a Rottweiler lived down the block from us. The dog was really very friendly, a nice dog, but there was this implicit threat in the way it played fetch with railroad ties. It never attacked anyone, but there was always the fact that it *could,* and that made the big, muscular dog a gleeful terror to us children.

It may have made me petty, but as I sat there scratching the ears of my massive Cornuprocyon, I kept thinking that, finally, my dog could beat up that dog. I couldn't help but smile.

I WALKED the rest of the way to the cabin, leaving my Volvo parked at the side of the road. Rick really didn't understand the concept that cars were *not* for destroying, and trying to keep my Sense up while driving was a dangerous proposition. I'd gotten lucky the first time; I didn't want to risk a playful ambush from the rear crushing my only means of transportation.

Originally, Uncle Herman's cabin was a small, one-room log building with an outhouse. I still thought of it that way, so it came as a bit of a shock every time I looked at it now. Over the summer, its occupancy had grown. Now it was a flat ranch-house style cabin, with full indoor plumbing and solar-powered electric. I honestly didn't know how Matt managed to set all of that up in the space of three months; I knew he hadn't summoned it in—his power never would have enabled that. He'd been in charge of the day-to-day administration of the Grove, though, and he'd done the expansion of the house. He'd even rigged a computer in his room with a number of runes that allowed him to summon internet connectivity.

Looking at the cars in the driveway, I saw that Matt, Amy, and

Nielsen were all here. Full house. I took a breath, enjoyed my freedom for only a moment, then reached for the door handle.

"...the function of this particular phrase?" The voice of Thaddeus Nielsen cut through the inside of the cabin as soon as I opened the door. His nasal timbre had the high-pitched tones of contempt, and it sent a chill up my spine; that voice had once pronounced a death sentence on me in the same detached tone.

Now it was Andrea who suffered under Nielsen's wilting verbal lash. It didn't appear she'd broken any of his bones or burned the place down, so on the whole I thought she was doing far better than I had when facing him down. Instead, she sat there, staring off into space.

I'd never seen Andrea with her Sense lowered, but I liked to check. Before addressing Nielsen I closed my eyes and raised my Sense. Instantly, it flooded the cabin, making me intimately a part of everything therein. As always, Andrea's Sense met mine, already raised.

The Sense takes effort to maintain. It's a physical burden to use it to manipulate anything, but even simply keeping it up requires a level of mental concentration that comes from practice and freedom from distraction.

Every single time I checked, Andrea's not-inconsiderably-sized Sense was up. She went through her life in a fog of the Sense, never pausing to revert to normal human interaction. She felt *everything* within twenty feet of her all the time. She hadn't looked up when I'd walked in because she hadn't needed to. She had Sensed me before I'd laid my hand on the latch.

I'd rescued Andrea from the physical danger, but I had a long way to go to pull her away from the emotional damage she'd suffered at the hands of Cythymau.

Upon rescuing her, I'd immediately expected the grateful damsel in distress to simper with gratitude. That's what rescued damsels did, right? After all, I'd risked *everything* to free this beautiful girl from the clutches of an evil demon. Grace had *died* covering our retreat with that bomb. I'd sacrificed my teacher for this girl.

Leading up to the rescue, I'd had daydreams of her falling in love with me for my heroism, following me about like an imprinted puppy with gratitude fostering in her a desire to serve my every, stupid, masculine whim.

Now I knew better. Turns out, you don't just spring back from thousands of years of abuse. Andrea hadn't been a prize to be won by my gallantry; she'd been a wild animal to be set free. She had her own problems to deal with.

So it wasn't really a shock that Andrea remained still, not reacting to Nielsen's question. He sighed, and then continued in his condescendingly officious tones. "Ms. Rothstein, the Grove has graciously agreed to your temporary membership. However, there are some very pressing concerns about you, including the fact that you may be an unwitting, or worse, a witting agent of Cythymau. Assistance in understanding and interpreting our enemy's techniques would go far toward proving your continued usefulness to, and therefore ensuring your continued membership in, the Grove system."

I'd heard this speech before, and my anger flared. My talk with Nielsen months ago, when he'd announced to me I was no longer eligible for membership in the Grove, had sounded almost exactly the same. Less than a minute later, he'd opened fire on me. I knew this was a very polite, but very definite, threat. The Grove didn't let summoners live outside the system.

Thaddeus had just threatened to kill Andrea.

Over the line.

I brought my Sense back up and stripped Thaddeus of anything on him containing a rune or the ability to make one. It wouldn't neutralize him, but it would kneecap him. I placed his gear in a neat little pile outside the cabin. He brought his Sense to life immediately, trying to grasp for his gear back.

Nielsen was a very skilled, precise, and lightning-fast summoner. Without his runes, though, it was a Sense-on-Sense fight. Skill and precision went out the window at that point; Sense-on-Sense had all the finesse of an arm-wrestling match, and I had the bigger biceps.

"Nielsen, *enough*. You are the Grove Director of Spokane, but you have abused my hospitality far too long. You will not come to *my* house—"

"Your house? This is the headquarters of the Grove, and I am its director."

"Get a new headquarters, then. This cabin and the land around it are in *my* name. You are in *my* home. And you have just threatened the life of *my* guest. Leave. Now."

Thaddeus stared at me. I sent a quick tug on the bond between Rick and me, and a *whoomph* sounded from outside for emphasis. Thad got the picture immediately, and exited with as much pride as he could carry.

I'd had enough of Thaddeus Nielsen. He had gone after my life, now Andrea's. He'd always been a self-righteous menace, but now that he'd gone back to threatening lives, he had to be dealt with. There was really only one thing to do about it. I left Andrea sitting in the front room, what used to be the *only* room, of the cabin, and went down the hall to find Matt.

"YOU GET a phone connection on that thing?" I asked my comrade-in-arms.

Matt was a summoner, but just barely. He'd escaped Rick's attack on the Spokane Grove by being insignificant. His Sense was tiny and weak. He could summon a piece of paper, maybe. He could summon light. Sure, he was an apt pupil of Grace's in runework, but he simply didn't have the strength to pull off Grace's flashier summons.

Every corner of his room overflowed with bits of paper, most of it piled in stacks. His desktop computer sat covered in sticky notes, each with a rune phrase or two on it. Next to the computer, a mini-fridge hummed away, filled (no doubt) with both blood and some sugary caffeine-bomb to keep Matt at his keyboard at all hours.

"I can hook you up through the net, yeah," Matt said. "Or you can use the satphone."

"Satphone?"

"Satellite phone. Much better reception around here than cell towers."

"Isn't that expensive?"

Matt shrugged. "Not too bad. I keep it here for emergencies. You need it?"

"Uh, sure. Not really an emergency, but there's a call I need to make. You may want plausible deniability on this one."

Matt's face blanched. "Robert, I thought you were done picking a fight with the Grove. You and I both know no good can come of it."

I sighed. "Not the Grove. Well, not me. Technically. Do you really want to know more?"

Matt was a smart guy; he kept his head down, didn't make waves. I liked Matt a lot, but he'd never have the balls to get on the front line. Rear-echelon work he was great at, and that meant he did what the Grove told him.

"You know," he said, exaggerating his level of casualness, "I think I am going to head back to the stove, make some coffee. You with me?"

"Nah," I said. "I'm going to hang here for a bit." Matt nodded, leaving the room. I reached for the satphone.

"Detective Frank Allen."

"Uh, hi. Detective Allen? This is Robert Lorents."

Silence from the other end of the phone. "Lorents? Why are you calling?"

"Well, actually I have a tip for you. You're still running the summoner investigations for Spokane County, right?"

Detective Allen gave an exasperated chuckle at this. "In name only. The anti-summoner movement has gotten way out ahead of the Spokane County Sheriff's office. I'm the next best thing to a patrol officer, now. It's the Feds who are really in charge."

"Well, okay. But my tip is for you."

"You're going to rat on a summoner?"

"Is this a secure line?"

"Ah, no. We can talk in person later. Give me the info, I'll make sure the right people get it."

"His name is Thaddeus Nielsen. That's N-i-e-l-s-e-n. He's driving in from somewhere in North Idaho now in a black sedan, license plate number AHF4032." Allen had been out here before; he knew that "somewhere in North Idaho" meant this cabin.

"Got it. You know I can't keep him away from the Feds, right? I have to pass this info up the chain. You're an anonymous source, as far as I'm concerned, but he's going to Federal custody, not State. You know what happens to him then?"

I did. This was a man who had tried multiple times to kill me, who only *stopped* trying to kill me because Rick held him hostage. This was a man who would try, eventually, to kill Andrea.

"Yes, Detective. They kill him."

And I wouldn't have to.

ANDREA

OKAY NOW? Everything was *okay* now?

I'd listened to that bullshit once before. A demon robbed me with those slick, slippery words. I wouldn't make the same mistake twice.

I could feel the blood surge through Skinny as he struck a smug, heroic stance in front of Stuffy, pointing toward the door. Stuffy's blood pressure rose in response, throbbing like a too-loud drum under his skin.

As I watched, Stuffy's face flushed. He opened his mouth, raised his finger in the beginning of a counterpoint gesture, then seemed to think better of it. Closing his mouth, dropping his hand, he turned and walked slowly out. His footsteps struck measured beats against the polished grain of the hardwood floor in contrast to his hammering pulse.

Skinny strode out of the room, apparently not wanting or expecting a reaction from me.

Good. I'd get a head start before he missed me and tried to bring me back. Naggy still puttered around the kitchen, sipping her coffee. She muttered to herself about the disagreement between Skinny and Stuffy, so it was unlikely she'd notice me leave. Stocky sat across from me and typed on his ridiculously small computer, not paying attention. After a few moments, he closed his computer and headed after Robert.

Of all the humans here, Stocky bugged me the least. He didn't talk much. I liked that. But in a face-off against Skinny, he'd be useless to me.

I needed to run right now, but... Stuffy hadn't actually left yet; he stood outside by his vehicle. I didn't want him to observe my escape.

But if I didn't go now, someone would detain me. My freedom wasn't something I could take a chance on. I'd just left captivity, and staying was too big a risk.

Quietly, I slipped through the door and back outside. The Cornuprocyon still lurked out here somewhere, waiting for unwary prey. Skinny might have believed the demon was tame, but I didn't. In my experience, all Cornuprocyons were ruthless and deadly hunters. To escape its detection, I'd have to clear the vicinity fast.

I marched down the front path toward the road, ignoring Stuffy in the driveway. In a pinch, I knew I could overpower him to make my escape, but I didn't want to make a ruckus unless forced.

"Andrea." Stuffy hovered near his vehicle with the door open. "I'd like to continue our conversation back at my apartment. If you aren't busy"—he glanced significantly toward the empty road where I was headed—"would now be a good time?"

No. No more listening; no more talking. I turned to *communicate* that to him physically, but instead I saw his vehicle. It would get me away from the cabin fast—faster than fleeing on foot. Even if Stuffy tried to stop me from striking out on my own once we got away from here, preventing me would be much harder. Fewer people. Less resources. He had a smaller Sense than mine. One-on-one *he* would be at the disadvantage, if it came to it.

I walked toward the passenger door, ignoring Stuffy's startled expression. I slid in to the vehicle, and tried to not to hyperventilate over how close and small the interior was. My nervous energy hummed with nowhere to go. On my lap, my fingers clenched into fists, turning my knuckles white.

Keep cool. Breathe. Breathe. Hold it together, Andrea.

Stuffy seated himself behind the wheel, closed his door, and fastened himself in.

He turned the key in the ignition, glancing over at me. "Here," he said, quickly leaning toward me, reaching over me for something in the car. I couldn't help shrinking back farther into the seat, but there wasn't enough room to get away. Not able to completely dodge or avoid him, my breath hitched.

Out. Outside the metal box, open ground waited. But cars moved faster than people.

Much faster. Faster away from Skinny and the Cornuprocyon threat. The heat and smell of Stuffy hung in front of me much too close. *Don't lash out. Don't kill the best escape route.* I held my breath.

"I know they weren't prevalent when you were here before, but you really should wear a seatbelt." Stuffy grasped a strap next to me and started to pull it across the car toward him.

Across *me.*

PANIC. Cythymau's gleeful hooting laughter drowned out my surroundings, belying my Sense. I couldn't breathe, couldn't think. I struck out at Stuffy's wrist with the heel of my hand. He swore, dropping the cursed strap.

Using my Sense, I stripped the whole strap mechanism out of the car, dropping it into the gravel outside. The threat vanquished, I could finally take a deep breath.

Cythymau wasn't here. I had my own will. I *needed* this vehicle's speed. It needed a driver. Stuffy. Don't kill Stuffy.

Stuffy stared at me, holding his smarting wrist. Then at the place where the strap mechanism used to hang, his eyes wide.

"What was—"

"No straps," I said firmly.

His breath exhaled on a long "Oooooooooooooookay," but the muscles in his shoulders tensed further. "Okay," he said again. "No straps."

He put the car into gear and we pulled away from the cabin, rolling down the gravel roadway. The gasoline flowed down a hose into the engine, collided with a spark, exploded outward, fighting for freedom, but the engine contained it. The pistons churned, the axle rotated, and finally the rubber of the tires sent gravel scattering. It was all one long chain reaction.

The engine consumed the gasoline and transformed it, pushing the vehicle forward, fueling the inanimate steel and plastic cage around me. After enduring and enduring, oil finally broke free to the earth's surface, only to be trapped again, refined, altered into a commodity that burned away into nothingness in a matter of seconds. Like me, gasoline was a power source to be depleted, so someone else could reach their goal.

I knew the gasoline wasn't sentient; it couldn't feel itself being used up, but I didn't feel truly alive anymore either. We were both ghosts of long-forgotten things that life had left behind.

The vehicle moved, but I held myself very, very still. I focused on resisting the urge to fling open the door and run out into the trees, hiding myself in the heavily forested landscape past the road's shoulder.

"I won't ask why you decided to come with me," Stuffy began, and I groaned.

Again, this was a half-truth. He was always talking at me and asking questions. I never said much or answered, but he did it anyway. Most times, I didn't even pay attention to what Stuffy said when he spoke.

I did this time, though, because I had no choice. Listen, or run screaming from this murderous-but-speedy metal box.

"...but I'm glad you did. I don't ask you all these questions about Cythymau for my own amusement, you know." Stuffy's eyes were fixed on the road. I glanced over at him, trying to keep the disbelief off my face.

"I understand that you're coming out of a horrific situation, but I desperately need intelligence about the things I'm asking you. Based on what I've managed to get out of Robert, the rune forms and methods Cythymau employed appear to be variants on archaic summoning practices that were used here for a very short period of time and then abandoned. The examples we have of anything resembling the rune structures used by Cythymau are fragmentary at best."

I yawned widely. Maybe Stuffy would take the hint. He threw me an irritated glance, but kept talking.

"You have more knowledge in your head about those rune forms and what they mean, what their potential uses are, than exists in all of the Grove libraries. You could be instrumental in helping us decipher their purpose and use. We need to understand them to better protect this Weave from demons like Cythymau in the future."

I snorted. So many falsehoods humans spoke. Cythymau had been a power unto himself. The demon had died, so this Grove would never face a like power again. Which was to their advantage. If *that* demon had lived, this Weave would have ceased to exist as they'd known it. He would have remade it.

Skinny's master had denied me my chance at revenge, my chance to have vengeance over my living nightmare. I knew I probably wouldn't have fought Cythymau and lived. Mutually assured destruction was the best and most likely outcome. Regardless, I would have made Cythymau hurt, made him bleed for forging me into his weapon.

Whereas Skinny's master had put herself between *that* demon and everyone in this Weave, I had only been intent on the demon's destruction.

Skinny's master had traded her life for this Weave. I wasn't going to offer to sacrifice myself to the Grove. Been there, done that, lifetimes ago. It hadn't worked out well for me. This time, I wouldn't make the same mistake.

Stuffy heard my snort; I could tell by the way his jaw tightened and his muscles tensed, pushing down the gas pedal. I'd never give Stuffy or any of his ilk the means to emulate Cythymau. If that knowledge got out, a thousand power-mad fools would want to exploit it. They'd trap and enslave those they could, then turn and war with each other.

I wasn't stupid enough to offer to strap myself back down on a rune-covered stone slab like I'd never left.

Nothing that came out of Stuffy's mouth could convince me that *he* or the Grove needed to rival the self-styled "god" who'd held me captive. He kept talking.

"I've sent copies of Summoner Moore's transcripts to supposed rune experts back east, but so far their progress has been disappointingly small, to say the least. But your assistance could change everything. No doubt you picked up a lot of knowledge in your extended stay in the other Weave. I expect you are at least familiar with if not fluent in archaic rune forms. You have intimate knowledge of Cythymau and his world that no one else can match."

Stuffy's voice had begun to heat with the strength of his passion for this subject. His blood pumped faster and his words came quicker. My wary hackles rose anew, and I drew my knees up, folding my arms over them.

The only truth here was that I had knowledge he wanted.

He tried a new angle. His voice became calm and measured as he took a couple of deep breaths to steady himself. I could tell by his suspiciously regular breathing and rigid shoulder muscles that he was consciously holding himself still, trying very hard not to spook me. That frightened me by itself, and my arms reflexively tightened over my legs.

"You could be a great asset to Groves throughout the nation, and I've made sure that those higher up the Grove command know that. If you cooperate with me in this matter, your position in the Grove would become very secure. If you keep withholding information, it will get harder and harder for me to guarantee that. There are those who think that if you aren't willing to share information with the Grove, you become a greater liability to the rest of us. If you value your security, you should re-think your attitude so far."

Stuffy tried to mask his emotions from me. More lies. Yet another deceiver trying to use me to gain power.

My vision fragmented and my skin crawled with waves of pins and needles, no matter how hard I tried to force down my jittering nerves. The "me" I'd begun to rebuild, the thinking me, shimmered like a mirage about to be swept aside. Adrenaline flooded my limbs and my hands shook with the need to strike out at something.

Flailing for a calm refuge, I let part of my Sense focus on the life coursing through the trees flashing by in the evening gloaming outside the window. For a fraction of a second, the sap flowed through each tree, one after another. Serene. Without demands. I hugged the hazy blur around me, trying not to fly apart.

"Not interested." I managed to push the words past my clenched jaw.

Stuffy made no vocal sound of displeasure, but his hands tightened on the steering wheel and a fine sweat broke out on the back of his neck. His agitation grew, engaging his adrenal glands, electrons firing rapidly in his brain. I shut out as much of Stuffy and the car as possible from my Sense, focusing on the life that sped past outside.

Breathe. My lungs expanded and contracted much too fast, ignoring my attempts to slow them down. Sweat misted on my skin. Must be still, like a mountain. Mustn't let on how close I was to breaking and throwing myself out of the vehicle.

"Let me tell you a story."

"No." I just wanted to get to our destination, finish running away from all of these humans who claimed to look out for *my* interests.

"Hear me out anyway," Stuffy insisted. Hunching in the seat, I turned my body to face out the window.

"I had a sister, once. Talia. You remind me of her, especially that wary attitude. You both have a trust problem. You don't want to rely on anyone but yourself. That'd be all well and good, if you were a normal person, one of the bland neighbor kids who would never interest demons like Cythymau or accidentally cause international incidents. If you were one of those kids, the worst thing that could happen to you is you might piss off a sheriff or two and end up in the county clink. But you aren't. And my sister wasn't. Now she's dead."

He spoke as if I didn't know about things in the world that could hurt me. My *trust problem* came from everyone else hiding another agenda. How young did he think I was? I had been in Cythymau's cave for longer than Stuffy had existed.

Stuffy blew out a long breath as I remained silent, but in the end, he kept speaking.

"The Groves are in turmoil right now. Summoners are systematically being captured, detained and exterminated in numbers that haven't been seen since the outbreak of anti-summoner witch-hunts in the sixteenth and seventeenth centuries. Summoner Moore's actions have sent more summoners to death row than can ever be washed out with the death of one demon, even one named Cythymau."

I wasn't stupid. I knew from what I had seen with my own eyes that Skinny and his mentor had been sent to Cythymau's Weave alone. Stuffy had no idea of Cythymau's power or capabilities at all, and yet he still harped after every scrap of knowledge I might have while simultaneously underestimating its potential.

The very fact that Summoner Moore prevailed against *that* demon at all was impressive. I owed her my freedom, as did every other summoner in this Weave. Stuffy thought this "government crackdown" was the worst thing that could have happened to this Weave going back for centuries. I rolled that thought around in my head. It elicited a slightly itchy feeling in my eyes that made my lips twitch. Stuffy was so... naïve. Wrong, and naïve.

"I need more from you," Stuffy continued. "Summoner Moore may not have meant to start a witch hunt—despite all evidence to the contrary—but that's what happened. All actions have consequences, whether intended or not. You need to trust that the Grove has your best interests at heart, but this includes protecting all Grove assets, including you. Whatever Cythyamau put you through over there, you already made it out, and you *can* do something to help the Grove protect its own right now."

Stuffy still had a very idealistic view of the world. I envied him that. He had principles, but not much else.

Yes, decisions and actions had consequences. Very, very bad consequences. And people died over and over and over again, and you became part of the weapon used to torture them. Doing nothing in this situation was definitely much better.

I leaned my shoulder against the glass of the window, fighting the urge to fling open the door and bolt out into the green shrubs and trees flashing by the car outside. Unfortunately, Stuffy seemed to take my new body language as a signal that I was actually listening.

"I loved my sister, but I was too late to help her. I'm not too late to help you, but you need to let me. To the Council, you're an unknown that could do a lot of damage to an incredibly precarious situation. We need something that proves your indisputable value to the Groves as a whole. You *have* knowledge that can guarantee your position in the Grove is secure no matter what happens, or how the factions might shift. Think about it. Please."

Panicky again, I pushed myself away from the door and fumbled around, looking for the window crank. I needed more air. Stuffy noticed my dilemma and muttered something under his breath. He toggled a small lever on his side of the car that caused little gears in the door to fire. My window abruptly opened six inches before stopping.

"Since you don't have a seat belt on, opening it further wouldn't be safe," he explained. It was a weak excuse but not worth fighting over. Now that I knew which gears controlled the window, I could use my Sense to move them, or eject the window glass from the vehicle completely. The air was more important. I submerged as much of my face as possible in the airflow, heaving in great gulps of it in an attempt to calm down.

I watched scrublands and wheat fields fly by before subtly changing into houses, apartments, and stores. When the darkness outside became punctuated by streetlights, I realized that we had truly left the empty forest lanes now. The road under the car's tires had changed from gravel to pavement a while ago, but with the streetlights my fears came flooding back.

With streetlights came communities, people—more humans who would want something from me and expect me to be like them. Or try to imprison me when they found out I wasn't.

"Let me out." The words escaped my lips before I even knew I was going to utter them.

"What? We're not quite there yet. Please hold on."

"I need out now." I gritted out between clenched teeth. My

suddenly thundering heart wasn't going to calm down until I was moving.

"It's really not a good idea to—"

I wrenched open my door, tucked my arms in, and flung myself free of the vehicle.

ANDREA

USING MY SENSE, I siphoned off some of my momentum, so I landed a little softer. Not *a lot* softer.

My shoulder hit the pavement with a jarring bounce, and pain flashed up my collarbone. Brakes squealed as Stuffy tried to bring the car to a stop. I attempted to tuck-and-roll less than successfully. My knee hit the road next, not quite in line with the rest of my body. I heard my sweats rip. Pain flared in my leg. I gritted my teeth. Holding my body in a tighter line, I plucked more kinetic force from the traffic to bring my tumble under control. I rolled upright, jumped up onto my feet, and then scanned the vicinity for my nearest escape route.

And looked straight into the eyes of a startled grandmother peeking out of her house on the edge of the street. More lights flicked on. Curtains opened as other people peered out of doors and windows. So many humans, so many eyes. All focused on me. My muscles froze. The car behind Stuffy honked, and the driver rolled down his window.

"What the hell!?" he yelled. "Is that girl crazy? Was she trying to get herself run over?"

The woman I'd originally seen peeking out her door moved out onto her porch.

"You OK, honey?" she called. "Do you need help? I'm happy to phone whoever you need." She pulled out a cell phone and ran her finger down the screen to unlock it. More neighbors started moving out onto their porches. More cars rolled to a stop behind Stuffy, honking, attracting even more attention than before. So many humans, all looking at me, moving closer.

"Andrea," Stuffy said through the still open passenger door, "I don't—"

In the car was better than out, after all. The car was still faster at running away. Faster than me. Too many people here. Stuffy would know somewhere we could hide. By myself, I had no idea where to run—not with this many people already watching me so intently.

I jumped back in the car, slammed the door behind me, and stared straight ahead. My heart pounded in my ears. "Drive." Better the devil I knew than the multitude of strange ones.

Giving me a long look, Stuffy shifted the car back into gear.

"I should have some gauze and some iodine for your injuries at my place. Let's see if we can get there without any more surprises, shall we?" I gave him a reluctant nod, and the tires of the car once more hummed on the road.

I closed my eyes and tried not to think of anything as the car traveled away from the horde of humans—far too slowly for my taste. When we reached the small, horseshoe-shaped apartment complex that Stuffy called home, I almost struck out on my own anyway. If I hadn't started a ruckus a few blocks distant... But at least this place had four walls and a door. It would have to work for now.

As far as hiding places were concerned, Stuffy's home was not ideal. It was surrounded on two sides by other buildings, forming a U with a small, scraggly courtyard in the middle, and at least six other units with more humans living in them. His apartment was in the building farthest from the parking lot, the bottom of the U, but on the far left. The complex was all one level, with only one set of neighbors close enough to bother me. When I stood in his small kitchen, I could Sense his neighbors in their apartment through the walls. I retreated back to the living room and perched myself on a footstool in its exact center. This spot gave me the maximum amount of isolation from the other humans who kept invading my space. I knew that even though I could Sense them, they couldn't see me, but I still couldn't relax here.

Stuffy moved in and out of my range too as he puttered around the apartment, finding the first-aid kit and then a clean washcloth. He came over and acted like he was going to try and fuss over me himself. I took the washcloth and small metal box and retreated to the exit, ready to find a different hiding place if he forced the issue.

He put his hands up in a gesture of surrender. "Suit yourself. I'm going to cook a frozen pizza because I'm hungry. You're welcome to have some when it's done."

I nodded, just so he'd shut up. Skinny and Stocky were crazy about the food, but honestly, counting down the minutes before I could leave had my focus. I sponged off my wounds with the washcloth. The skin around the abrasions had turned purplish with bruises, but the scrapes themselves could have been worse. Gritting my teeth against the burn, I splashed some iodine on both of them. Next, I dug a bandage out, cut it in half, then wrapped one half around my knee, the other around my shoulder.

By the time I figured out how to use the little metal clasps and had gotten the bandages to fasten securely, intriguing smells were starting to come from the pizza in the oven and my stomach rumbled noisily.

I reconsidered my decision to run before eating. If I ate first, I'd be able to run for longer after I left... Also, the bread and spice aromas starting to permeate the apartment smelled heavenly.

Stuffy was just cracking the oven to check inside when I felt the Weave change subtly in the apartment. Ignoring my knee's protest, I dropped into a crouch to deal with whatever demon had decided to disturb the Weave.

Stuffy had his back to the disturbance, and kept puttering in the kitchen, pulling out a drawer and fishing through its contents. For a fraction of a second, I considered warning him, but if his Sense was so weak that he couldn't feel the shift in the Weave, he probably wouldn't be much use to me in a fight against a demon either.

A small birdlike woman in a dark gray business suit suddenly took form, standing between me and Stuffy. I frowned. She felt hollow and insubstantial to my Sense—nothing more than a typical summon that created a hologram. It had been one of *that* demon's favorites, but not really difficult or threatening by itself. She wasn't really there, just a complicated projection of light, movement and sound.

I didn't want to go back into the kitchen because of Stuffy's neighbors, but standing next to this mirage when I couldn't see what was on the other side wasn't comfortable either.

"Ahem." The apparition cleared its throat. "I trust this is not a bad time, Director Nielsen? My apologies for barging in unannounced, but matters have become serious enough that the Seattle Grove wanted me to update you as soon as possible." The phantom glanced my way. "It appears that I have made your other guest uncomfortable."

Stuffy turned smoothly from laying the steaming pizza on the counter. The pizza was fairly standard, covered in tomato sauce, cheese, garlic, basil and some type of pungent, spicy-smelling meat. The apparition couldn't really affect anything here, but it would probably distract Stuffy long enough for me to sneak off—*after* eating. My mouth salivated at the thought, confirming my plan of action.

"Ms. Miller. No apologies are necessary. I'm sure Andrea meant no offense. Like many of us, she is wary of strangers in these uncertain times. Andrea, may I introduce the Seattle Grove Historian, Ms. Annalisa Miller? She has been instrumental in helping me ensure the continued security of the Spokane Grove since the events of a few months ago. I assure you that we have nothing to fear from her."

I gave Stuffy another nod and a noncommittal grunt. In my experience the most "helpful" people usually had the worst agenda. The aroma issuing from the gently steaming pan drew me across the room against my will, skirting around the phantom of the small historian.

I drew up short as I crossed, aware I'd come uncomfortably close to the strangers in the next apartment. But the pizza really did smell delicious.

"May we speak privately?" the phantasm asked.

"If possible, I would prefer to speak here," Stuffy said, stiffly. Whoever this intruder was, he didn't appear happy to see her. His next words descended into cold formality.

"I do not wish to leave Andrea alone; she still has some difficulty adjusting to new surroundings. I am sure you can understand." His tone changed to a slightly wry timbre as he handed me a plate topped with a triangular slice of pizza. "If you are worried about confidentiality, I assure you that Andrea is very skilled at keeping her own counsel."

The phantasm walked closer to Stuffy. I accepted the plate and retreated to my original spot in the living room, hoping they would both leave me alone and continue their conversation over there.

"I'll defer that decision to you as the director of the Grove." The small bird-like woman crossed her non-existent arms over her body stiffly. I guessed she didn't approve.

Like I cared one way or the other. I would be out of here soon. I poked the slice. The cheese was melted and golden, and a little too hot. I used my Sense to inspect the slice and the toppings for signs of foul play. Stuffy might be crafty enough to try a fast one. Gingerly picking it up, I took a bite. A spicy, salty, and savory flavor burst across my tongue. For lack of anything better to do, I continued to watch Stuffy and the mirage converse.

"Thank you. Please speak freely. I assume it must be something of importance, since sending a note would not suffice." Stuffy sounded even more like his namesake than usual; his words clattered in the room like ice cubes.

"Indeed," she answered, not to be outdone. "The Seattle Grove has tasked me with keeping them updated on any progress you may have made on being able to calm this anti-summoner fervor down, seeing as you are at the epicenter of the current crackdown."

I picked part of the spicy sausage off my pizza slice and rolled it up in some cheese before popping it in my mouth. It was almost better without the bread on the bottom. I chewed thoughtfully.

Stuffy gave the apparition a bland look.

I wiped my sauce-speckled hand on my pants. Messy but flavorful.

"I'm sure I've made all progress that may have been expected," Stuffy said. "OOOI thought the Council was gravely against one director going off and unilaterally making decisions with an event of this scale. That was certainly my impression when the Council removed Director Moore and asked me to take her place. You can be assured that I am doing everything in my power, but explicitly by the book."

I bit down on the naked crust and tried to remember the last time I'd eaten bread. Usually I favored foraging for my own food in the forest, but I had to admit that Stuffy's food offering made me crave eating even more.

The phantasm frowned. "I agree that it was the unwise actions of one director in an attempt to protect this very small Grove that led us to this point, but surely you can't mean to do nothing."

"Oh, I'm *not* doing *nothing*. But I fail to see how any overt action on my part would ameliorate the situation. What is the Seattle Grove suggesting I do, exactly?"

The woman in the image rubbed her arms uncomfortably. "The Council is actually divided as to appropriate action." She cleared her throat. "Some of them agree that it is best to go as deep underground as possible until this blows over. They advocate the closing and abandoning of "suspected" Grove facilities and businesses and the dispersal of the assets and members to new Grove locations, preferably in other cities and states. However, there is a counter-contingent."

Blah. Blah. Blah. People talked so much. I finished off the last of the slice and licked my fingers. There was still a pan over by Thad with six more slices. It held my attention. This conversation could keep going for a while. Maybe I could stay a bit longer.

"A counter-contingent?" Stuffy's heart rate spiked and his voice sounded strange, like he was having trouble swallowing a bite of the pizza. But his was still on the plate untouched, so maybe not. If he wasn't eating it, he probably wouldn't mind me taking more. I *could* just summon the whole pizza and be out the door, but the disturbance in the Weave might actually draw their attention to me. Not worth the risk.

I stood quietly and started edging my way back toward the kitchen, allowing the woman who wasn't really there a wide berth.

"Surely they can't be advocating a head-on fight with the U.S. government. That's madness." Stuffy's voice still sounded strained and clogged. His adrenaline spiked, and I Sensed the goosebumps that suddenly covered his skin.

More importantly, he'd turned away from the counter with the pizza to more fully face the phantasm, giving me an unguarded pathway to food. I walked slowly and carefully in that direction.

"Is it madness, though?" The woman spoke now. "Is it sane to stand still and do nothing while our friends, neighbors, and families are exterminated? Governments who've targeted a group of people for extermination like this in the past were all eventually overthrown. Maybe it's past time that summoners take action to counter how we are treated by an ignorant and intolerant government. Before more families have their parents slaughtered, their siblings incarcerated, and their neighbors and friends targeted for interrogation."

"How much traction can this counter-contingent have? Are you seriously saying the Seattle Grove is considering taking on the resources of the U.S. government?"

I carefully lifted a slice of the food from the pan with the server utensil. Stuffy made a new gurgling noise and groped behind him for the counter. I froze, afraid he was about to turn back toward me, but his eyes remained fixed on the small female projection.

"No, not the Seattle Grove by itself. However, the Grove system as a whole is capable of defending itself far better than most groups that become a target for genocide," she said. "Up until now, we have chosen not to, given the already prevalent negative view of our people, in order to have a chance to live relatively unmolested by the government. After Grace Moore's actions, the government is no longer willing to leave us that option. The Grove leadership can't afford to do nothing anymore."

As long as she kept talking, I'd probably be OK. I bit down thoughtfully on the pizza, allowing the flavors to roll across my tongue and quench my hunger. After everything that had happened today, I understood Skinny and Stocky's obsession with the food better. The triangle slices made it convenient, and the spicy, cheesy toppings were strangely satisfying. If I stayed here while I ate it, I might even be able to sneak a third, maybe a fourth piece.

Stuffy wasn't doing all that well with this conversation, actually. His face had been flushed as he listened, but now it seemed rather pale, even though his heart still raced. I relished for a moment that Stuffy was apparently enjoying the conversation with this visitor as much as I usually enjoyed our little "talks." It seemed like poetic justice.

"What remains now is the question of how we will decide to act, not *if* we will act. As the sole person in charge of leadership at 'ground zero,' with a little savvy you can be instrumental in the Grove's future, the era about to be ushered in. You can influence whether summoners become empowered to emerge from the shadows in this generation or remain the target of every government agency and conspiracy from here to the North Pole. That option, I hardly need to point out, puts the very Weave in danger. If we don't have even the limited freedom we've enjoyed in the underbelly of society, maintaining the Weave will become almost impossible."

I could Sense more humans starting to slip up to Stuffy's door. They wore matching dark uniforms with stiff vests and strange firearms that I didn't recognize. They were crouched, moving deliberately to either side of the threshold even with the door closed. I glanced over at Stuffy. He didn't seem concerned, or even to notice. His attention was still focused on the woman. Two more humans came up to the door with a long, heavy, cylinder. I tensed, dropped the last of my pizza back onto the plate, and wiped my fingers nervously on my pants. Had someone followed us after I jumped out of Stuffy's vehicle?

"Even if you are correct, and we have to find an alternate way forward," Stuffy continued arguing with the birdlike woman, "I am against the use of force. The Groves exist to protect, not to be some kind of tool of vengeance for all the times we may have been wronged or persecuted. People fear us because our powers *should* only be used with great caution."

The two humans outside swung their cylinder at the door. It splintered open, rebounding off the wall with a bang. Stuffy broke off his conversation, spun toward the noise and stared. The summons of the birdlike woman hung in the air for a fraction of a second longer before blinking out.

One of the humans outside lobbed a small, oblong object into the room: some kind of weird-shaped ball with metal on one end. It rattled across the floor and exploded into a flash of light that rattled the windows and made my eardrums ring. The brilliance of the flash left me unseeing, and my ears felt like I'd been plunged underwater. Only my Sense told me the humans were charging into the room, still crouched to make themselves smaller targets.

Any doubt that these humans might leave me alone vanished. That weapon had been meant to disable everyone in the room and give them the advantage. It hadn't contained enough concussive force to permanently damage me. I might be blind, but my Sense still told me exactly where they were; their pounding hearts and overworked adrenal glands thundered in my head in concert with my ringing ears.

They'd picked the wrong adversary to capture this time. They fanned out as they advanced, attempting to block off the exit.

My throat vibrating with a shout of defiance, I streaked forward. One of the humans discharged his firearm, trying to stop me. I stripped the kinetic force away from the bullet with my Sense just before it reached me. It rattled to the floor at my feet. I hurtled into the intruder on my immediate left. He reacted to my counterattack too late. My fist connected solidly with the side of his jaw, whipping his head to the side. His teeth scraped along my knuckles, ripping my hand up, but I didn't have time to stop.

The human to his immediate right tried to grapple me, but I

ducked through his grasp and kicked out with my heel, taking him in the solar plexus. I shifted my weight forward and drove my fist upward into his neck. He staggered back, choking.

My eyes and ears still muddled from the earlier explosion, I only partially saw the flash that sent multiple bullets into the air toward me from the two remaining attackers. The bullets would be tricky to handle, but my blood was up. No matter what new adversaries showed, I wasn't going to be captured today.

Stuffy suddenly appeared in front of me on the edge my Sense, catching one of the bullets high in his left shoulder. It tore into him and burrowed deep, leaving a mess of raw nerves, severed blood vessels, and mutilated flesh in its wake. I didn't expect it; I froze for a fraction of a second. On autopilot, I stripped force away from the blanket of projectiles hurtling toward me; the rest of the bullets fell, clattering harmlessly to the floor. Stuffy crumpled to the floor too, his blood starting to leak out of the ugly wound.

Stuffy wasn't up to my level. He hadn't been a threat to any of them without runes. I'd assumed this was another ploy to capture summoners for nefarious ends. But they'd just used lethal force against someone who couldn't defend himself. That meant a to-the-death engagement. These humans' goal was to kill.

That's what the demon—what Cythymau did. And I knew Cythymau's methods very, very well.

I'd been fighting the wrong way. I'd been trying to fight like a person, with concern for human life.

If these people had come to Stuffy's door peddling death, I could certainly reciprocate.

I closed my eyes and focused my Sense on the hearts pounding in the twenty feet around me. Of the six hearts I could Sense, only two needed to keep beating: my own and Stuffy's. The rest I piled in front of me as a warning to any humans who might try to challenge my expertise in this arena.

These particular humans wouldn't bring death to anyone ever again.

ROBERT

I HUNG up the phone and left Matt's room, feeling pretty pleased with myself. The Feds were a problem for all of us; Nielsen getting picked up by them would come as a blow, but not a shock, to the Groves. I wasn't sure who we'd get as his replacement, but I'd cross that bridge when I came to it. There was a distinct advantage in having a direct line to law enforcement; especially law enforcement still hungry to prove itself dedicated to the pursuit of summoners.

I sauntered out to the main room, expecting to see Andrea seated where she had been. Instead, I found Matt sitting in her place, a stack of papers in one hand and a steaming mug of coffee in the other. He mumbled to himself, something about fourth-quarter projections and option values. Matt was a business student, and his study material could sometimes get pretty arcane.

"Where's Andrea?" I asked him.

"She left with Thad," said Matt.

"Left? With Nielsen?"

"Yup."

"Why?"

"Dunno."

Panic began to set in. If Andrea was with Nielsen, she might be getting caught up in whatever kerfuffle I'd just sent Nielsen's way. I was trying to *protect* her; why in the world had she left with *her greatest threat?*

I sprinted down the driveway. From my right, I saw Rick running parallel to me. I spun and shouted "No!" at him, sending my chastisement through our link and letting him feel how stern I was about this. He stopped short and shot me one of his sad-puppy looks, but I didn't have time. I'd need to make it up to him later, but now was something of an emergency.

I jumped in my Volvo and raised a cloud of dust peeling out. While I drove, I kept checking my cell phone for reception, cursing myself for not grabbing Matt's satphone when I left his room.

It took ten long minutes before I was in range. I punched in Allen's number as quickly as I could. No answer. One other number to try.

"Carlenos here."

"Captain! Robert Lorents. How are you?"

"Robert? You know anything about this bust going on?"

"Umm, maybe. I kinda gave Allen the tip."

"No shit? Why the hell would you—"

"Is this a secure line?"

"No. Shit. OK, then—what are you calling about?"

"I need Allen to call off the bust."

Carlenos chuckled. "Can't do that. He gave the intel to the Feds; it's their bust now. He's in getting interrogated as to his source, which he claims is anonymous."

"Has it happened yet?"

"Nope. They're getting their team in place; they're going to take the bastard in his apartment. Um, Robert? What are *you* going to do?" That last question was asked with all the calm and concern of "Good Cop" trying to talk a confession out of a suspect.

"A friend of mine is with the target. I just don't want to see her getting in any trouble."

"Grace is there?" Carlenos asked, hopeful. I choked for a moment; there had never been a full conversation between the cops and me about Grace's endgame.

"No. Grace didn't make it out of that blast back at the gym. I think you knew that, really."

"Damn. I figured, but you can't blame a guy for hoping."

"Look, Captain, this friend of mine? She's kinda…delicate. Been through a lot. I don't want to see this thing go south, but I'm gonna do what I've gotta do to get her out of there."

Silence on the other end of the line.

"You know I should be sending in backup with you telling me that."

"You call for backup and so do I. This turns into a pitched battle and I don't know what happens, but I know a lot of people die, possibly me among them, but definitely a *lot* of law enforcement. Come up to the cabin sometime; I'd love for you to meet my backup on more friendly terms."

"Robert, we've gone beyond what we should say on the phone." Dammit, he was right. But I still needed his help.

"Look, call off what you can, mitigate what you can. I'm not going to try to break up the bust, I just want Andrea out. If your office keeps call tapes, I'd destroy them." Not perfect security, but the best I could do with the tools I had.

"This friend of yours really worth that much to you?"

"I rescued her. She's under *my* protection. For so long as she is, I will do what it takes to protect her, and damn the consequences.

"You know who you sounded like there?"

"Who?"

"Grace."

Phone conversations are great. They allow one's eyes to water and one's face to break into a half-smile without the other person seeing it.

Using the address I managed to wheedle from Carlenos, I found Nielsen's apartment in one of three run-down-looking, single-story buildings formed into a "U" shape with a courtyard in the middle. A couple of streetlights illuminated the parking lot, and one more had been erected in the middle of the grassy courtyard area; they bathed the scene in a pale light. The parking lot sat at the open end of the "U," already coated in black SUVs by the time I arrived. That was *not* a good sign.

I pulled into the near area of the parking lot, trying to act like an everyday resident of the apartments. As I began to exit my vehicle, two men in black fatigues and body armor appeared, crouched down behind the short fence that separated the courtyard from the parking lot. They carried assault-style rifles and their faces were blanched white, even under the pale streetlights. Their chests heaved with the deep, hard breaths of driving adrenaline. One of them grabbed for a radio; that was bad sign number two.

Bad sign number three was the splintered door of the apartment on the far left side of the bottom of the U-shape.

I brought my Sense up, but I was barely in range of the men outside the home; I couldn't tell what was going on inside. I heard a wild, primal scream, and then gunshots. The man with the radio brought it to his lips.

Taking his entire radio would have been bold; my goal here was to stay under the radar. Instead, I pulled the acid out of his battery and deposited it below the topsoil of the front yard. The landlord was going to have some issues growing his grass out, but that wasn't my problem.

The fed spoke into his radio once, twice, thrice to no avail. He cussed and threw it to the side. More men were rushing from the SUVs; one stepped in front of me and held his hands out.

"Stay back, sir. We've got a situation here." Sir? Usually I rated a "son" from these officious-bastard types. This whole college thing really *did* make you older.

"Oh, I'm headed to that apartment. Over there." I pointed at one of the apartments on the left building, close but not too close to the action.

"Shots have been fired. We need civilians out of this area."

Crap. I couldn't do this without blowing my cover; not this way. I had to try something else.

"Sure, of course. Good luck," I said, my hands in the air, slowly backing away. More shots rang out before the chattering bursts of assault-weapons fire kicked in; what was *happening* in there? I backed away from the Feds, walked slowly around the corner of the block, and then sprinted around to the rear of the apartments.

Behind the apartment complex was a laundromat. I ducked inside the door and headed to the back, keeping my Sense up. In the far corner, out of view of the Feds, I managed to get about half of Nielsen's apartment into range of my Sense.

It would have to do.

Andrea stood in the middle of the apartment. To her right, Thad lay on the ground with a bullet wound, but he was conscious and starting to stand. One and a half Fed corpses lay on the floor in range of my Sense, but the pile of four hearts, formed in a pyramid with three as the base and one on top, gave me a pretty vivid idea that two and a half bodies lay beyond my Sense range. Andrea seemed almost preternaturally calm.

OK, that was a little disturbing. I'd always tried to avoid killing law enforcement when I'd come into conflict with them in the past. That's not to say I'd succeeded; I'd been responsible, indirectly, for the loss of several lives. Andrea, though, seemed to be using lethal force without hesitation.

Of course she was. The scene I felt—I *became*—with my Sense, churned my gut, but it figured.

I both heard and felt the shouts coming from the far side of the apartment. The Feds outside didn't know what they were walking into; they were mounting a second assault. Andrea wasn't moving; her fight-or-flight instincts, normally set to flight, had gone in the other direction.

A Dumpster sat at the back of the laundromat; whether it was for the laundry or the apartments, I couldn't tell, and honestly didn't care at the moment. I dropped it in front of Andrea, giving her and Nielsen cover from the bullets coming in the front door. I took a split second to arrange the paint spelling out "Waste Management" on the side of the Dumpster to say "You're welcome, boss" instead. Nielsen had already Sensed my interference, of course, but I still had to prod him.

There were two agents standing near the back door of the apartment, presumably to contain any runners. There wasn't much time for subtlety; I summoned the back wall off Nielsen's apartment and dropped it squarely on them. It pinned them, but they'd live.

There was a moment of shock as Nielsen and Andrea realized their opportunity.

Andrea took off out the back at a dead sprint. Nielsen wasn't far behind, but his shoulder caused him pain. Four more agents followed them, but as soon as they ran into my range, I took the bullets out of their guns and threw them into the garbage can beside me. They weren't much of a danger to Andrea, now. Hopefully, that'd make *her* less of a danger to *them*.

The entire chase ran out of range from my hiding spot in the laundromat. I couldn't tell what was going on in the pursuit, but I knew I had to get Andrea out of that situation. I wanted to leave Nielsen, but it had become apparent that Nielsen had, quite literally, taken a bullet for Andrea. Odds were he deserved a second chance as well.

Damn me. This was not the way I wanted things to go down.

My Volvo was still parked out front. That was a problem. I walked back around to it. The big man was still standing guard at the entrance to the apartment complex. As I approached him, a Valley sheriff's car pulled onto the scene, Captain Carlenos at its helm. The passenger door swung open as he pushed it.

"Get in," Carlenos said.

I looked at my Volvo, then back at Carlenos. I wanted to ignore him, to go after Andrea, but they were in no actual danger for the moment. I hopped into Carlenos's car and closed the door.

"What the hell is going on, Lorents?" Carlenos's voice was just this side of a growl.

"I tipped Detective Allen off to Thaddeus Nielsen, the man who took over after Grace died. Nielsen's already tried to kill me once, and then he threatened... my friend. I decided that he was best disposed of, and tried to use the Feds to do it."

"Look, kid." Back to being young again. "You are seriously playing with fire here. You think that Fed didn't know who you were? You've been showing up in proximity to reality terrorism events for a year now."

"Reality terrorism? Really?"

"Gotta speak the lingo. Call it 'summoning' and someone accuses you of being a sympathizer. Point is, you're on a watch list. You're young, and no one can say for sure, but you're definitely a person of interest. I've been trying to convince the Feds that you're a target; some sort of internal Grove revenge scheme to take out not only Herman Lorents, but all his descendants. I'm grabbing you right now because I'm here to offer you protective custody."

I nearly laughed. "Protective custody? Sounds a lot like the foster system to me."

"It's not; you'd get a new life in a new place. You tell the story about how Grace sent that big-ass raccoon-thing after you, how we nobly saved your life, et cetera. Tell them Grace is dead, which now has the advantage of being true, and give some basic details on Grove organization that everyone already knows. We take you away from here, protect you, give you a new life and a new identity."

"And if I say no?"

"Don't."

I stared at him until he cracked. "You say no, and you've gone from 'person of interest' to 'suspect.' Frank and I can't keep them off your back, and these guys find evidence where there ain't none, if you get my meaning."

"Captain, I appreciate what you've done. I really do. But I sacrificed far too much to save Andrea from a hellhole of a world, and I can't abandon her. I can't abandon Uncle Herman's place. I'm certainly not leaving Francine. I've made a life for myself here, and I'm not letting the Feds ruin that."

"Robert, the Feds *are* going to ruin it. The only question left is this: do you end up in a new life, or no life? That's it. You step out of this car, you step into the limelight. You'll be investigated as a suspected summoner. No one who's been investigated yet *hasn't* been found guilty. And you actually *are* guilty, though you're damn good at hiding it. You'll go down in flames. Frank and I will have to act like you tricked us, and honestly I don't know how well that goes over. It's a card we've already played once. I'm just hoping they think of me as a Barney Fife and not as a turncoat."

"What happens if they label you a turncoat?"

"I get executed, my whole family gets investigated. My wife gets executed, the kids go into the foster system."

I shuddered at that. "Captain, I can't take the offer. It wouldn't work anyway; that backup I told you about on the phone? He'll follow me if I'm away too long, and that wouldn't end well. You're telling me that I'm going to get outed as a summoner. It's a definite thing, set in stone?"

"If you say no, yeah, it's set in stone."

"Well, okay then." I took a deep breath. Grace's face flashed into my mind, and her voice from a different time, sitting over a garlic-laden table of food. *We're both going to die; are you ready for that?* I'd consigned myself to my fate again and again. This was just one more time, right?

"Captain, I'm sorry."

"You're still turning it down?"

"Yes, but that's not what I'm apologizing for."

"OK... what is?"

"This." I summoned the top off the container of pepper spray on his belt. Not the lid—the top. An unstoppable, aerosolized mist of pepper spray began filling the cabin of the cruiser. I used my Sense to deflect the particles away from me, then opened the door and rolled out of the car.

The big, lurking fed outside had begun moving at the popping sound of the exploding OC can. I might have been able to explain that malfunction away, but my goal here had suddenly become "flashy" instead of "subtle." I summoned the engine block out of his cruiser and brought it smashing down on his cab. The impact was flashy, but I centered it on the passenger side; Carlenos got a bump on the head as he fumbled for the door handle, but was not knocked out. Half a second later, his door flew open and he rolled out, coughing and clutching his eyes.

That would allay any suspicion. Three months ago, Grace had put a bullet through his leg for the same reason; Carlenos needed to stop getting himself into these fixes, really.

Time for the ol' razzle-dazzle. If I was doing this, I may as well do it big and bold, get as many Feds headed after me instead of my fleeing friend and director. I didn't want to get lethal, which was why I avoided calling Rick; that wasn't a line he was capable of walking. I did, however, want everyone looking at *me*.

The first thing I did was disarm every federal officer capable of taking a shot at me; there were six in the parking lot.

I saw another two coming out of the house wearing latex gloves, presumably for evidence collection purposes. They were out of range for the moment, and they paused at the doorway of the apartment, gawking at the scene for a moment before reacting. I needed something a little more spectacular.

So I de-engined every SUV in the parking lot, transporting the engines thirty feet in the air and letting them fall.

I am a summoner; that is to say I can move matter and energy from point A to point B. I can't create anything; if I throw fire, I have to get the fire from *somewhere.*

Rick was a generator of kinetic force, but I needed something to give me that force to use. A set of three falling engine blocks were just the thing; the engines fell thirty feet, but gently settled to the ground as I pulled their force away from them.

I spread that force out into a wide pattern, slamming into each of the four Feds in the parking lot hard, but not sharply enough to do real damage. Each agent was knocked off his feet.

The two from the apartment drew their pistols and opened fire on me, but bullets were of little use. It's possible to ward a bullet against summoning, but in order to do that you had to *be* a summoner. The government fanatics simply didn't have the resources to stop me with small-arms fire.

The bullets zinged harmlessly past me. I was sweating with the effort of keeping my Sense up, but hours of force-ball catch with Rick had improved my stamina out of self-preservation. The armed Feds compounded their mistake by approaching me as they fired. When they hit forty feet, I felt them enter my Sense. Then they were mine.

Summoning on the human body is something of a no-no. I'd done it, once, with catastrophic results. After seeing her neat little pile of human hearts, I had a feeling that Andrea had done it earlier today with *intentionally* catastrophic results. Had I wanted to, I could have ended both of those Feds before they fired their next shot. They didn't know it, of course; the Sense rarely ranges out to forty feet and most summoners don't rely on theirs nearly as heavily as I do. These Feds were seeing something new out of a summoner; no rune tags, no blood, just raw power.

And it was frightening them.

Time to add humiliation. Summoning into or out of the body is unpredictable without some serious medical training; summoning away someone's clothes is a prank any junior high student would respect.

I disarmed the Feds and stripped them naked for good measure. I sent their belts back at them, but wrapped each around the ankles of its owner. I grabbed a rock and flung it high, using its descent to garner more force, which in turn yanked tight the belts, causing the naked Feds to fall to the ground in front of Nielsen's apartment. I summoned each of their shoelaces to my hand. Those I used to manually tie their arms behind their back.

"Boo!" I said, leaning down into one man's ear as I snugged the knots tight about his wrists. He flinched, and I chuckled at him.

Time to get out of here; the four Feds in the parking lot were beginning to regain their breath. I'd made enough of a point. I ditched the Volvo; it would only bring more cops. Instead, I took off on foot.

Last spring, I'd watched Cythymau send a summoning of light to create an illusion. It had been a fascinating move, and one Matt had been working on with me. Matt's derivations of light-summoning involved the light in fiber-optic cables, but I'd been working on a different application. Robert Lorents disappeared around the corner, but the person who then casually walked to the bus stop was a tall, slightly balding chubby dude in a beer-stained tank top and filthy jeans.

I waited patiently at the bus stop for half an hour. By the end of the ride back to the STA Plaza, I could barely walk from the effort of maintaining the illusion. From the sirens going off around me, I knew the manhunt was on.

An hour in the restroom at the Spokane Transit Authority Plaza was actually very easy to pull off; enough drunks pass out in there to make it completely believable. I recuperated for that hour, regaining the energy to bring my illusion back before taking the bus back out to my dorm room in Cheney. I was going to need to collect my things quickly and get the hell out of there.

So much for the college life.

ANDREA

My shoes beat a rapid rhythm against the pavement as I ran away from the men trying to kill me. Ducking into the first alley, I welcomed the presence of its Dumpsters, broken cardboard, dim streetlights, dark shadows, and air of neglect. That meant few humans came this way. I needed to get where none of them would find me.

"Andrea." Stuffy's lungs labored as he struggled to keep up with me and get the words out. "Wait up, please." He was managing to stay in range of my Sense, but just barely. He fluttered on its edge like an annoying burr. On the other hand, that annoying burr *had* put his body between me and a flying bit of metal that could have meant his end.

Completely unnecessarily, of course.

I hadn't needed the help. I could've picked that little projectile out of the air way before it reached my skin. But he didn't seem to know that. He'd taken a wound for me.

Through my Sense, I could feel blood oozing out around the sharp bit of metal in his shoulder. He stumbled to one knee, panting. His presence in my Sense receded as I ran out of range. For a moment, I kept running, but my stomach twisted sourly. Those men had been trying to kill both of us. If I ran away and left Stuffy here as a diversion, some of the men would stop. Others might be at least delayed before coming after me.

A fraction of a second later, the implications of that thought hit me, and my headlong flight slowed. Leaving Stuffy behind as a sacrifice to this world's authorities was a coldly logical move. Something worthy of Cythymau, the puppet master himself. But when I escaped from that Weave, I'd sworn I'd stop letting that demon use me to hurt others. Generally, I preferred to guarantee that by not getting involved with anyone.

Leaving Stuffy here amounted to letting him get captured, killed, or perhaps worse. The only thing I knew about these humans was that they had no hesitation in using lethal force. With Stuffy weakened already, who could say they wouldn't stoop to torture or experimentation? Cythymau hadn't shied away from either when it suited his purpose.

If I left behind someone who'd attempted to protect me (even if rather stupidly) for slightly better odds at getting away, I was acting just like the thing I loathed most.

Piss.

Turning sharply, I ran back to Stuffy's side and pulled him to his feet by his uninjured right arm. His body swayed dangerously once he regained his feet, as though standing in a high wind. Muttering, I levered myself under his uninjured arm. My grip dug into his forearm, but I was pretty sure I could get us moving like this. At least I was until I started forward. He voiced a strangled groan; his face turned an ashen green even in our poor lighting. His knees sagged, pressing his weight down on me. If he couldn't at least hold up some of his own weight, we were cooked.

As he moved, the bit of jagged metal rubbed the muscle in his shoulder, tearing more flesh. I couldn't leave him behind, but we couldn't keep standing here, either. I'd planned to already be long gone.

I popped the small, damaging piece of metal out of his shoulder. It rattled onto the ground. Bright red blood immediately welled out of the bullet wound, drops splattering on the pavement where the bullet had landed. I panicked, slapping my free hand down on his chest to apply pressure instinctually.

Was removing it going to be worse? Having that bit of metal out of his shoulder should have been good, right? I shook my head, trying to jar my amorphous memories loose.

I couldn't remember. My memories of life before were broken, hazy, like strands of a discarded daydream. The horror that came after was much more real.

Unfortunately, so was the blood slowly oozing around my fingers. Too much blood on my hands. Why must there always be blood... I shook myself free of the grim memories that threatened to overwhelm my Sense. I lived. Stuffy lived. We were free for another day at least. And we needed to not be here.

I summoned a sheet from Stuffy's apartment and tore it into long strips, binding his wound as tightly as I could. It just had to hold until I could find him some medical help more skilled than me.

Repositioned under his uninjured shoulder, my smaller frame could just manage to hold his upright.

I grunted, struggling to bear Stuffy's weight and propel his straggling steps into something resembling a fast shamble. Every moment we stayed here, my urgency and need to be gone rose. I wouldn't be captured again.

"We can't be here," I muttered more to myself than him, trying to stave off the panic that threatened to swallow me. "We'll get caught. Past time to leave. You *must* find a way to run." To my complete surprise, Stuffy mumbled something into his chest and actually started to pick up his feet, allowing a faster pace.

Not letting the opportunity pass, I hunched over, taking as much of his weight as possible. Then I resumed my original trajectory, still at a much slower pace than I would have liked. But we were moving. An ear-splitting crash like a clap of thunder came from the vicinity of the apartment we'd just left, and then some marginally quieter banging. I had no idea what other weapons these men had, and I wasn't going to slow down to find out when they hadn't found us yet. If they did catch up, I would just have to fight free. Again.

We made it to the end of the long alley and ducked across the street behind some combination laundromat and deli. The electric lights cast patterns onto the uneven gravel behind its parking lot. The machines inside hummed. The air smelled strangely of meat and wet linen. I kept us out of the light as best as I could and breathed a sigh of relief as the next windowless alley swallowed us.

My life in this Weave was too long ago to tell me what to do next. I didn't want to turn into a cold-hearted monster like Cythymau, but I had no idea where to hide us, or how to find Stuffy the help he needed.

That wasn't true. I knew one place where they'd take Stuffy in and patch him up.

But that was last place I wanted to go right now. Hell, that was the one place where I'd been running from when I left with Stuffy. If I went back now, my ride in that rolling torture contraption, listening to Stuffy's rambling, had all been for naught. I'd be right back where I started, and everyone would know I had tried to run away.

Or would they? I had left with Stuffy. Stuffy was the supposed leader of their little pack, even if Skinny sometimes challenged that authority. It didn't look like Stuffy was in any condition to be ratting me out anytime soon.

Plus I'd be able to defy Skinny by bringing back the one person he'd banned from the premises. That did amuse me.

If Skinny or any of the others turned Stuffy away, then they were just as false as I'd always expected. If they didn't, Stuffy would get the best help there. And if they did turn him away, the woods were still a much better hiding place than here where there were so many people. I'd find a place to stash Stuffy and then go steal medical supplies if necessary.

Taking Stuffy back to the cabin didn't mean I had to stay there. It just meant breaking off on my own had been... delayed, a bit.

I huffed out a breath and hitched Stuffy's weight more firmly across my shoulders as I jogged through another deserted and distressingly open parking lot, making for an alley diagonal from the one I'd just left.

One last problem with my new plan: I hadn't actually paid attention to how to get back to the cabin. I hadn't thought I'd need that information. Oh, sure, my Sense had been up the whole time, so I knew the general direction, but landmarks or the best way to get back there without getting caught? Not a clue.

The obvious way to fix that would be to put Stuffy down for a second and perform a summons.

But that meant stopping again, and we were already desperately slow. I didn't even know how long it had been since I bolted out the back of Stuffy's apartment. The time seemed to stretch out like the rope in a hangman's knot whenever I tried to guess.

Regardless, right now Stuffy and I were slow, and slow meant more likely to get caught. I had to fix that.

I blew out a long breath. I didn't like it. In fact, I hated it. But I didn't have much choice other than abandoning Stuffy. I'd already dragged him with me this far. What was a little farther? I would *not* become Cythymau, ready to sacrifice others on a whim for my comfort and well-being. Defending myself was one thing, but intentionally inflicting unnecessary harm was different.

Scanning our immediate surroundings, I spotted two large Dumpsters in an enclosure behind a mini-mart, backed up against the neighboring building. It looked like there should be a large enough gap between the dumpsters and the back of the enclosure to hide Stuffy behind the left one and draw my runes behind the other.

I maneuvered us over to the enclosure, reached out and plucked the lock off the gate with my Sense, and shoved us inside as quickly as possible. Closing the door behind us, I sent the lock back to its original place. Next I propped Stuffy up against the back of the Dumpster. I straightened and stretched out my back. Anyone coming in would have to go around to the back in order to—oh, piss.

Little splotches of blood shone wetly on the pavement, trailing off where I had deposited Stuffy. I looked at the front of his shirt. The blood stained the cloth a garish red, streaking out and down from the wound, past his shirt, staining his left pant leg, and apparently dripping on the ground. Well, I could take care of the immediate vicinity easy enough. I stripped the blood off the ground and out of his clothes using my Sense. Next, I deposited it at the bottom of the Dumpster underneath trash.

Not that his shirt stayed clean. New blood bloomed slowly across the cloth of my makeshift bandage. I frowned. The wound appeared to be bleeding sluggishly, but I needed to try to bind it further so he didn't lose more blood. Quickly I sketched out Ansuz, Gebo, Nauthiz, interweaving their forms to create one single overlapping rune emblem, the only way I knew how. From Stuffy's extensive questioning, I knew this was not the way that humans here used runes. My only real rune training had been from watching the demon who held me captive. I didn't want to teach the humans Cythymau's ways. Fortunately, Stuffy wasn't in any condition to be picking up my secrets.

I grabbed blood to fuel the summons from the new stain on Stuffy's bandage. There hardly seemed a point in using my own blood when his was already being wasted. I focused my Sense on the rune emblem, and a long beach towel covered in pink stars and unicorns from the laundromat popped into existence under my hand. I bound it toga style over his left shoulder and around his chest. His pulse sped up and his shoulder muscles twitched with the pain of me tightening down the bandage. He groaned and his eyes fluttered, but he did not open them all the way. The grayish pallor to his skin really did not look very good.

I started sketching the rune emblem I would need to find the cabin, starting with Sowilo, Othila, and Kenaz. Centering that emblem in my Sense, I then started layering additional runes to summon the light reflections that would make my rudimentary topographical map. The layered runes acted like a filter for my Sense, allowing me to build a three-dimensional model with the returned light. It recreated the current topography, complete with rooftops, vehicles and roads. When I was done, I had a small hologram of the suburbs in front of me, which slowly melted away into country roads, and finally the winding drive to Skinny's cabin.

Using my holographic map, I could see which streets were

crawling with small vehicles or people. The men in black suits clustered around the apartment much to my south. Good enough. I could see where to take us, at least. Once we reached the forest, I could live undetected for years if necessary. This concrete hive of humanity was the worst place to be trapped.

Using my Sense, I checked for anyone outside the enclosure. All clear. Time to make for the city limits to our north. Fortunately, Stuffy did not live that far inside the city limits, and there were wide expanses of farmland between us and the cabin road. Once we got out of the immediate vicinity, it would be much easier to avoid any stray humans.

I crouched down in front of Stuffy. "Hey, we need to get moving again," I said. No response. I put my hand on his right shoulder and gave it a gentle shake. "Oy. Stuffy. We need to go." Still nothing. Wait a second, though. He didn't actually call himself Stuffy. The others called him something else. What was it, again? My brow wrinkled with frustration. I leaned forward so that my mouth was right next to his ear, since I couldn't yell or risk bringing unwanted attention.

"Wake up. We have to get out of here and get you somewhere safe." It went against the grain, but I ground it out between clenched teeth anyway: "Please."

Piss and shit.

His eyelids fluttered but he didn't open them. I put my hand to his forehead. His skin felt possibly a little cooler than mine, but not clammy. I thought that was probably a good thing, but I was new to this whole trying-to-rescue-people thing. I hadn't done that since... The small, pixie-like disguise Cythymau had used on our first meeting danced in my mind's eye. Couldn't think of that now.

Stuffy's normal appellation was something a lot more officious sounding. I'd hated it from the very first time I heard it. Something to do with the very repressive summoning castes here... Oh yes. That was it. "Spokane Grove Director Thaddeus Nielsen, you must get up. You have responsibilities to your Grove members." I didn't really know if he did or not, but it sounded like something he would say.

To my great relief, he reacted to the words. He was trying to stumble to his feet before he even had his eyes all the way open. I hurriedly took my position under his right arm, supporting his weight so he wouldn't topple over. He was upright, and I had an idea where we were headed. It wasn't going to get any better than this until we got out of the suburbs.

I unlocked the enclosure using my Sense and shouldered open the door, pushing our way out quietly. My hands were full trying to keep Stuffy moving; I replaced the lock with my Sense and took my first labored steps down the alley, supporting all of Stuffy's mass. He was rapidly becoming an unwieldy counterweight. His feet seemed to have trouble keeping up the shambling jog we'd managed before. If he couldn't stay alert, he was a lot worse off than I'd first realized, but I did still have some options.

I could barely believe that I was considering pulling them out for Stuffy—Nielsen's—sake. I'd sworn Cythymau's secrets would go to the grave with me. His magics were tainted. But I hadn't realized that people hunted summoners here. I wouldn't—*couldn't*—teach the knowledge I had. It was not something to be shared. But the evilest demon's magic could occasionally be used to protect. Even I knew that. It's just that usually there was a price. A high price.

Cythymau's voice floated through my mind. "Are you sure you want to save them? Even if it costs everything you have?"

I shuddered. I felt as though when I invoked his magics, used the skills that Cythymau had taught, that I invited him to exact another price from this Weave. To extract another price out of me, who had already paid with everything I had for what seemed like an eternity. But I would be the one using them this time. Not Cythymau. And I would not demand payment.

But still, the traces would be in the Weave, if anyone knew how to look. I doubted anyone in this Weave would hold that knowledge, but Visitors were a whole other matter. Better not to risk bringing this Weave to something's attention. I'd only use it if Stuf—Nielsen absolutely could not go on, and we were in imminent danger. So far, I hadn't seen any of the men who attacked us, but I didn't let that fool me. They were out there, and they were looking for us. It was only a matter of time.

EXHAUSTED, sweaty, my back and legs screaming in pain, I dragged Nielsen and myself through the straggling remnants of town and into a ditch that ran parallel between the roadway and the fields to our right. We should be able to follow it until we reached the foothills of the mountains where Skinny's cabin sat.

Several miles ago, I'd given up on propping him up from the right. I'd hunched over and levered myself underneath him, and now carried him piggy-back style. I stole all of the energy from the surroundings that I could to help keep him up there, but since that was mostly a light breeze and the occasional momentum from a confused squirrel or owl, we were moving no faster than a crawl.

I was good at enduring. I'd had lots of practice. It was the only thing that kept me snatching the little bits of energy with my Sense and putting one foot in front of the other. I was completely unaware of anything outside the twenty-foot ring of my Sense, my entire being focused on my slow trudge and not dropping Nielsen. His skin had gone cool a while ago; I'd summoned a blanket, wrapping him up in it sausage style. But I still worried. We had several miles to the cabin. He responded when I goaded him with his Grove responsibilities, but I wasn't sure, with our pace, that trying to get back to the cabin had been a good call. I didn't have any other ideas.

Even Cythymau's forbidden learning wouldn't provide medical care. That hadn't been high on the demon's priority list. But it could provide speed, and we were in the unpopulated fields between the city and the mountains. Sighing, I crouched and let Nielsen slide off my back so that he was resting seated against the side of the ditch with his legs splayed out in front of him.

Closing my eyes, I reluctantly drew the entwined runes into the dirt by my feet that would link my Sense back to Cythymau's world and exchange the field's sandy, dry soil for the runed stone dagger that changed my life so long ago. My skin crawled with remembered pain, the scoring heat as Cythymau traced it over my forehead, drawing the rune emblem that had tied us for so long. I powered the summon and felt the dagger's unwelcome weight in my hand.

A cloud slipped from its position over the moon, casting silvery light over where I huddled with Nielsen sprawled beside me. The runes accused me from where I'd etched them into the earth. Hastily I swept my sneaker over them.

I had hoped never to hold this artifact ever again. My hand prickled where it touched the engraved stone. *Please let him be conscious enough to help me with this, one last summon before the cabin.* I bit my lip. Once he knew I had this thing and could use it, he'd never stop hounding me. But his skin was chalky, with two high bright points of fever on his cheekbones.

In trying to save him, I'd already busted every single one of my resolutions since being brought to this Weave. I wouldn't become Cythymau. I would kill myself first. And since Nielsen had stepped in front of me thinking he was providing me protection, I owed it to him to at least try to get him back among his friends. I frowned. Friends didn't seem quite right. Allies, then.

Whatever.

"Director Nielsen," I intoned officiously, "one of your Grove subordinates requires your immediate assistance. Right now."

He mumbled something unintelligible. I moved closer, allowing him to brace his weight on my already aching shoulder. He stumbled to his feet and stood there in front of me for a moment. Ridiculously, since I was about to wield it, I hid the dagger behind my back.

He shook his head, obviously trying to clear his senses. He looked up and only then seemed to realize who had addressed him. "Andrea? Who needs help?"

He paused. "Are you...um...err...asking me for help?" He stared at me as he asked, as though I had just grown another head in front of him and he didn't quite believe it or something.

Was I? I supposed that might be a fair interpretation of my words. But only because I was trying to save him, too. I hadn't been sure how much of our escape he was actually conscious for. It must have seemed like some kind of bizarre, delirious dream. He definitely had the fever.

I pointed at the bloody bandage on his chest. "We need to get back to the cabin so you can get that treated. But I can't carry you anymore. I need your help with a different summons, so I can get us back to the cabin."

"Oh," he said, his brow wrinkling in confusion. "You need help summoning? I don't know if I can power anything right now. I'm a little light-headed, actually. But I'm willing to try. Definitely," he added, when I didn't immediately respond.

I threw a hand up asking for silence. I thought I'd heard—

Whoomph.

The large Cornuprocyon Skinny called Rick landed a short distance away and regarded us, his coat bristling. I tensed, watching it warily. Great. This was the last thing I needed today. Nielsen's right hand still rested on my shoulder; the pommel of the stone dagger dug into my fingers and the small of my back. No doubt Skinny had sent him to locate me like some kind of over-hyped hunting dog. I didn't want a full-on fight with this thing.

The *whoomph* sounded again as Rick leaped and landed closer to us. I expected that if he attacked one of us it would be me, seeing as I had run away and all, but when the Cornuprocyon released a blast of kinetic energy, it was clearly meant to barrel into Nielsen, narrowly missing me, but tearing Nielsen away from me and knocking him flat. I redirected it with my Sense, noticing that it was hardly full strength. Rick must have been sent out to find and not kill. That was a little reassuring, I supposed, but not really. I hated anyone who tried to confine me. But Skinny and the Cornuprocyon went everywhere together. If it was here, Skinny should be nearby. I could use his help getting Nielsen back to the cabin *without the dagger.*

Rick huffed out a breath in what sounded suspiciously like disapproval and lumbered closer. I stared. Cornuprocyons *didn't* walk. They pounced on their prey suddenly from above, or blasted it with force. What the heck was this thing up to?

While I stayed frozen, exhausted and dumbfounded, the Cornuprocyon slowly sidled up right in front of us. Once he was in the range of my Sense, I looked for signs he was readying an attack—he could impale us by lunging, release bursts of kinetic force, leap suddenly, or even try to claw one of us. He got right up next to us and crouched to put his large face and snout on level with us in a manner that would have been comical in other circumstances. Involuntarily, I took a step backward. Nielsen, dependent on me for his balance, took the step with me to avoid falling over.

The Cornuprocyon rumbled, putting his nose right next to Nielsen, who also froze. Rick snuffled; Nielsen toppled over, landing on his butt and skidding about two feet. Or at least that's what seemed to happen. A fraction of a second too late, I realized the Cornuprocyon had judged he wouldn't need much to knock Nielsen over, and essentially let out a sneeze of kinetic force.

Rick proceeded to place that large snout between us and waggle it, so I backed up. After he'd done that a few times, Nielsen was sitting by himself several feet off. The gigantic beast settled deliberately down on its haunches between us, rumbling rather menacingly at Nielsen. Rick's large, spiky back loomed in front of me, so I circled to try to get around where I could at least see Nielsen. The forest of quills circled with me, always ending up between me and Nielsen, while Rick continued to vibrate threateningly.

After we had done this dance for a few moments, I bit my lip in consternation. The Cornuprocyon was essentially herding me, keeping itself between me and Nielsen. Rick directed another small kinetic blast of displeasure at Nielsen, and this time, I stole it with my Sense. I skidded to a halt in front of Nielsen and spread my arms wide.

"Hey," I yelled at Rick, "Stop it! He's already hurt."

The Cornuprocyon looked back and forth between us, confused.

"Where's Skinny?" I demanded.

It cocked its head at me.

Oh, piss. It probably didn't even understand half of what I'd said.

Obviously it had picked up on the fact that I didn't like it blasting Nielsen with force. Not much more than that.

"Where's Skinny?" I reiterated. "He needs to get his ass over here, because I'm a bit cheesed off right now."

Rick shook himself and lumbered toward me at a slow walk. Then, just as freakily as before, it started trying to herd me away from Nielsen again. "Stop that," I snapped, then paused. If I assumed it was engaging in this bizarre behavior because it actually wanted me to follow it, instead of just having a mindless desire to eat me, this might actually be useful. I eyed it distrustfully.

Cornuprocyons could be controlled, but they fed on summoners. That was a fact. And Skinny didn't have a full bond with this one. Heck, even I could feel a slight tug on my Sense when I was near the giant creature. That didn't mean I trusted it.

"You want me to come with you?" I asked, braced to have to fight at any minute.

The Cornuprocyon's whole frame shivered and bounced in excitement when I asked the question. Then, in what I took to be an answer, it started trying to herd me away from Nielsen with renewed vigor.

"Nielsen is hurt. He comes too," I said.

Rick's quills immediately stood up on end as he rumbled in disapproval.

"Nielsen comes, or I don't." I crossed my arms over my chest and glared straight into the beast's gleaming red eyes.

It whined and shook its head in distress.

I held firm. "Both of us go, or neither of us do," I repeated.

The Cornyprocyon rolled and brought its head right up next to me in what could only be called a beseeching, puppy-dog manner.

This beast was like no other Cornuprocyon I'd met. There was no doubt now; it had understood what I'd said and was trying to get me to change my mind.

"I mean it."

The Cornuprocyon huffed out a long-suffering sigh and rolled onto its feet. It leaped a small distance away and then waited, looking at me over its shoulder.

I guessed that meant I'd won.

I looked down at the runed dagger still in my hand. This wasn't needed, for now. I bent quickly, drew the runes, blooded the figure, and sent the dagger back where I'd found it. A small puff of dirt settled on the ground where it had been.

Shouldering Stuffy's awkward weight once more, I heaved a sigh. With the Cornuprocyon's kinetic leaps to help, we should get wherever the Cornyprocyon was headed in short order. I just hoped for Nielsen's sake that was the cabin, or somewhere else with medical supplies. At this point, I was too exhausted to even try to guess whether Skinny would be waiting, expecting to be greeted like a hero. He apparently liked that kind of thing.

ROBERT

I KNEW something was wrong as soon as I saw the cop standing at the front door of the bus. Directly beside him stood Jeremy, my former SARTWAP partner. My throat went dry as the line to disembark progressed. My illusion had yet to be tested at this level of scrutiny.

Still, the balding, drunken Spokane Transit Authority traveler, complete with scruffy facial hair, received no more than a cursory glance from my partner as the cop waved me off the bus and onto the pavement next to the Pence Union Building.

As soon as I stepped off the bus, I looked to my left, up the hill to the red brick monstrosity of a building that was Streeter Hall. The parking lot of the dorm itself was filled with law enforcement officers, most of which were manning a yellow tape line cordoning off Streeter from the rest of the world. Cop cars from the EWU police, the Cheney police, the familiar Spokane County Sheriff's office, and the black, unmarked SUVs parked in the street outside the dorm blocked in the student vehicles in their actual parking spaces.

Most importantly, the Feds were shuttling boxes in and out of a van. I couldn't see the red evidence tape sealing them shut, but I knew it was there. Those were my belongings, and the Feds were already loading them up.

A perimeter had been set up around the dorm, and so the street in between the PUB and my temporary home was filled with students in states of dress ranging from bathrobes to fuzzy pajamas to fully clothed. All of them gawked at the spectacle.

Perfect. I could almost hear Grace's sardonic tones. I took a moment to wish for her presence, once again. Futile. Instead, I steeled myself.

The Spokane Transit Authority is not exactly the fastest method of transportation in the world. Add that to my power nap in the Plaza, and by the time my bus arrived back at the PUB, the Feds had gotten a several-hour head start on my getting back to Cheney. And, of course, SARTWAP. The student patrols blended in, but I already knew the faces. I didn't see Clem himself, though I wish I'd been a fly on the wall when that pompous ass heard about me. As it was, his minions were scouring the campus along with law enforcement, looking for the former mole in their organization.

I was pretty sure that the televisions across campus would be plastered with images of my face and nigh-hysterical reporters declaring my scuffle with the Feds as a "Sign that the End was Nigh" or some such.

Cheney wasn't the wisest place for me.

Even with my power nap, my knees had started to wobble. The effort of keeping my illusion up pulsed pain behind my temples like the most sadistic drumbeat ever imagined. Every step off the bus caused me to draw a panting breath, and I had to grit my teeth as the sun assaulted my light-based construct, forcing me to double down on my effort. I had maybe a couple minutes more of this before I simply collapsed; if the Feds found me now, there was no way I'd be able to engage them meaningfully.

Still, all my most valued—and useful—possessions were in my dorm room. A box of notes, left by my Uncle Herman, which I'd been slowly putting together. Last spring, I'd even managed to summon Uncle Herman's spirit, though I'd done some pretty nasty damage to the Weave when I did it. He'd set me on the road to decoding those notes, getting me more comfortable with the shifting between worlds.

Also included in my most valued possession was the Grove Book given to me by Grace. A book that recorded her family's guardian spirits, and the specific rune sets to summon them. A book left to me, by her, in case of emergency. I wasn't sure how her ancestors would react if someone who *wasn't* a Moore called them in from the afterlife, but at some point I might need to take the chance.

Most importantly, she'd put rune sets in that book for me to summon help in case of emergency. It had been a precaution of hers before our big fight with Rick last year; now I was in an emergency, and I needed every ounce of help I could get.

This wasn't going to be easy.

I had no idea whether the one box I was after—the one containing Uncle Herman's old summoning notes and Grace's Grove Book—was already loaded into the van, but I had to assume that it was. That box was a bonanza for the Feds; it would have been the first thing they'd looked for, and I was betting it was the first thing they'd secured.

So. Box in the van. No appreciable cover anywhere within forty feet of the vehicle—no nooks, crannies, or buildings to hide in. And after one fight with the Feds and hours of maintaining an illusion, no energy for a confrontation. The direct approach wouldn't help me now.

What would Grace do?

This was her type of situation. Energy reserves depleted, on her knees with the weakness of it, she'd taken out a powerful demon and an entire army of his minions. Surely if she could do that, I could move one measly box out of a van. So how would she do it?

First problem—I needed cover. If I wanted to try anything, I needed to be in a place where no one could see me. Since I couldn't get the van in range of my Sense, anything I tried would have to be an old-school rune-based summoning.

Mentally, I kicked myself for not seeing this coming. If this had to be a rune job anyway, there was no use coming here. I should have thought of using runes *before* stepping into the middle of an investigatory hot-spot, but I spent so much time relying on my Sense that using runes hadn't even occurred to me. I could hear Grace nagging me for my stupidity and shook my head. No time to punish myself now; I just needed to get the job done.

The PUB was largely devoid of people; presumably they were mingling with the crowd, watching my belongings get packed away. I entered the PUB and immediately ducked into one of the many alcoves in that building. I stepped in looking like a balding, drunk STA patron, and stepped out in the guise of an overweight college kid. I couldn't hold it for long, but I didn't have to. All I had to do was make it to the music building.

In high school, I'd found safety in the band room. The normal halls of the high school teemed with people willing to scoff at me, to make me feel less of myself. In the band room, my saxophone could keep me company, could sing praises to me in a voice that only I could draw forth. The band room stood as something of a sanctuary.

Now that I was in college, there was an entire *building* of such sanctuary.

I took the trek across campus as quickly as I could without being conspicuous. I hadn't been wrong about my face being everywhere; posters had been tacked to bulletin boards, showing (of all things) the school photograph from my last year of high school. Campus cops patrolled the brick pathways, looking at students with the expression of men who didn't expect to find anything.

And yet the students went on. Most of them treated the sudden flood of law enforcement as nothing more than a mild nuisance, and strode past them on their way to class, or lunch, or the library, or wherever. It amazed me, once again, how life for everyone *not* me simply... went on.

The effort of maintaining my illusion felt like a thousand nails driving into my brain, but I gritted my teeth and held it until entering the familiar territory of the music hall. The department was equipped with sealed-in, sound-insulated practice rooms. Lockable, no windows, and a sound buffer—they were the closest thing I had to a fortress. Once inside, I twisted the lock. Alone at last, I let my illusion vanish. The nails receded from my brain, leaving me feeling light-headed and slightly giddy with relief.

The practice room was nothing more than a closet with a chair and an old, upright piano. On top of the piano was a notepad, but I didn't see a pen around. I don't carry runes with me; if I run into a situation, my Sense is usually enough to get me out. In short, I had paper, but nothing to inscribe my runes with.

Improvisation time. The pianos in the practice rooms are relics of the sixties. They're not impressive collector's pieces by any stretch of the imagination, but they're still kept meticulously in tune by the music department. To look at him, the old piano in this room was a normal, wooden, upright piano, battered by use. But generations of music students had used him to create beauty. If he could talk, he could give us a history of melodies from the fingers of hundreds. He was a blue-collar workhorse of the sublime, a beat-up shell over a flawless harmonious core.

So I winced at my sacrilege as I opened the piano and broke one of his hammers free from the forest within. I made sure to pull a low-A-flat hammer, a note seldom used, but I was still ruining the perfect ability of this instrument to create sound. I whispered an apology to the old man as I did it.

The broken wood of the hammer's attached dowel cut into the foam sound insulation tile in the booth easily enough. I scratched the runes onto the wall. I needed something pretty specific, and I didn't know the exact location of it. The phrase I used was therefore lengthier than most, and described the box in several different ways, just to make sure I got the right one.

I had no blood other than mine, so mine it would have to be. I scratched the shattered end of the dowel into the back of my hand. It hurt more than my perhaps overblown masculinity will allow me to admit, but it freed enough of my blood to coat the runes.

Then I leaned against the wall, my bloody hand resting on the runes. My mind rebelled at the idea of bringing my Sense back up. My instinct to avoid the pain I knew would come with it warred with my conscious knowledge that I absolutely needed this. I took several deep breaths, gained control of my monkey brain, then brought my Sense up.

A thousand needles pierced my head, dropping me to my knees. I kept my hand on the runes, but my arm now extended up past my head, and my torso slumped into the wall. Focus. I needed to push past the pain and focus on the runes, on the box at the other end of them.

My Sense brought its stream of awareness hammering through my brain. I became everything within forty feet. All of a sudden, the music coming from other practice rooms, sealed to prevent this very problem, hit my musician's mind in a cacophony. Each was surely lovely in its own right, but I could not hear the trees because of the overwhelming rush of the forest.

Focus. Deep breaths.

Using runes is never easy for me, but doing it with a torrent of noise and in excruciating pain is almost impossible. Almost. I sought the runes out with my Sense, the blood pulsing them to life. I forced my Sense into them, slowly crushing my awareness into that small phrase, and finding its target on the other side. I grabbed it, pulled it through.

The box appeared beside me, and I passed out on top of it.

I HONESTLY DO NOT KNOW how long I spent sprawled on my box of summoner's relics in the practice room. The practice room nap is a long-respected music student's tradition, though, and I was left undisturbed. I awoke to the pain in my hand, and looked down to see pus forming around the cut I'd put in my flesh. My blood on the wall had dried to a crusty brown.

Most importantly, my box of notes and Grace's Grove Book were all there. Now the exit.

I'd had some rest, at least. It must not have been enough, though, because bringing my Sense up brought the stabbing nail-pains along with it. No way could I hold an illusion up for any length of time. I needed a different way of doing this.

I had my cell phone on me, but I'd also seen enough spy dramas to know that it was probably being tapped. It was a cheap burner-style phone, no GPS to track, but if they knew the number they'd be on me.

However, there was a tuba player three practice stalls down with a cell in his pocket; I snagged it with my Sense and made a call.

I knew the fosties' line would be watched. They probably had my whole call history from the dorms printed out. There was a number, though, that wouldn't appear on that sheet. My high-school friend Jake and I hadn't spoken since I'd started college. We'd drifted apart over the summer, so with any luck he'd be low on my "known associates" list. Still, he'd been my stalwart companion for a long time prior to and throughout high school. I hoped he would come through one more time.

"Yo, who the fuck is..." The voice on the other end of the call came through crass and stable, with a hint of surprise.

"Jake, it's me."

"Oh fuck. Fuck. Robert? Shit, man, you fucked up. You fucked up big. Do you know that—"

"That there's a massive manhunt out for me? Kinda why I'm calling you on a borrowed celly. I need help."

Silence. I was asking Jake to become an accomplice. The fact that the line stayed dead quiet for thirty to forty seconds after I said that told me he comprehended the severity of what I asked.

"You don't sound so good, man. You OK?" He was buying time to think. I couldn't blame him.

"Yeah, for now. Look, if you want to steer clear of all this bullshit, I get it. I can try—"

"Fuck it, naw. Only live once, right? What do you need, fucker?"

I took a deep breath and hoped I hadn't just gotten my best friend killed along with me. "I need a lift. I'm in a practice room in the music building on campus. I need to get the hell away from this town, and I need to do it on the down-low. Can you borrow your folks' car, maybe give me a ride?"

"Fuck that, man, I got wheels of my own these days. Let me get my shit together and we can roll out. Be there in a half. Where you gonna be?"

After a brief tutorial on campus geography, we hung up. I had half an hour to kill.

The hallways outside the practice rooms were lined with instrument lockers. Fighting the pain of my Sense, I tried to find a tenor sax, but there were none within the forty feet boundary. I settled on the biggest case I could find, which was (regrettably) that of a French horn.

Undignified, and not the least bit jazzy. Not the sort of instrument I would normally be caught dead with, but it would have to do. There was no time for my woodwind snobbery.

I grabbed the shell of the case only. The internal, padded lining I left cradling the French horn. It was the hard, leather-wrapped wooden shell I was looking for. Much like a mobster with a violin case, I needed storage for my contraband that wasn't a cardboard box half-crushed from a college kid passing out on it. I transferred my papers and Grace's Grove Book to the case. I scratched at the tile, removing the runes by doing further damage. Then I sat back down and waited.

JAKE WAS as regular as clockwork. Not regularly on-time, mind you, but it was a sure thing that, if he said it would take him half an hour, you could expect him in forty-five minutes. When that time stretched into a full hour, I started to get worried. I should have used the time to rest some more, gain back even a small part of the energy I'd need if Jake and I got into a situation getting clear of campus. Instead, I spent the time worrying about him. What if the Feds had been monitoring his lines too? What if they were simply searching all the cars coming into town? What if—

My musings were cut short by a sudden knock on the door. I braced myself to bring my Sense up again to check the identity, but when I heard a muffled "Yo, fucker, we doing this?" through the sound insulation, I sighed with relief and opened the door.

Jake looked at me, shook his head, and tossed me a gray hoodie. It had no decorations, and it smelled as though it hadn't been through the laundry in weeks, but I shrugged it on without comment, bringing the hood down over my face. Jake's eyebrow raised when he looked at my French horn case.

"Branchin' out from the sax? I guess that's cool, fucker."

I let it slide. We could deal with the indignity of the French horn thing later. "Let's just get out of here. It's a little too hot for my tastes."

"Word."

We slipped silently out to his car. It was a red Japanese compact, with some rust showing around the back and bumper stickers containing such wisdom as "A Day Without Sunshine Is, You Know, Night" and "Haters Gonna Hate" interspersed with various graphic representations of a marijuana leaf and the obligatory "Coexist" formed out of religious icons. I took these in without comment; I honestly would have been surprised to *not* find such decoration on Jake's first ride.

The car coughed its way to life like a lung cancer patient on his last legs. An ominous clanking noise resonated through the cabin as we pulled into the streets of Cheney. I looked at Jake with one of my eyebrows raised, but he simply shrugged and turned up the stereo.

If I had to guess, I would say that Jake's car stereo was worth about as much as the car, perhaps more. He had cranked it up, heavy on a bass beat. Over that beat, Eminem rapped about Vicodin or something, but the sound bypassed my ears altogether, finding root in my skull and my chest. It effectively drowned out the grinding of the car's slow, torturous death with quasi-musical ignorance.

Conversation was, thankfully, suspended in light of the pounding stereo. For the first time since the showdown, I could relax, and think on what I'd done. Initially, I let myself be angry with Thad. After all, if he hadn't been such a prick, I wouldn't have called the cops on him. This was all his fault, right?

But as we drove and I let myself relax, that anger ran its course. In its place came the certainty that, once again, the thing completely fouling my life at the moment was me. One minute I'm a college student. The next I'm the subject of a manhunt.

Once again, I could almost hear Grace scoffing. *Brilliant.*

We took the back route out of Cheney, avoiding the campus entirely in favor of a longer trek out to I-90. On the freeway, the car maxed out doing about 50 in a 75, which explained Jake's timing getting to me. Still, we made it clear of the town without being accosted by the cops.

It wasn't much, but it was enough. I settled in and buried myself in the music as Jake drove toward the safety of Uncle Herman's cabin.

ANDREA

THE MOON PROVIDED SOME LIGHT, but not that much. I navigated by keeping the Cornuprocyon's large bulk just ahead of me in my Sense.

Time compressed into a continuous blur. My arm, back, and leg muscles strained with the effort of keeping Nielsen on my back and myself upright, while constantly siphoning kinetic energy from the Cornuprocyon's leaps. Sense the force, coil it into a spring to fuel my own movement, leap forward, snatch more force to cushion our landing before repeating the process. The demon might seem to be accommodating right now, but I didn't trust him enough to try to seat either of us in the forest of spines. Even Skinny, as much as he tried to say that the demon was completely safe, had never tried that trick. That said, if I fell behind Rick, even for a moment, there was a good chance I would crash in a spectacular catastrophe. If that happened, this whole ordeal would be for nothing.

The process of Sensing and summoning became automatic, almost mechanical. I was so focused on maintaining momentum, I didn't realize at first when the mammoth demon came to an abrupt stop. I probably would have kept going, except Cornuprocyons don't generate energy while resting and there was nothing there for my Sense to grab when I reached out to pull it away to fuel my next leap.

Flailing wildly, I just barely managed to keep us on our feet and not cartwheel end over end from the sudden stop.

Dazed, I looked up and confirmed that Rick had, in fact, led me back to the cabin. The Cornuprocyon sat at the end of the drive, looking at Stuffy/Nielsen disapprovingly, his club-like tail twitching. Tough bananas for the overgrown guard, um—dog wasn't appropriate —thing.

Grunting, I used the last of my strength and levered Stuffy more fully onto my back, then staggered my way up the last of the drive. Stocky's minivan was pulled up on the grass beside the cabin.

Light spilled from the windows into the night, letting me know that I had in fact managed to bring Stuffy back where there might be help. Not that I'd really expected them to be gone, but the sight of the cabin casting its bright aura in the dark forest felt more welcoming than I expected.

I was only about twelve feet from the door when Rick huffed and bristled, before suddenly leaping to place himself right next to the outer wall of the cabin.

He brought his head down in front of the door, turned to place his snout at my level, and sneezed, blowing my hair back on a slightly damp wind. I really didn't want to think about what that moisture meant.

"Let me through," I said, hitching Stuffy's increasingly painful bulk up farther on my shoulder and trying to distribute the weight more evenly through my aching feet. "I am taking this man inside and getting him help. Right now."

Rick's tail twitched dangerously, almost taking out several of the funny-shaped dishes and antennas on the roof.

"Also, if you destroy his cabin, Skinny will be super-not-pleased."

Rick stilled his tail, letting me think for a second that I might have won. Then the beast reached past my shoulder with the tip of his nose and pushed at Nielsen where I still held him, knocking me off-balance.

Rick rumbled deep in his chest.

"Look," I said, exhausted, with no patience left in me for this stupid, overgrown carnivore's opinions on what might make Skinny angry. "I'm tired, I'm hungry, and Stuffy may be dying. So either you and I can throw down right now, or you can let me through the damn door. No matter which one of us wins, I'm pretty sure the winner will be in deep shit with your master, and honestly, I think it's pretty clear that I don't care if I piss him off right now."

The beast ceased growling, but huffed another uncertain, whining breath at me.

"That means you lose, buster," I gritted. "Now, *get out of my way.*"

He snorted one last time, but removed his head from blocking the door.

I stumbled the last twelve feet on protesting legs. Fumbling to open the door, I braced myself to fight the occupants for Stuffy's admittance. But as the door swung open, the couch in the living room stood empty. Matt's laptop lay skewed on the coffee table as if he'd gotten up in a hurry.

"Hello?" I called, curiously deflated about getting no reaction to my absence or the wounded burden on my back. Here I was, back at the cabin, and no one cared. The same cabin I had sworn to leave behind earlier today.

Or possibly yesterday, depending on what time it was. My hike out of the city hadn't been fast by any stretch of the imagination. Strangely, that passage of time made me feel a little better about things.

"I need help here. Stuff—er—Nielsen's hurt." Both my eyes and my Sense told me no one was in the front room, hallway or kitchen. They must be in the rooms in back, or outside.

Still no one answered my call. After all the grief Naggy, self-proclaimed den-mom, had given me about talking more and asking for help, this was the reality. Me, and what I could do, as per usual. I should have seen it coming.

I slouched Stuffy over to the couch using a crab-like skittering motion, and tried to lay him down gently. Seriously, my body wasn't used to these kinds of strenuous physical demands, and the fire racing up and down my spine indicated I had almost reached my limit. Stuffy hit the cushions with a groan, so I may not have been entirely successful with that "gently" thing.

As I stood up and stretched the kink out of my back, Naggy hit the radius of my Sense, moving fast from the back offices by the kitchen. Her arms were full of paper. She hit the front room and dumped it all in a pile in front of the wood-burning stove, a few papers still clasped in her fist. She hit the kitchen next, and took a carton of butcher's blood from the top shelf in the fridge. She walked quickly into the living room and sat down at the small side table.

Stocky followed close behind her, setting down several filing boxes. Neither of them spared Stuffy or me even a cursory glance.

"Umm," I tried again. "I could use some help here with him." Naggy looked up. I gestured at Nielsen's pasty skin and bloody shirt.

She raised her eyebrows. "What the hell happened to him? I wish I could do more but... The first-aid kit's on top of the fridge. Use it. There's no time." She sat down and began scribbling furiously. She signed it with a flourish, lined up a tidy rune phrase, blooded it, and her Sense twitched it out of range of me, already headed to its alternate destination in the Weave. Naggy began writing another missive without even pausing.

Stocky started shoving papers from the boxes into the stove. He spoke without pausing in his task. "Took you long enough to come back. If you're going to patch him up, you better do it now. Robert's been outed to the authorities, and the Feds could be here any time. I can't believe they aren't here already." He said it like it should mean something to me. I stared at him blankly.

He glanced at me, shaking his head in irritation while continuing to shovel paper into the flames. "The authorities. Like cops. The same kind of people that put that bullet in Director Nielsen. We're just cleaning up so they can't find anything on us here, and then we'll be gone. Do what you got to do, but do it fast. As soon as Robert gets here, we're clearing out for good. And if he doesn't get here soon, we'll have to go anyway. He'd better hurry his ass up."

I blinked. The men from Nielsen's apartment were coming here? I turned and walked into the kitchen to look for the first-aid kit while I tried to process Stocky's words. The others here weren't going to fight to keep their territory. They were running, just like me. These Feds must be pretty powerful to make three summoners and a Cornuprocyon pull up shop.

I chewed that thought over in my mind. This place wasn't safe either. Stocky, Naggy, Skinny, all of them were in the process of abandoning it. Leaving it behind. Now they wanted to escape, too. From "Feds."

A squat white box with a red first-aid symbol on it sat on top of the fridge where Naggy had said it would be. I reached up and pulled it down.

Cythymau had usurped all authority anywhere he went. Were these officials as corrupt and ruthless? They *had* shown a willingness to kill.

As had I.

I felt the men's heartbeats echoing in my head again, hollow and ghostly. I shouldn't have done that. I just wanted everyone to leave me alone, let me live freely on my own terms. And Nielsen—I couldn't leave him behind to get captured if this place was about to get invaded, too.

I owed him. Sure, maybe not as much as he thought. But he had put his life on the line for me. I couldn't ignore that.

I padded back out to the living room. Stocky was still shoving papers into the stove as fast as it could consume them. It seemed a strange thing for a summoner to do, but none of these people made sense to me.

Naggy kept writing letter after letter, piffing each one off with a different set of runes. Even I could guess that she was alerting other Groves to the recent events or Stuffy/Nielsen's injuries. Anything else could have waited until we left the premises.

I stripped off Stuffy's bloodstained and bedraggled shirt, frowning at the angry wound with its puckered scarlet mouth and ring of purple bruising. There was a bottle in the first-aid box marked "antiseptic", so I took some wadded gauze, drenched it in the stuff, and then strapped it to his chest tightly with a roll of bandaging. It wasn't pretty, and it wasn't anywhere close to what a doctor might have done, but at least it didn't look like it was about to fall off.

I was just packing the bottles back into the box when I heard a car clanking its way up the gravel driveway outside. It was beyond my Sense range, but that didn't stop me from jumping to my feet and crossing to stand by the entrance. I stood where the door would open and allow me the best strike at whoever might come through. I waited tensely for the car to cross the boundary of my Sense.

Once the vehicle was in the range of my Sense, I breathed a sigh of relief. It was hard to imagine that assassins would allow their equipment to degrade to such a rusty bucket of bolts. Plus I recognized the passenger.

The vehicle pulled to the top of the drive. The engine spluttered out. Skinny and the stranger got out of the car. "Thanks for the ride, man." Skinny said. "You can come in for a minute if you want."

"Naw, fucker. I've already seen more than enough of this summoning shit for a lifetime. I'm up to my eyeballs in the fuckin' slop, and that's more than I want. No offense, but the farther I get away from here, the happier I'll be. You know I always got your back if you need it and all that, but meeting your summoner family would just finish making this super weird. Plus, if shit totally gets fucked and goes sideways, I don't want the cops to finger me next, wanting the who's-who-of-summoning or some such jazz. Can't tell what I don't know. Take care, fucker."

"I'll catch up with you after this all blows over, Jake." Skinny slapped the other guy on the back. The stranger waved and climbed back into the vehicle. Skinny stood in the doorway with his hand on the knob, watching him leave, until the car pulled out of range of my Sense. Then all I could hear was the rattle of the engine and the gravel crunching under its wheels as the car pulled back out.

Skinny wasn't really a threat by himself—he was more annoyingly over-protective and proprietary—so I moved to finish packing up the first-aid kit. I supposed I was going with them, at least until Nielsen could fend for himself a little better.

I didn't really have anything in the room I'd occupied for the last few months except a few clothes that Naggy had picked up at a thrift store for me. I should probably take those with me, even though keeping them or leaving them really didn't mean much to me. Everyone here had made it very clear that they preferred when I remained clothed at all times.

I wadded the clothes into the bottom of a grocery bag and wandered back out to the living room just as Skinny came inside.

He looked frazzled, exhausted like me, with his hair standing up at all angles and dark bags under his eyes. He probably wasn't in any shape for a fight, but I crossed to stand in front of Stuffy just in case, folding my arms over my chest to show I meant business. I'd already challenged his pet Cornuprocyon on Stuffy's presence here, so in comparison Skinny wasn't nearly as intimidating.

He scanned the room, taking in the chaos: Naggy busily writing, Stocky shoving the last of his boxes of papers in the stove, and finally Nielsen, reclining behind me with his clumsily wrapped wound. I thrust out my chin at Skinny, daring him to comment on my disregard for his earlier ultimatum. Stocky got up and exited the room, returned with an armful of laptops and a square of cloth.

Finally, Robert grunted and shook his head, turned and walked deeper into the cabin.

Well, that was anticlimactic. I had been expecting at least some kind of an argument.

Stocky walked over with the large square of fabric and tied it into a triangle, which he proceeded to make into a sling for Stuffy's injured shoulder. *Finally.* Someone was actually living up to all their talk about help. When he finished, Stocky handed me a sweatshirt without comment and went back to the stack of laptops, pulling out the hard drives. It took me a moment to realize the shirt was for Nielsen. I carefully pulled it over his head and slipped his uninjured arm through the sleeve. It was roomy enough to leave his injured arm and sling inside the shirt without too much constriction.

A loud impact assaulted my ears. I looked over to find Stocky taking a large hammer to the laptops' innards. Bits of metal and wire flew out from the drives. He heaved a sigh. Naggy looked up and echoed the sigh. She piffed off her last note and put down her pen.

"Well," she said, "I've warned everyone I can that this Grove is about to be the epicenter of an even bigger shit storm. I think it's about time we find a port before that storm hits." She walked over to where Nielsen lay with his eyes closed and put her hand against his forehead. "He doesn't feel clammy. That's something, at least."

Skinny walked back down the hallway and into the room with a box of miscellaneous clothes and an instrument case full of summoning stuff: runed bracers, some kind of handwritten notes, and a small black book stuck out haphazardly from the top.

"Matt, are you done with those hard drives?" Naggy asked Stocky. Seeing as he was the only one that had actually lived up to their promises, I decided to try and remember his name going forward. Not Stocky, then. Matt.

Matt nodded forlornly, looking at the debris scattered over the cabin floor.

"Why didn't you just summon them and your files over to a safehouse?" Skinny asked. "You've spent months on developing all of that."

"You know my Sense isn't strong enough to move much more than one piece of paper at time, and alerting the other Groves needed to be Amy's priority. There's just not enough time for me to risk not destroying our tracks. Plus, I wasn't sure if you'd make it back here before we had to leave. I've got my personal laptop and a backup comp in the van, so I won't be totally cut off. Better to be safe than sorry."

Naggy sighed. "Well, anyway, we're all as ready as we're going to be. Time to get the hell out." She laboriously drew a set of runes onto the table, and then blooded them by dumping the rest of the cow's blood unceremoniously over them.

A bottle labeled "VODKA" in plain block letters, a rag, and a pile of miscellaneous paper rubbish popped into existence on the table's surface. Unscrewing the bottle cap, she looked at Matt. "You're driving the van, right?"

Matt shrugged. "Might as well."

She picked the vodka up, tipped her head back, and took a long pull straight from the bottle. Then she stuffed the rag in the bottle so that the bottom of the fabric was immersed while the majority of still hung out. I continued to watch as she shook it to make sure the rag was firmly lodged, then nodded at everyone. The others started to move toward the door. Matt held it open and motioned for me.

I helped Nielsen to his feet for what felt like the millionth time that night. His eyes were open just a slit, and I thought he was conscious, but he hadn't said a word this whole time. We limped toward the door together. Skinny and Naggy followed us out. Matt helped me deposit Nielsen in the van and get him strapped in.

Not that *I* was going to wear any of these straps, but in Nielsen's case I'd make an exception; he'd flop around every time the van hit a curve.

The remaining three just stood and stared at the cabin for several minutes. I hadn't thought to ask before where we were going, but watching the three of them gaze at the cabin, it had finally sunk in that they didn't expect to come back here at all, ever.

"You remember that time Grace summoned in duck curry from four different countries so we could compare and contrast? An 'education,' she called it." Skinny laughed tremulously and cleared his throat. "She was totally crazy about that shit. It's my Uncle Herman's cabin, but I always remember Grace and her food when I'm here now. God, she kind of sucked at games, though."

"Yeah." Matt smiled. "Never knew where any of her lessons were going to end up, really."

"Here," Naggy said, holding the cocktail out to Skinny. "You should have the honors. It's your house." I blinked. Everyone referred to the place as Uncle Herman's. I had taken Skinny's—Robert's—possessiveness as pure bluster. The grim, grieved set of his jaw as he looked at the Molotov he'd been handed told a different story.

Robert stowed his box of belongings in the van, and Matt backed the vehicle a good way from the building.

Robert stood gazing a few moments more at the cabin and sighed.

Digging around in his pocket, he pulled out a lighter and flicked it to life with his thumb. He touched the flame to the cloth hanging out of the vodka bottle, then wound up his pitch, and let it sail in a long beautiful arc through the cabin's open doorway. It shattered against the far wall, releasing a sheet of hungry flame.

ROBERT

No matter what it is that's burning, there is something intrinsically beautiful about fire. I'm pretty sure it's a holdover from our caveman days. Thag, who loved staring at fire, was probably more likely to build one and learn to use it than Thog, who ran away from it. It stands to reason that Thag was safer, as the fire would cook his food, keep him warm, and frighten away predators. Consequence: twenty thousand years later, we find fire pretty, verging on hypnotic.

The fact that it was Uncle Herman's cabin that threw off this glowing, hypnotic light also helped keep me staring.

Sure, time was of the essence. The Feds were closing in, and we needed to go.

Even so, I couldn't help but stand and stare as the flames lapped away at the last vestige of my childhood. The snapping crackle lulled me down into a relaxed state. I could vaguely hear Matt behind me, slamming the doors to his minivan. But that mattered less than the inferno before me, giving me a brief preview of the hell the Feds claimed was my destiny. This glowing pyre of my youth left me feeling hollow and numb, staring into the flames.

It could have been hours, but it was more probably mere minutes before I felt a soft tap on my shoulder. I turned away from the hypnotic display. Everyone but Amy and me had already claimed their seats in the van. Matt was behind the wheel. Andrea and Thad were on the bench in the back.

"It's time." Amy's voice was high and tense, but her face wore the mask of a comforting smile.

"Yeah," I said. "One last thing, though."

I gave that ever-present bond between Rick and me a tug, and heard the crashing of the great Cornuprocyon through the woods. The *whoomph*, a sound that only a year ago inspired so much terror, brought a smile to my lips. He landed in front of me, his eyes fixed on the burning cabin behind me and his ten-foot club of a tail twitching behind him.

Amy backed up several steps. I scratched his nose.

"We need to leave," I said, slowly. I've never been exactly sure how much Rick understands when I talk to him. It wasn't the sound of my voice; Rick never responded to anyone else's verbal commands. But when I verbalized, it forced the words into thought, and I'm pretty sure he got the gist of those thoughts over the bond.

He twisted his head to the side and looked at me.

"We have to go. The Feds are on their way, and we can't be here anymore. We're heading to the south, to another place. There's all kinds of open space down there for you. I'm sure you'll like it. But I need you to go underground, and I need you to meet me there."

Rick nudged his nose into my chest. I moved my hand behind his ear and stroked him calmly. "It's going to be okay, but I need you to go underground. You remember how you did that before?"

Rick performed a quarter-turn away from me and pointed his nose at the ground. Another *whoomph* sounded, and a spinning cone of force sent rocks and dirt flying around us. It opened a massive tunnel in the ground, big enough for an oversized Cornuprocyon to fit into. Rick craned his head back to look at me.

"Good boy. Meet me down south."

Rick snorted as he trundled down into his hole. Another *whoomph* sounded from within, much quieter this time. Behind the

Cornuprocyon, the earth collapsed as he covered his trail. My friend was safe, and away.

"To the south?" Amy asked. "Isn't that a little general?"

"He'll follow the bond," I said. "Close enough."

I took one last look at the licking flames. I wanted to make a poetic exit, to say something profound. But Uncle Herman had one last trick to play. As I opened my mouth to say my last goodbyes, a light breeze kicked up, filling my face and my lungs with a barrage of smoke. I broke into a coughing fit, as did Amy. It was fitting; my uncle may have been crazy, but he never went much for the drama.

"OK," I said after I'd recovered my breath. "Time to go."

THERE'S an odd sensation to driving at night as a fugitive. The road is filled with travelers moving to and fro on their business, and from the outside I knew our van resembled every other one. Still, the darkness through which our headlights cut a path seemed more of a threat than a comfort. Every set of headlights approaching became a potential cop in the nervous recesses in my mind. My heart raced and my mind spun visions of our inevitable final showdown.

And who did I have with me? Nielsen, whom I'd been *trying* to take down, now lay on the back bench. Andrea, whom I'd tried to save from Nielsen, was on the bench seat next to him, holding his wound and talking quietly to him. Matt kept a blank look on his face as he drove, and Amy, in the passenger seat, stared at her feet.

One mistake, one bad decision, and I'd endangered us all. Out of the five people in this van, and the one Cornuprocyon in the earth somewhere behind it, three of them did *not* deserve what I'd done. I knew I had the burden of fixing it, and I struggled with figuring out how.

From the labored breathing elsewhere inside the minivan, I was not alone in my thoughts.

"So... Plummer," I said half-heartedly. I turned my head to look at Matt, hoping he would pick up the conversation.

"Yeah."

"Why Plummer?"

In response, Matt half-turned his head. "Amy, can you pass Robert his new documents?"

Amy reached into my seatback and handed forward a manila envelope. I cracked it and looked inside.

"What in the world is this?"

"Your new identity," Matt said. "Congratulations, you're officially a member of the Coeur d'Alene tribe."

"I'm... what?"

"By federal treaty, you're now legally an Indian. And we're going onto treatied Indian reservation land. It presents all kinds of jurisdictional roadblocks. The Feds *can* still come after us if they find out where we are, but it'll slow them down a bit."

"Since when do I look like an Indian?"

"You don't. Fortunately, in order to be a member of the tribe, you only need to have a little of the blood in you. I've been working up this paperwork as proof for all of us as part of a contingency plan. We'll hole up in Plummer under our new tribal identities."

"This doesn't seem a little, I don't know, racist?"

"If it helps, I declined any share of tribal revenue. We're only exploiting the jurisdiction."

"Yeah, but using the words 'tribal' and 'exploiting' in the same breath just feels so... wrong."

"You're a wanted terrorist. What we're doing isn't going to damage the tribe at all, and we're only going to be there a couple of days. We need to bounce identities several times through multiple jurisdictions if we're going to do this right." Matt's voice stayed calm and level.

"Jesus, man. How much time have you spent thinking about this?"

"What else was there to think about? It wasn't exactly hard to see this coming. You have a thirty-foot spiky deathball for a pet. Eventually, we were going to go on the run. I figured the way I could best be of use would be setting up our escape."

"Yeah, but... how?"

"My Sense is only good enough to move around pieces of paper or flashes of data. That isn't great in the front-line fights with demons, but I can get a lot of paperwork done very quickly, and insert it directly into the system without all that fuss about presenting proof to a clerk."

My mind reeled at the possibilities. The Feds thought *I* was the dangerous one, but Matt's ability to manipulate the system from the inside should have terrified them far more than anything I'd done. I wasn't the real danger to our society; this calm, docile, red-tape-o-mancer next to me could destabilize entire economies if he chose. I thumbed through my paperwork idly, not reading it. I grudgingly had to admit that I was impressed.

Matt, sensing my discomfort, turned on the radio. His taste in stations ran parallel to his taste in everything else—dull and informative. The dulcet tones of Spokane Public Radio's announcer filled the car, telling us about a number of independent, artistic, and doubtless enriching experiences taking place this weekend around the Spokane area. Some even sounded mildly interesting, though not when compared to a desperate flight for my life. After the arts calendar, though, the announcer switched over.

"In local news, a showdown between the Spokane Police Department and a gang of evil reality terrorists occurred early this afternoon in the Spokane Valley. Police warn that the terrorists have escaped and are at large. Anyone with information as to their whereabouts should call 911 immediately. Known associates of the terrorists, including notably, the former foster parents of one Robert Lorents, have been taken into custody for potential reality terrorism activities as well."

It took my mind a moment to process that, but when it did my blood ran cold.

"Robert?" Amy said behind me.

I didn't respond. My fosties had been taken. People who had no involvement in my "reality terrorism" were going to take the rap. After all, the cops couldn't arrest *nobody* after a brawl like we'd had. If they did, it would look like they'd *lost*.

My hands clenched, released, clenched again. Something had to be done.

"Robert?" Amy asked again. "You OK?"

I was decidedly not, but I still didn't respond. Matt began shooting me quick nervous glances, trying to keep his eyes on the road. Nielsen's breathing was labored in the back, and Andrea had been markedly quiet for most of our trip. I was the only combat-effective summoner here, and even I was on my last legs.

"No," I said. "I'm not. But let's get you all somewhere safe first."

"Somewhere safe" turned out to be a single-wide trailer home on the outskirts of Plummer, Idaho. If you don't know Plummer, just imagine a large lumber mill. Now scatter some houses and a grocery store around it and add a diner. That's what Plummer looks like.

The trailer itself was furnished and the kitchen stocked with mostly canned and dried foods. Matt shrugged when I looked at him. His quiet foresight continued to impress.

Andrea dragged Thad to the couch. He was still hurting, and he looked to be fading in and out of consciousness. Her head twitched nervously to look at everything around her, like an animal forced into service from the wild.

Matt went to the freezer in the kitchen and pulled out a paper container, then slipped it into a waiting microwave. Thirty seconds later, he opened the top and passed the cup to Amy; it was blood of some sort. Amy began writing notes again, firing them off to Council members, asking for help. I was betting it was hopeless; the Groves didn't like to send actual *help* to us, but Amy clearly had more faith than I. Instead, I went for the Grove Book left to me by my mentor.

The pages were filled with runesets for various spirits and ancestors. I didn't know Grace's ancestors, with the exception of one I'd met briefly. The spirits were one of Grace's favorite tricks in battle, but the effort and time it would take me to summon them made it less practical for me. I double-checked to see if Grace had recorded *herself* as a guardian spirit, but no such luck.

In the back there were some scrawled runes. I copied them down on a piece of paper. Amy's cup still had blood in it, so I used that to smear my runes.

"What's that?" asked Amy from behind me.

"Grace left me these runes in case of emergency," I said. "It was her last line of defense for me, a set of runes to get me help if something happened to her. She gave them to me last fall when Rick first showed up. Not sure who they get ahold of, but I figure now's the best time." I sat in a floppy chair next to the couch, a burnt-orange thing clearly provisioned from a secondhand store.

I needed this. Grace had never *actually* let me down, and this was her ace in the hole. I brought up my Sense and began the painstaking process of putting it through the runes.

The summons was, typically, complicated. It had a very specific set of runes for location, and another for destination; two summons strung into one. Essentially, it was a combination meant to both grab a target *and* send it. I am not sure how long it took to navigate my Sense through those runes, first to the target, then to the destination, but my concentration was complete. By the time I finished, I could tell I'd done everything the runes laid out, but I still wasn't exactly clear on what that was.

Still, my fosties were in custody. It was time to bring in the big guns, and whatever Grace had left me as a reserve would certainly be one of those.

Behind me, Amy burst into a startled laugh.

"What the hell is so funny?"

She handed me a letter. I presumed that she'd gotten a reply back from one of the Groves, but when I started reading I knew what had happened.

AMY—

I just picked up this new apprentice. He's a complete schmuck, and a total loose cannon to boot. He's pretty strong, but he's also a reckless, stupid kid who could possibly kill us all in a fit of hormonal spite.

If you're reading this, it's because I'm dead and this idiot has actually figured out how to use runes well enough to summon it to you. We're going to pick a fight with something exponentially more powerful than us, so it's long odds either of us make it out, but you're reading this, so he did and I didn't.

The Groves are going to hate this kid, which is why I think I like him. Do me a favor and try to keep him alive, will you?

Grace

I SANK into my floppy chair, my mentor's message in hand. "Well," I said. "Shit." A hysterical giggle forced its way past my anger. Even in death, Grace managed to make me feel immature.

Amy hadn't been there last fall. *She* was my last line of defense, and it was a political line, not a physical one. She was chuckling, and I couldn't help but laugh. I'd risked my life to get that rune phrase out of my dorm room, and it was completely worthless.

I owed Grace one for that. Too bad I couldn't—

Oh, I thought, looking at Uncle Herman's box of obscure summoning notes. Notes which had already helped me summon one spirit. *Right.*

It was going to be a long night.

UNCLE HERMAN'S box was a headache even when I wasn't completely exhausted and pressed for time. Now, stumbling through his notes, I had to put my frustration to the side. I didn't let any of the others in on what I was doing; I knew they'd object. If he were in better shape, Thad would have probably tried to stop me with lethal force.

The bedroom off the living room contained cots and large potted ferns on a dark, cold linoleum floor. Matt had apparently picked up the folding cots in lieu of full-sized beds for our sleeping quarters.

I made a mental note to ask him about the ferns.

I'd stolen the remainder of the cup o'blood for this and traced out a series of runes on a pad of paper. Grace hadn't put her signature into the Grove Book, so I was largely playing this by ear. I was pretty sure this summons would get me into deep trouble with the Grove, but at this point I simply didn't care. One more demerit on my record would hardly be noticeable. I blooded the runes.

Then I slammed the Weave. Generally, that's a bad idea, because you don't know where you're getting your summons from. Also, it tends to do a decent amount of damage to the Weave itself. This time, I didn't care *where* my target came from; only one existed. I'd fixed the Weave before; I could do it again. This time it was worth it.

My Sense struggled in the runes, crashing its way through our Weave and into another to grasp wildly for its target. I got hold of her for a moment, slipped, grabbed again. Not my cleanest performance, but it got the job done.

Grace appeared on the other side of one of the potted ferns, clad in a one-piece swimsuit. A floral-print sarong sat on her hips, and a wide-brimmed hat covered her head. There was a large, bright flower behind her ear, and her eyes were hidden by a mammoth pair of sunglasses.

Not what I had been expecting.

She removed the ridiculously oversized shades and looked me over. Then marched toward me, her shoulders set and her nostrils flaring. "Just who do you think you're summoning?" she demanded in her most commanding tone. My creative impulse obviously hadn't impressed her. She jabbed a finger at my bellybutton. I twitched in response.

It was good to see her again. Even angry, her presence in the room comforted me. When Grace was around, I could believe everything was going to be all right.

That said, an emotional breakdown would have been absolutely bad form. I decided to go for disarming humor instead. That usually had good odds with her when she was in these moods. I leaned forward and, doing my best country-boy goofball routine, said, "Hullo, Grace."

It took her a moment of staring, but eventually she let out a long-suffering sigh. It wasn't the laughter I wanted, but it was something. I needed to keep working it.

"I can see I called at a bad time. Nice hat."

Instead of saying anything, her eyes dipped to her swimsuit and back. I wanted to say something about the suit—the situation *demanded* I say something about the swimsuit—but I held back. I finally went for the straight play.

"It's... good to see you."

That finally got a verbal response. Grace's hand went to her hip, and her voice came out less angry and more matter-of-fact. "Look, I never really had time to go into it with everything we had going on, but Ancestral Spirits have to sign up for this kind of thing. I never did. It's good to see you too, but you can't just go summoning any spirit willy-nilly like this. How did you even figure out *how* to summon me?"

"Uncle Herman. It wasn't easy, if you're worried that some other summoner might do the same thing." I wasn't about to admit to Grace that it had involved doing a relatively large amount of damage to the Weave. She might be dead, but she'd still find a way to make me pay for that.

"No, Robert. That lovely thought hadn't occurred to me. But I guess it has now. Thanks for that. Since you've got my attention, why don't you tell me exactly how you managed to summon me without a Visitant Pact, and then I'll go back to my 'vacation,' and you will never do this again."

"I can't do that. I mean, I can tell you how I managed to summon you, but you can't go back. Not yet. Please."

Her response came faster than I expected. "I'm sure I'll regret asking this, but why not?"

I had her. I knew I had her. It was a relief; finally, someone could tell me what to do in this situation. Finally, I could ease the responsibility of these people behind me pressing down.

"Because I need your help."

ANDREA

ROBERT REALLY WAS JUST as stupid as I thought. Maybe even more so.

He'd slunk out of the main room trying to act nonchalant, but his heart was pounding, which piqued my curiosity enough to command my attention. He'd then proceeded to painstakingly erect a sound-muffling barrier in the room before his next act of outrageous buffoonery.

He punched through the Weave with enough force to send shockwaves through reality in all directions. Naggy and Matt remained oblivious as he clumsily brute-forced a spirit into this Weave, leaving a gaping, sucking hole between us and the spirit's previous location. My jaw sagged. Not even Cythymau would have opened such a ham-fisted hole in reality. It stuck out in my Sense like a big, nasty, purpling wound. He should have known better. What if something else came through, or it started sucking things out of trailer? I looked at the potted plants, checking for signs of their impending doom. The fronds swayed slightly, but they didn't immediately gravitate toward the hole. Balance between Weaves was pretty delicate, and Robert hadn't sent anything back yet. It wasn't really my problem to deal with, though. I shouldn't have to clean up his messes.

I glanced at Matt and Amy. They were still discussing the events of the day in low voices, as if Robert hadn't just torn a gaping hole in the next room. His barrier might cancel sound, but it didn't affect my Sense. Theirs must have been smaller than I'd thought possible, or somehow totally inactive, if they hadn't felt that. If I gave Robert a few minutes, maybe he'd take care of it on his own. Instead he stood, animatedly defending the stupidest frontal assault to rescue his fosties I'd ever heard to the newly-summoned spirit.

"You want to *what?!*" Apparently I wasn't the only one who thought Robert was full of BS.

The voice reverberated in my Sense. Naggy and Matt didn't even look up. If they had any true skill with their Senses at all, they should have been able to detect both the giant rend in the Weave and the unexpected Visitor. I shifted in the orange floppy chair I'd claimed, glancing toward the door of the small bedroom even though I didn't really need to. My Sense told me that the exclamation came from the small, swimsuit-clad entity he'd summoned. Even in spirit form, I recognized the dark eyes and black, longish hair of his ex-mentor, Grace, from their incursion into Cythymau's Weave.

"Do you really need me to tell you what a bad idea this is?" The diminutive woman put her hand to her forehead and stared at Robert under her spread fingers. She took up so little space in my Sense. She seemed even slighter than I remembered. Much too small to have taken out *that* demon on her own.

"Hey, it's no worse than some of your plans," Robert said.

"Yeah, and we know how well that *last one* worked out for me." She quirked an eyebrow at him.

My mouth opened. Were they talking about the plan to rescue me? Had she just cracked a *joke* with her own death as the punchline?

"Well, in fairness, I did kind of drag you into that situation before you could prep anything better." Robert ended this statement on a self-deprecating laugh. Grace put her hand on her hip and shook her head at him, frowning.

"I think that just makes my point. You like to go off half-cocked. One of these times you are going to get yourself killed. I took the hit last time, but that only works once. My shift on the front lines is over."

She seemed very blasé about dying.

"With the time dilation between Cythymau's Weave and ours, you know I couldn't wait." Robert crossed his arms over his chest.

"I knew you *wouldn't* wait. There's a difference." Grace tapped a finger onto Robert's chest, pushing him back gently.

Wait. The way they were talking, it sounded like coming to my rescue *had* been Robert's idea. I'd always assumed that he'd stepped in to take the credit after his mentor paid the ultimate price.

Robert staggered slightly, unfolding his arms to regain his balance. "Come on, Grace. If I'd waited, Andrea would have had to deal with being Cythymau's pawn for at least decades more, with no guarantee that we'd ever actually get the firepower we needed or come up with a better plan."

My cheeks heated. I *hated* Robert's heroic posturing. Decried him for it. Now it sounded like I'd been the one acting like an arse. I'd never asked him to rescue me. I didn't want help—didn't trust it. But no matter how my mind skittered around the thought, I couldn't deny he'd done me a great service.

Grace planted her other hand on her hip. "Oh, I'm pretty sure anything *other* than what we did would have been a better plan. Who knows, I might even still be alive. I'm not bitter or anything, and I'm glad we got Andrea out, but the plan we used was a piece of shit. I *died*, remember?"

Robert made an indignant sound. Grace cut him off with an up-thrown hand. "It was my own cockeyed, last-ditch, do-or-die solution; I'm not trying to lay blame here. I'm enjoying the afterlife thoroughly. Truly, it's a vacation worth dying for, so there's that. *Except* I apparently now have an occasional problem with snot-nosed kids who don't know how to let their elders rest in peace."

"Hey, I'm not that disruptive. You'd think you're not even the least bit happy to see me."

"Well, despite the unorthodox summons, I *am* glad to see you. But *now* I'm going to be worrying that you want to come join me. You do remember that even with me blowing myself up, Andrea's rescue was a pretty close-run thing, right?"

Robert scuffed the sole of his shoe against the cheap, builder-grade trailer carpet. His heart pumped faster, telling me he was actually a lot more distressed by the turn in conversation than his body language to Grace conveyed.

"As if I could forget any of this? I admit the end part of rescuing Andrea didn't go as planned, but you didn't *tell me* what you were planning to do. I'm still pissed at you for making yourself the epicenter of a nuke with no warning, by the way. That was a low and dirty trick."

"Well, we both know you wouldn't leave without your damsel in distress, and by that point every other scenario ended up with all of us dead or under Cythymau's power. Dead seemed vastly preferable, all things considered. I kept the death count within acceptable boundaries."

"Acceptable to *you* maybe," Robert muttered.

Grace went on, either not hearing him or ignoring him. "I'll be damned if I'm going to let all the time and effort I spent on you go to waste. I had a good life. Now you and Andrea go out and do the same." She gave him a wink and giant grin. "Not that I think you'll take my advice, but try, *just try*, this one time to listen to me and do this the smart way. Plus, you look like hell. I hope you'll at least get some sleep before you try this superhuman act of sheer bravado. You aren't much help to anyone if you get caught. You know, basic stuff like that."

"Speaking of not getting caught..." Robert coughed awkwardly. "I kinda outed myself to the Feds and had to burn down Uncle Herman's cabin." Grace covered her face with her hand as Robert added, "I don't suppose you had a back-up plan for something catastrophic like that? Matt apparently worked some kind of hustle with the paperwork to get us this place temporarily, but I don't think it'll work long-term."

Grace's lips curled into a grin at the mention of her other apprentice. "Isn't Matt's talent for altering paperwork just delicious? He's a bright boy, that one. Those goobers who told him he didn't have the talent to be a summoner should be shot." Grace wagged her head in denial.

"Well, Rick probably ate whoever it was during Cythymau's original attack," Robert pointed out. "So I doubt they'll be belittling the talents of any other summoner-born children."

"Well, since I'm here, I suppose I could help," Grace conceded. "Temporarily, at least."

Robert's old mentor was kind of a kook. I got up and walked closer to the back of the room, intrigued by the dynamic that seemed to be developing between them. Grace and Robert didn't embody the relationship I'd expected from a Grove summoning master and student.

"Regardless of how awesome you think *Matt* is," Robert said, a little acidly, "his hiding spot is only going to work against the Feds, which I imagine is exactly one-half the institutions out to kill us after this last stunt. Do you have anywhere else set up we can go? Somewhere the Groves might not know about? You mentioned your family before or something. I tried the emergency summons you left in the back of your old Grove book, but it just sent a note to Amy. Thanks for that glowing assessment of my talents, by the way. Nice to know that *Matt's a bright boy,* and I'm a hormonal wrecking ball."

Robert crossed his arms across his chest and pouted. Actually pouted, just like a little kid. My mouth dropped open.

"Aw, c'mon." Spirit Grace punched him in the shoulder. "I wrote that right after I met you. You *were* a hormonal wrecking ball back then. Now I know you much better, and you're a mostly-controlled wrecking ball. A wrecking ball I obviously think has a lot of potential, by the way, or I wouldn't have put my ass on the line for you. But I mean, come on. You just told me you're going to storm a detention facility at an unknown location, with an unknown number of opposing forces, to break your fosties out. That doesn't exactly lend itself to any subtle interpretation. Are you telling me I haven't made a correct assessment of your normal mode of operation?"

There was a moment of silence as the two of them stared at each other. A bizarre itch tickled the back of my throat; I realized I might be going to laugh. I cleared my throat rather hurriedly, and was saved by Grace picking up the conversation again.

"Anything other than wrecking ball really doesn't fit. Tell you what. Take it as a compliment. Most people don't have the *juice* to back up a wrecking ball analogy."

"A safe house?" Robert's voice sounded a little strained as he tried to steer the conversation back to his original question.

"Oh, yeah. Things have gotten that bad with the Groves, huh? I have one, but it's one I set up back when I moved to the Seattle Grove, which means it's in their boundaries. It's a great little place up on the Olympic peninsula. Lovely area." She paused and put her hand back on her hip, "Of course, that's assuming you don't get captured trying to save your fosties, and live long enough to use it."

"I'll be careful. I won't get caught."

"Uh huh. Be sure that you don't." Grace reached for something on her arm that wasn't there, then swore. "I can't get used to that," she said. "No rune board. I need a map. I'll show you where the safe house is."

Robert painstakingly drew out the runes and clumsily summoned a map. "You're getting better," she said. "That only took, like, two minutes."

"Yeah, I'm slow," Robert admitted. "It's frustrating."

"No, I mean it. Just a few months ago you would have ended up slamming the Weave to get that thing."

"Yeah, well, some of your lessons actually did stick, you know." Robert shot her a grumpy glance.

What a total lie. He still hadn't done anything with the giant gaping hole he'd torn in the Weave not five minutes ago.

"Always nice to have that affirmed is all." Grace smiled and spread out the map on the floor. She went down on her knees in front of it and motioned him down beside her. "OK, so see, here is Seattle, and here is Olympia. You're going to head north from there on 101. Take highway three through Shelton. The safe house is here, outside the city limits, but still within striking distance of a *truly* amazing little bakery. Once you're on the property itself, it's nice and secluded, plus there are lots of state parks and empty land around for, you know, whatever covert activity you need to do." She got to her feet and dusted off her hands. Robert rose with her.

"Well, I know I can't change your mind, but I really wish you would reconsider this," she said.

"Francine put up with me when I was a real prick, you know."

"Yeah, I know."

"I can't just leave her there."

"I know that, too. Be careful. Be smart."

"I will." Robert hugged her impulsively and then released the summons. His old mentor vanished like a wisp of smoke. He stood in the room, staring at the place where Grace had been. His tear ducts fired and his chest gave a trembling hiccupping movement. He took a deep breath, bracing his abdominal muscles against the traitorous tremor. After a few minutes of struggling with his own breathing, he slowly started fixing the hole he'd torn in the Weave with his summons. He was lucky nothing had wandered through it during his long conversation with Grace. *I* wouldn't want to play those odds, but I wouldn't have dragged something through willy-nilly in the first place. When he finished, Robert poked his head out the door of the room.

"I'm exhausted," he said. "I'm going to bed. The rest of you probably should too. Tomorrow I'm going to go get the fosties, and then we're all headed to Grace's old safe house over by Shelton. 'Night."

I sat back down in the floppy orange chair and chewed over all the information I'd accidentally learned. Robert might actually have half a leg to stand on when he claimed to be my rescuer. Of course Grace still got the final credit in my book, because without her I'd still be a glorified summoning battery in Cythymau's cave, probably with Robert beside me. But on the other hand, it had become very obvious during the conversation that Robert had actually paid a high price to secure my freedom. And now I was thinking just like Cythymau, evaluating my circumstances in terms of costs and payments.

Exhaustion dragged at me. I headed to bed, wanting to escape my doubts and second thoughts.

I woke up feeling less exhausted, but no more sure about Robert. I checked on Nielsen; he seemed to be doing OK, but what did I know? My medical knowledge was about thirty years too old, and had spent centuries being buried under arcane lore during my stay in Cythymau's Weave.

Matt was sitting in the small kitchen, a stack of bowls, pile of spoons, carton of milk, and bag of generic cereal in front of him. He poured the milk over his cereal as he waved me over. I took a bowl and the chair opposite him, then proceeded to build my own slurry of frosted cubes and milk. I dreaded the chalky flavor of the frosting, but the cubes of cereal were better than nothing. I dug the spoon in and scooped some up, but let the spoon hover for a few seconds before letting it return to rest.

"So." I couldn't believe I was going to ask this. "Did Ski—er—Rorobert leave yet?" The words came out low and hesitant, but I had asked. I wanted to know.

"No. Not yet." Matt didn't ask *why* I wanted to know. I liked that about him. He didn't bug me, and he didn't try to pry things out of me. He didn't seem to have any expectations of me, and since everyone else here obviously had ideas about what was best for me, I found his neutrality refreshing.

I had picked up yesterday that Robert planned to confront the men in suits, but I wasn't clear on why. I pushed the cereal around in my bowl.

"He's going to confront the same men that tried to capture or kill, uh, Nielsen and me?"

"Yeah."

"Why?"

"They're holding two people that he considers family. And they wouldn't be in trouble if he hadn't exposed himself to the police, so he feels directly responsible. He's determined to go get them back."

I pondered this. It sounded like this kid just had a complex about rescuing people. His mentor was right: he was going to get himself killed.

I finally raised the spoon to my lips and bit down on the mushy, sweet blob of wheat. Yep, the flavor of this cereal really hadn't changed while I was gone.

I was still sitting at the table plowing through my lackluster breakfast when Naggy came out and took the third seat, leaving the fourth for Robert.

"He's still here?" she asked, rubbing sleep out of her face. She grabbed a bowl and dumped cereal into it with a lack of enthusiasm.

"Yup," Matt answered.

"Good. He can't do this."

Matt shrugged.

"He'll get himself captured and/or killed for no good reason," Naggy predicted, with a jab of her spoon for emphasis. "I already lost my best friend over his stubbornness. Now he's going to throw his life away doing the same thing. And Grace's death will be meaningless."

"That's not true," Matt said. "Grace died taking out Cythymau."

"Whatever," Naggy muttered. "Even in that stupid 'emergency' note, she asked me to look after him. How am I supposed to do that when he won't even *listen*? This is bullshit."

"So go with him," Matt suggested. Naggy rolled her eyes.

"You know I can't. Either one of us would be more of a handicap than a help. Might as well kneecap him while I'm at it."

"You could try that."

She let out a short bark of laughter. "If it was that easy, we wouldn't even be having this conversation."

"True." We took a few bites of mushy cereal in silence.

Robert came in, took a couple handfuls of dry cereal, threw them back, and reached for the milk jug. He drank straight from its mouth, which was gross, but nobody else said anything. I wasn't planning to stick around long enough to need to use the milk again.

"I'm going to do this thing," he said, "and I'm taking Rick with me as backup, so I'll leave the van in case you guys need it for anything."

"Don't do it," Naggy said. "We can find some way to help your fosties that doesn't require you to take on the authorities head-on."

"What else am I supposed to do? Do you have a different plan?"

"No, this just isn't safe, and it isn't right," Naggy reiterated. "Look, Grace asked me to look after you, and you're making it really difficult."

"Yeah, well, Francine? She looks after me too. I can't just let her get tortured because of me. I don't want to be responsible for more deaths. Unless you have a better plan, one that actually gets them out of fed custody, I'm going to do this."

Naggy's lips compressed into a thin line, but she shook her head.

"Thought so." He threw back another handful of cereal. "Catch you guys on the flip side."

He exited the trailer with a swagger that was belied by the amount of nervous tension I Sensed in his muscles. He wasn't any more sure about what he was doing than the rest of us.

We sat at the table staring at each other until Naggy abruptly got up, mumbling that she had to go check on Nielsen. She didn't make it out of my Sense radius before tears started rolling down her cheeks. I thought Matt hadn't noticed, but he looked straight at me.

"You could go after Robert, you know. Maybe between the two of you, you'd actually have a chance of saving his fosties. Amy's not wrong. He's gonna get himself screwed, even if they don't kill him outright, and Grace would have hated that. That punk was totally the teacher's pet, even though he seems to doubt it."

I stared at him. My island of neutrality had vanished. Even Matt wanted me to go get re-trapped with Robert.

"Why would *I* care what Grace would have hated?" I asked harshly, jerking to my feet. Stomping out of the trailer, I let the screen slam behind me. Then I stood outside, at a loss.

The trailer was ringed by the tall pines on the edge of the trailer park. I walked over to them for something to do, and found a fallen branch. It was covered with lichen and moss, and felt dry against my palm. Sitting in the tall, dry grass, I could pretend that I was alone—not twenty feet away from the tin can holding Naggy and Matt. I started stripping the lichen, moss, and bark off the branch to give myself something to do.

Robert was going to go confront the authorities. No, more than that, he planned to force them to give up his "fosties." That meant he was going to try to defeat them. I shivered.

I needed some kind of protection, in case whatever he did brought the Feds down on me. Looking at the smooth, naked branch in front of me, I started peeling wood away with my Sense. The unneeded material fell away, revealing a small rune emblem. I began making another as I thought.

If Robert tried to take the Feds on one at a time, he might even succeed. Individually, he was pretty strong. But that didn't sound like what he was going to try at all. These authorities had resources.

Even if I hadn't been paying the best of attention, I had been around this Weave long enough to know they had anti-summoner drugs and task forces. To take them on in their own territory was the height of stupidity. He hadn't even tried to come up with a better plan to reduce their advantage and take them off their game. No wonder Grace called him a wrecking ball.

As I pondered, more and more tokens formed under my fingers, until I had the full complement. I summoned a thin ring of wood out of the branch, fashioned it into a bracelet band, and suspended the tokens around it using my sense and a bit of wire I stole from Matt's emergency supplies. The forms of each rune emblem shone clear in my Sense, allowing my fingers to find them quickly. All told, there were about forty archaic emblems on the bracelet, and I should be able to defend myself pretty well in most circumstances. I wouldn't be easy pickings for anyone now.

I slipped the bracelet onto my wrist, admiring the deep patterns in the wood. The dark gloss of the grain glistened against the skin of my wrist, and I had a moment of wondering what the heck I was doing.

Was I actually thinking of putting my newfound freedom at risk after several millennia of slavery? For a kid who had barely seen eighteen years in total, and was going in with the stupidest pissing rescue plan on the planet? I mean, he was going to try and take on a superior force head-on and beat them into the ground, which would take a lightning-fast, precision attack.

I just didn't think he had the chops to do that. He might be a wrecking ball, but a wrecking ball's damage rarely has pinpoint accuracy.

Matt and Naggy both said he always did his own thing.

He'd gotten his last partner killed. I didn't want to end up like Grace, no matter how posh the afterlife might be. Fuck this. Fuck him. I needed to take care of myself.

ROBERT

MY FIRST ISSUE WAS TRANSPORTATION. Oh, sure; the minivan was right there. I can't honestly say it didn't tempt me. But I didn't want to foul up Matt's escape plan. I had a duty to my foster parents, but I didn't want the others getting hurt because of me.

Well, maybe Thad. But even he wasn't worth sacrificing Andrea, Amy, and Matt for.

If I took the minivan, I'd be leaving Matt's plan high and dry. No sense spoiling all that work. Matt, however, was not an offensive thinker. Given time, he could apparently vanish us off the earth, but staging an emergency rescue op was asking too much of him. Amy had been in some intense situations with me, including an incident with a wine-fueled maenad, but she was more hindrance than help in raw combat.

Andrea was... a wild card. It was clear—terrifyingly clear—that she could throw down if she chose to. Only months ago, I had considered her only in the abstract. She'd been my damsel in distress, the beautiful girl I would rescue from the clutches of the evil Cythymau. Then I'd met her. As it turns out, thousands of years of abuse and enslavement don't turn you into a grateful beauty—they just make you crazy. Taking her into a violent situation *might* have provided me with much-needed backup. It also might send her into a complete murderous rage.

Not worth the risk.

I began to walk down the gravel road. It wasn't a solution to my transit problems, but it was a start. I'd figure something out later.

Suddenly, an explosion of rock and gravel erupted from the road in front of me. The dirt flew and the rocks rained down. A gaping hole had opened up in the middle of the road. An orange snout snuffled its way out, followed by the rest of my overenthusiastic pet's head, poking its way out from the ground. Rick's tongue lolled as he looked at me, and the earth began to shake under my feet. I envisioned his ten-foot club of a tail twitching back and forth in his tunnel, slamming into the walls of earth around him.

"Hey, bud," I said, holding my hand out. "I see you made it."

Rick nudged my hand with his nose. I obliged him by giving him a scratch.

"You know, I'm going to head back into town. These folks are safe, but I may need a little backup. You want to come?"

The frequency of crashes coming from the tunnel increased as Rick's tail wagged. I took that as a yes.

"OK, but I need you to stay low. Don't come out unless you have to, but be ready to throw down if I need you. Oh, and *don't* hurt my foster parents. You hear me, boy? *No* hurting Francine or Donald. *No.* OK? Good boy."

Rick tucked his head over his shoulder and rotated himself around. His tail flashed free of the earth like a whale putting on a show for tourists, then he was gone. I wasn't going to be alone for this one; that was a good sign.

A COUPLE OF MINUTES' walk brought me to the one block that constitutes downtown Plummer. By this point, I was exhausted. I made my way to the bar on a hunch, and was rewarded by the sight of a couple of cars parked outside. Presumably, their owners had passed out elsewhere, having made the prudent decision to walk or catch a ride home after a Friday night of heavy drinking.

Perfect.

I didn't know how to hotwire a car, but I didn't need to. I circled the building, my Sense up, feeling the interior of the bar. Sure enough, there was a key rack inside, behind the counter. A key with a Chevy logo hung from it; I summoned it. I placed good odds that it belonged to the beat-up Chevy compact in front of the bar.

I was already a terrorist. In comparison, car thief just didn't seem as bad. With any luck, the owner would spend the morning hung over in bed, and I'd get several hours before this thing was reported stolen. It's not that I was particularly *proud* of stealing this man's car, but I promised myself I'd get it back to him. And the situation here was pretty dire.

The inside of the compact reeked of cigarettes. The upholstery was torn and the radio had long since been removed, presumably to a pawn shop somewhere. A luxury ride this wasn't, but on the other hand, I was a beggar, not a chooser.

Then I headed north, back to Spokane. It was time to pay a visit to an old friend.

THE STUDIO APARTMENT WAS SPARTAN-LOOKING. The walls had no decorations, and the kitchen area shone with the kind of cleanliness that makes you wonder if anyone had ever actually *cooked* there. There was a twin bed in one corner, and a small television mounted to the wall, attached only to a cable box. The one concession to comfort, a poufy leather recliner pointed at the television, occupied the center of the room. Another corner held a desk with an ancient computer whose case boasted of the sixteen megs of RAM contained inside. The desk chair had no armrests and no headrests.

An upright standing freezer stood next to the kitchen counter. My curiosity-inspired glance inside revealed a massive fortification built entirely of frozen dinner boxes. That answered the question about the kitchen usage, if nothing else.

I knew that Spokane sheriff's detectives were underpaid, but I didn't think they were *this* broke. Detective Allen lived this way by *choice,* and it showed in how meticulously he kept the room.

I took the poufy chair, pointed it at the door instead of the television, and sat down gently, waiting for the good detective to make his entrance. I'd hoped to catch him in his apartment, but a glance at the calendar above the desk showed that he was due off-shift in little over an hour.

Best to wait.

I rested my head on my arm in a sinister-looking pose. This was not the apartment of a man who wanted company, and I was pretty sure Detective Allen wouldn't be thrilled to see me. No sense wasting the moment.

The problem was in the chair. It was large, and it was fluffy. The experience was like sitting *in* a cloud, but without all the dust and water. I'd spent a short night on a cot; within a couple of minutes that chair had pulled me down into wonderful sleep.

I awoke to the sound of a service .45 being cocked. Blearily I blinked my eyes, bringing the barrel into focus. I woke up much faster. The adrenaline hit me, but I controlled it, channeled it, and brought my Sense up.

Most summoners don't have the Sense radius of Andrea, let alone me. Thad was considered powerful at eight feet. So most cops are trained to deal with rune-based summoning, because relying on your Sense to protect you from bullets only works if you've got the radius to do it. All those beliefs had been reinforced by Grace, who had shown Allen nothing but rune-based summoning. In short, Allen hadn't been in a straight-up confrontation with me since I'd been trained.

I disarmed him by removing all the bullets from his gun, hiding them under his mattress. I added a pile of important-feeling wires from the insides of his cell phone and radio but left the gun and the casings intact, leaving Detective Allen none the wiser about their location.

"Good morning, Detective," I said casually. "It's nice to see you again."

"Lorents. What in the holy fuck are you doing here?" I'd never heard Allen swear. Of course, I'd never seen Allen truly *angry* before, and judging by his flushed face and strained tone, I'd put him there with this little home invasion.

"You owe me one."

"*I?* I owe *you?* How exactly do you figure that?"

"Well, technically not me. You owe Grace for that stunt she pulled drawing suspicion away from you last spring. She's dead, though, so now you owe me. I'm here to collect."

"No dice, kid. She was paying me back for covering your ass, a move which I am strongly reconsidering at this point. There are law enforcement officers who are *dead* because of that little trap you set, and you used me to do it. I owe you for that, and nothing else."

"Oh, bullshit. You think I *wanted* to get people killed? I tried to get you to call it off when I realized Andrea had gone with Nielsen. You and I both know that if you hand me in, the first thing I do is rat on you. We're in this together, like it or not."

Allen stared at the floor as he considered this line of logic. "Not if you're dead. A reality terrorist just broke into my home. If you won't get out, I will execute you right here and now."

"Detective Allen, I'm here, and there's some information I need. That's all."

Three *clicks* sounded from the Colt. He really would have done it—noted. Predictably, he went for his radio next. He shouted a request for backup into it, then shook it a couple of times when no response came.

"It's just you and me, Detective. How's about that info?"

Allen strode past me and sat down on the side of the bed. I stood up and used my Sense to reverse the recliner to face him. He looked at it as I sat back down in it, his face whitening.

"You really are the crazy bastard they say you are. I had a lot of hope for you, kid, but you're a reality terrorist through and through. You damn near killed Carlenos with that pepper spray."

"I'm sorry about Carlenos, and I am a summoner," I said. "But my foster parents aren't. I'm going to get them, and I need you to tell me where they are."

"Why should I help you? Either way, I'm screwed. I help you, I'm aiding a summoner. I don't help you, you frame me anyway. Seems I've got nothing to gain here."

"Well, there's the moral high ground. We're talking about two innocent people being held prisoner."

"How do I know they're innocent?"

I met this with a long stare. Allen looked away first.

"Fine. They're not summoners. They're being held as 'persons of interest.' That means county jail, not up at Airway Heights Correctional. Top floor, east wing. Highest security area there is. They'll be in the pod there. Satisfied?"

I was. I slipped my hand under his mattress and grabbed his clip along with the lone bullet from his chamber, then handed them to him. "Yes, Detective. I am. Here's your ammo back; I can't fix your phone or radio." He took the ammo and immediately reloaded his gun, but then holstered it under his left armpit.

On my way out the door, I looked back over my shoulder. "You know, Frank, I had a lot of hope for you, too."

I left before he could respond.

THE SPOKANE COUNTY JAIL is a mammoth, bizarre building. It rises ten stories above the ground, with the standard narrow slit windows and brick-like appearance from three sides. Like a man-made geode, the south side has a great semi-circle cut out of it, lined with black glass. Presumably this is a form of solar heating, but it gives the jail an ominous, almost fantastical quality. To house your prisoners in an obsidian pillar just feels like classic villainy.

I used the illusion of a chubby, middle-aged woman dressed in a halter top and shorts meant for much younger women to wait outside the jail. She blended in. This was next to the parking lot on the west side. Deputies and staff passed in and out, using a keycard to access the door. The keycard would beep, and then after several seconds the door would open.

I waited for a uniformed deputy of the tall-and-lanky persuasion to exit, and about forty-five minutes later one obliged. He was tall and thin, like me, with light reddish-brown hair cropped short. There was something about his face that struck me as hauntingly familiar, but I couldn't place it.

He left the building and headed into the parking lot. In my illusion, I followed him to his car, a green four-door in reasonably good shape. Using my Sense, I burned a rune into the underside of the back bumper of his car. He drove off without noticing me.

I didn't need to follow him; I just needed to get a bearing on that rune. Even with my limited abilities, it was easy enough to get a general direction. It took some driving around, but I eventually found the green car parked outside a shabby apartment in the bad part of Brown's Addition. The parking slots were labeled, and judging by the location of the green car, I could find my deputy in apartment number twenty-seven.

I let my illusion slip as I approached twenty-seven. Keeping it up was stressful enough, and I had other things on my mind. I reached the door. It was locked, but I simply used my Sense to remove the doorknob, the deadbolt, and the chain lock on the far side. I then strode into the tiny living space.

The lanky deputy had already removed his uniform and was sitting on a ratty-looking loveseat wearing plaid boxers and a stained white t-shirt. He had an unopened beer in one hand; the other held a bottle-opener. Communications first. I took his cell phone from his trouser pocket. He didn't appear to have a landline.

Then I went for menacing. Unlike Allen, this guy didn't know me. His preconceptions came entirely from the media. I put on my best bad-guy grin and bore down on him.

"Hello, Deputy..." I paused, my voice trailing off into a question. He mumbled something, but I couldn't hear.

"What was that?"

"Rosen. Deputy Rosen." The name took me by surprise.

"Rosen? Any relation to—"

"To the Deputy Karl Rosen you helped butcher a year ago? Yeah, he was my younger brother. I'm Calvin Rosen."

Crap. Karl Rosen had given his life during the conflict with Rick last year. He'd been a rookie, a nervous kid just following orders. I had liked him. His loss had obviously had an effect on Deputy Calvin Rosen here. I didn't want to pick on him, but some things had to be done. I steeled myself to intimidate him, even though on the inside I just wanted to give the guy a hug.

"Here, let me get that for you." I summoned the cap off his beer and into my hand. I tossed it towards the trash with a little underhanded flip. "There you go. Drink up, Deputy."

He stared at his beer, and the hand holding it began to shake.

"I'm heading to the top floor of your jail. I'll be leaving you without communication, and I'll be leaving you tied up. I just need your keycard and we'll be all good here. No one gets hurt."

He had more intestinal fortitude than I initially gave him credit for. I'd assumed that he would cower before me and let me go about my business. Instead, he screamed "Fuck you!" and chucked his still-full beer bottle directly at my head.

I snatched it out of the air. For extra style points, I grabbed the spilling beer and replaced it in the bottle. Calmly, I placed the bottle on the counter. "Deputy Rosen. Calvin. Can I call you Calvin? I still think of your brother when I think of Deputy Rosen."

Calvin didn't respond.

"You know how your brother died, Calvin? Has anyone ever told you the full story?"

"You and that bitch friend of yours killed him off, that's what I know." Calvin's voice was rough and angry. I couldn't blame the guy.

"That's the official story, yeah. Reality is a little more complicated than that. But do you know what he was doing?" I tried to keep my voice calm, professional.

"Fighting that beast you summoned."

"Nope. Rosen never engaged in the fight at all. He was helping the wounded, getting them to safety. He and I were getting people into cover; we moved guys *together.*"

"*Bullshit.* Karl was no traitor."

I sighed. "Nor am I, Calvin. I was in that fight, sure. But I wasn't fighting *against* the deputies who were there. Ask any of them, they'll tell you the truth. Grace and I are the reason so many lived."

Calvin glowered at me. I don't think he believed me, but he wasn't saying anything.

"Anyway, this one deputy got in trouble, pinned in a car. He managed to get free, but he couldn't move. It was too dangerous—the Cornuprocyon was between us and the deputy. I stayed put, tried to bide my time. Your brother ran out to get him. Maybe if I'd gone with him, covered him, he'd be alive. So you're right, in a sense. Karl died because of me."

"And now you're here to take me, too? You're a real son of a bitch."

"Nope. Think of it as returning the favor. I'm going to make sure you *live* through this one." I grabbed some duct tape from the hall closet and began binding his hands and mouth. He didn't struggle, but before I got his mouth taped shut he managed to ask one more question.

"Live through which one?"

I shook my head and placed the tape over his mouth. Some questions are better left unanswered.

ANDREA

I WASN'T GOING to try to run away on foot like I had last time. That had sucked big time. This time I would secure my own transportation. Matt's van stood in the gravel drive beside the trailer. I paced around outside until my Sense found what I needed. The van's keys vanished off the small end-table holding fake potted plants and popped back into existence in my hand.

I didn't know why Matt thought the artificial greenery everywhere was necessary. Ageless, unchanging, unable to rot away, the plants reminded me too much of my time as something not quite alive on Cythymau's stone slab. I gave the fake monstrosity a slight nudge with my Sense to cover where they'd been.

I fingered the keys, weighing them in my hand, feeling their sharp ridges. I had ridden in that van on the way here and had managed to get through the drive without a major panic attack. Of course, I had been exhausted at the time, but I thought I could probably handle the confines of the larger vehicle again, especially if I was the one driving.

Back when I'd lived in this Weave, I'd had a vehicle... maybe? I groped for the frayed memory tickling the back of my mind.

"I can't believe you spent all your savings on that—junk wagon." A small smile curled the corners of my lips. That was right. I'd owned a

1972 Chevy station wagon. And my—someone? Someone had not approved. My smile fell away as I shook off the incomplete thought. Surely driving a car should be a lot like riding a bike. Even with a few millennia intervening, the muscle memory would still be there, right?

I opened the driver's side door and slid behind the wheel, feeling slightly guilty. No one came bursting out of the trailer to stop me, but they probably assumed I was going to save their precious Robert. Nielsen was still wounded, too. But once Matt and Naggy realized that neither Robert nor I was coming back, they'd leave for a new safe house and be free to find a healer, so he was in good enough hands. Plus, I would never give Nielsen the knowledge that he wanted. It was probably better to take myself somewhere else before he was well enough to start pestering me again.

I scooted the seat forward, adjusted the mirrors, pressed my foot down on the brake, but couldn't find a clutch. What the heck?

I tried turning the key in the ignition, waiting for it to click and refuse to turn over, but the engine rumbled to life and the radio crackled, announcing, "You are listening to SPR, Spokane Public Radio."

I ignored the radio.

Step 1: the engine was running. Step 2: I needed it to move.

Upon inspection, the shifter looked simpler than I expected. It was to my right on the driving console, but it only had four options. D, R, N, and P. There were no numbered gears at all. It was currently in P, so it made sense that gear should be used when the vehicle was at a stop. I remembered that N meant neutral, so the drive gears weren't engaged. Keeping my foot on the brake, I moved the lever until it hit the R and tentatively took my foot off the brake pedal. The car lurched backwards.

R. Reverse.

Check.

I should have remembered that. Expecting it this time, I lifted my foot from the brake, let the van roll backwards, then had to quickly correct when I turned the wheel the wrong way and almost swiped the van into the trailer. Spinning the wheel the other way, I realigned the van, hit the brake, and shifted it up to the only option left. It slewed into drive with a jarring hitch. I rolled away from Matt's trailer and the little park on the reservation. At a little bit faster than a speed-walking pace. Piss and shit.

We hadn't seen much traffic on this part of the reservation. Right now I was triply grateful for that small mercy. If I had to deal with traffic, this would already be a catastrophe. No doubt I would have crashed the van and killed myself before I even reached the boundary of the trailer park.

Biting my lip, I pressed down on the gas pedal. The van leaped forward all at once. Cursing, I fought with the wheel to keep the van on the road, swerving into the left lane and back into my own before getting the speed under control.

So I was a bit rusty, but my brain was essentially somewhere around 2,000 years old. I guessed I should have been glad the memories were there at all. The last thing I needed was some new type of dimensional old-age dementia on top of all my shell shock.

I drove the first few miles with my hands braced widely on the wheel, my knuckles white. The first speed limit sign freaked me out, since I abruptly remembered that the number on the sign needed to match the number the needle pointed to on the dash. Otherwise authorities would pull you over. After being gone for so long, I couldn't remember exactly what the relationship between those authorities and Feds might be, and I didn't want to find out. I pressed on the brake until the numbers matched, ignoring the honking cars behind me. I wasn't getting pulled over, not today.

After the next few miles passed uneventfully, I felt like I was finally getting the hang of the whole driving thing. I didn't really understand how the transmission worked without a clutch, but as long as the vehicle kept me moving me forward, I wasn't going ask any awkward questions. I didn't want to jinx it.

Somewhere around mile ten or fifteen, I started paying attention to the radio. It was telling some humorous narrative about a night of chickens. I only started paying attention halfway through, but it seemed like a fun story. I'd forgotten that some humans made their living telling stories. It seemed so far removed from my life of survival, running, and fear. So innocent. Some people did nothing with their days except make up lies for others to find amusing.

I bet they never woke up unable to move, unable to talk, unable to do anything as their Sense was used against their will, often to kill, maim, and torture. Some days, I had been able to keep control of a small fraction of my Sense to use for myself—subverting some of the summons to my own purposes, using my small influence to cloud Cythymau's grasp over his beasts or weaken his understanding of what went on in that Weave. Without my full potential, his power weakened and he became blinder than he thought.

The day when that boy and his master came through the portal had been one of those days. I had managed to hide some of their entrance and actions from Cythymau, blending them in behind the vibrations of his own beast-bonds. That had turned out to be a few good days.

I had expected, once I got off that stone slab, that I would regain control of my Sense, and for the most part I had, but the input from the Weave never stopped. I had been nearly mad with the overwhelming amount of information still trying to cram itself into my head when I'd been released from that stone slab. In the welter of conflicting sensations, I'd tried to stab Robert. I remembered that.

But that didn't mean I had to return the favor and try to save him this time. It didn't. His master had already given him another chance. It wasn't my business what he decided to do with the life she'd bought for him.

"More suspected reality terrorists are being brought in for questioning at the Airway Heights Detention Center in Washington State." The crackle of the radio voice cut through my thoughts as the program switched. "The staggering influx of accused reality terrorists at the facility is raising concerns among the local residents about their safety and well-being, should even just a few of these radicals get loose. It is estimated that at least 400 new arrivals to the detention center have been processed so far this month. NPR's special reporter has spoken to officials on the scene, who are anxious to reassure concerned citizens that every precaution is being made that these people remain unable to summon and are absolutely not a threat to Airway Heights residents. While they would not confirm whether the summoners are being kept sedated at all times, they maintain that any risk of one escaping has been evaluated and contingencies have been put in place. No security issues are anticipated among the detained. They urge the public to report any suspicious activity that may lead to the capture of more of these domestic reality terrorists."

I frowned. "Domestic reality terrorist" was some pretty strong language. Summoners had never been well-tolerated by the government in this Weave, but back in my time they'd just been called summoners. None of this terrorist, enemy combatant stuff that kept cropping up since I'd been back. The government really did appear to be stepping the propaganda up a notch. And four hundred new summoners detained this month? How were they containing so many in one place, exactly? That many summoners should have been a powder keg waiting to go off, not something they could urbanely reassure the public wasn't a problem.

I had been avoiding these authorities on principle because I didn't want to get killed, captured, or tangled up in this Weave's power struggles, but maybe it was time I saw what they were really capable of.

I pulled the van to the side of the road and summoned a map using my shiny new charm bracelet. Airway Heights itself was really easy to find. The detention center wasn't marked, of course, but I could deal with that later. It looked like I would be running away with one last stop to view the detention center.

I started the van up and pulled out into traffic with much less difficulty the second time around. I was really starting to get the hang of this driving thing.

UNEXPECTEDLY, once I got close to Airway Heights, the roads to the Detention Center were marked clearly with large signs that gave approximate mileage, and told you which exit to take. You could just follow them. It was almost like they were *advertising* where to go for anyone who drove a car.

This immediately made me suspicious. The only reason to announce the location of this large detention center would be to trap potential rescuers, right? I mean, their own people should already know where it was, so the signs would be redundant. I squinted at the latest sign, which read "Airway Heights Detention Center, 1 Mile." There could be any number of traps set up for vehicles on that road. It would probably be like walking up and knocking on the big bad wolf's door while knowing he was inside, probably with an accomplice ready to jump you once you stepped across the threshold.

I took the exit before that one and ditched the van in a grocery store parking lot that looked like it had a lot of vehicles coming in and out. One more shouldn't be noticed for a few hours at least.

Now I was on foot again, which I really didn't like. But there was no other way to get within range of the facility and be sure they hadn't noticed.

I slipped through the brush and ditches at the edge of town, sticking to the tall grasses, striking out cross-country. I wanted to come out close to the main gate where the trucks and other vehicles would have to unload their cargo, but not right on top of it where they'd presumably have guards and surveillance. In fact, they'd probably have some kind of surveillance at least fifty feet out from the barrier around the facility, to deter and track potential escapees. I did not want my face on any of those cameras. I was not looking to trade Cythymau's prison for a new model.

The perimeter of the facility was a five-foot concrete barrier topped with chain link and razor wire. There were little black dots placed periodically at the top of the fence that I assumed were surveillance equipment. Two guard stations flanked the gate. In the middle of the yard stood a guard tower with the shapes of two heavily armed guards inside. I could see that trucks were still driving up to the gate, but from sixty feet back where I was, it was impossible to distinguish any details.

I crawled forward slowly on my elbows, trying to get as close as safely possible before triggering the summon on my bracelet to capture the light in the detention center's yard. That would bring it to my eyes, improvising my own binoculars. Hunkering down in the weeds, I pricked my finger and smeared my blood across the rune form.

The scene in the yard below came into sudden and uncomfortable focus. The latest truck through the gate pulled forward. Two orderlies in white jackets ran out to meet it. They yanked open the back doors and handed down an IV stand, which was attached to a man swaddled in some kind of mummy-like restraining outfit and strapped to the gurney with straps that crisscrossed over his chest and held him horizontally at the shoulders, waist, and below the knees and ankles. His eyes appeared to be open, staring sightlessly upward. The orderlies finished handing him off to guards, who checked something on a clipboard and waved for him to be wheeled inside. They repeated the process for another individual, then another, like some hugely obscene parody of a production line. None of the summoners were conscious; their eyes always stared up at nothing, the guards moving them around like so much cordwood—except that these logs looked to be hooked up to lots and lots of drugs. And they just kept coming. The first truck carried twenty-six summoners on gurneys that were all wheeled through the large, double-reinforced door of the building.

I admit, my first instinct was to mount a frontal attack in true wrecking-ball, heedless-of-the-consequences, apprentice fashion. A quick count of the guards, surveillance, and orderlies convinced me that wouldn't be an option. Even assuming the guards' guns were loaded with normal bullets and not whatever narcotic cocktail was being used to subdue the summoners in that courtyard, I couldn't take them all out before they tackled me and shot me up by force with whatever that crap was.

I stopped counting after the sixth truck in the same hour. This facility, whatever it was, held far, far more than four hundred summoners. I mean, I'd seen over one hundred fifty dropped off in the last hour. Even assuming they only accepted new summoners during business hours, that meant an average of one thousand summoners a day.

Which led me to another problem.

There weren't that many summoners in the population at large today. Especially not in the area surrounding Spokane and Airway Heights. Even assuming that this facility was getting all the summoners from the central northwest region, that number seemed high.

I might be rusty about the specifics in this Weave anymore, but even I could tell that number would be impossible to support for any sustained period of time, which meant... just mathematically speaking, it was impossible that all the people being cycled through this facility were summoners. It was also impossible that the facility was holding more than a thousand new prisoners per day. Some of them had to be going elsewhere. I waited around, trying to catch some prisoners being released, or to see where some prisoners might be sent.

Gurney after gurney went in, truck after truck dropped off and exited, but no prisoners came out from the main building. I changed the focus of my summon and tried to find an auxiliary gate they might be using for prisoner transport or release, but came up with nothing. The only apparent way in and out of that facility was the gate I had been watching for the last few hours.

My stomach tied in a hard, cramping knot. I was looking down into the very pit of hell. Cythymau would have been very capable of this kind of blatant disregard for human life and free will, but I hadn't expected to see it again so soon. To literally be fifty-five feet away from its walls and gaping maw ready to swallow me back up.

My skin broke out in a cold sweat. I cut off the summons and started backing away slowly on my elbows until I was well out of viewing range of the facility, deep among the brush and bushes in the middle of nowhere, my arms and torso scratched and bleeding from the rough, uneven ground. I stumbled to my feet and started running full out, headlong, not caring if I was even pointed in the right direction to get back to the van. It was as though Cythymau had somehow turned the authorities of this Weave into mini versions of himself and sent them here just to taunt me. All that was missing were the runes and the gleefully spooky, mad laugh I'd listened to for millennia, both waking and in my worst nightmares. I finally shambled to a stop when I had no more breath left in me, and promptly lost all the cereal I'd eaten that morning into the bushes.

I stood up, wiping my mouth on the back of my hand, wishing I could do something about the sour taste.

My stomach settled slightly and then dropped down into the soles of my feet as I realized that *that* was what Robert was headed into. His fosties had been taken. I had to stop him before he tried to storm into that hell alone. Or a similar one. This couldn't be the only facility.

I knew better than most the consequences of biting off more than you can handle, even if you believe you have the best of intentions. And the scene at that detention center wasn't going to be leaving me alone anytime soon.

I might not like Robert. He could be a pompous asshole. Even if my worst-enemy slot had been open after Cythymau, I wouldn't be able to send anyone to a living hell like that.

I did a quick summons, looking for Robert. He was to the north, not at the detention facility. Possibly he hadn't put whatever his plan was into action yet. I had to get to him in time. I ran back to the road, checked both ways for traffic, and seeing none, sprinted for the van. I might not be sure what I thought about Robert and company, but I knew for sure that I was one hundred percent against what I had just witnessed happening at that detention center.

ROBERT

THE FIRST CASUALTY of battle is, of course, the plan. I had Calvin Rosen's keycard, and I was wearing his face and his clothes when I stepped up to the employee entrance. What I didn't have was an answer for the crackling voice coming over the small speaker next to the door.

"Cal, didn't you just go off-shift? What're you doing back?"

My mind swam. Why *would* Calvin be coming back? There should be a reason, but the existence of the question itself sent my mind into a panic. "A panic" is exactly where you don't want your mind if you're trying to come up with a clever story.

"Uh-um..."

"Cal? You okay out there?" Genuine concern. That was a little calming—they were thinking something was wrong with Cal. Good enough, for now.

"Uh, yeah. Yeah, fine. Just... um... just left my cell phone behind. Need to come in and snag it." *Christ, Robert,* I thought to myself. *You're a foster kid. You can do a hell of a lot better than that.* Too late now. The lie was out, and if there's one rule about lying, it's never change the story once your opponent has it.

Cell phone. Stupid, stupid lie.

The door popped open. I walked into the dark maw of the jail. My Sense was up, but my eyes still blinked in the darkness as they adjusted to the dim light of the hallway. It was unpainted cement, ugly as sin, and lit by bare bulbs in cages every fifty feet or so. Interior decoration was not exactly a high priority in jail design.

The hallway led me into a large control room. Monitors lined one wall, watching the building from every possible angle. They were marked in some code of letters and numbers, and to the jailers watching them they formed a coherent picture of the jail. They'd installed their own version of a Sense on this building, and without knowing their code, I couldn't track it at all.

A fat jail deputy with blonde hair and a mustache swiveled his desk chair around to face me. "Hey, Cal," he said. "Welcome back. I'm not seeing a cell phone in here."

I looked around the control room. There was an exit opposite the room I'd entered, but it was a heavy steel door, presumably held shut by hydraulic systems. I *could* get through it, but my cover would be entirely blown if I did. I wasn't aiming for a running battle up ten stories and down again. Subtlety was my friend here.

"Well, maybe I left it upstairs. Care to open the doors, let me check?"

The fat deputy looked at me for a while. "Cal, you didn't go upstairs. Your whole shift was in here, remember?"

Crap. I let my illusion drop; it wasted energy I was going to need. I might not have been aiming for a running battle, but then again, no one ever said I was a good shot.

The deputy's hand slammed into a red button on the control panel. A general alarm blared. Throughout the jail, steel doors slammed shut automatically, giving a percussion beat to the *hraaaat, hraaaat* sound of the buzzing alarm. On one of the monitors behind the deputy, I watched some poor inmate fall onto the cement floor, leaping out of the way of the crushing auto-slam feature.

I rolled my eyes at the deputy and summoned the steel away from the door leading out of here. I formed it into a tube, wrapping the good deputy up in the center. A surprised "Erk!" echoed up from the door.

I moved. Speed was going to be very, very important. Illusions might be useful, but they wasted entirely too much energy. One male and one female deputy were already running down the hallway toward me.

Jails are, essentially, fortified structures. That said, they're designed to hold people *in,* not out. The guards running at me didn't have guns drawn because *they didn't have guns.* That was a fabulous security feature if all the people in jail with you are unarmed, but it made them useless in a fight against me. Guns wouldn't have helped them *much,* but still—those batons weren't going to do anything, and I think both of them knew it. Yet they charged on.

I remembered a couple of mall cops running past me in an opposite direction. Those two beautiful bastards had gotten themselves killed simply to buy a couple of seconds. They must have known it, much like these two, and they must have considered the cost one worth paying. I didn't want to hurt anyone if I didn't have to; they didn't deserve that.

I didn't stick to the hallway. I could Sense the stairwell on the other side of the wall. I summoned a portion of the wall out and placed it across the hallway, essentially blocking the guards' charge. As they ran up to my barricade, coming within my Sense, I summoned one of their radios.

"Control, Control—can we get a status? Where is he?"

I heard the next line in stereo as the guard *with* a radio, the woman, responded both within my Sense and into the radio. "He's taken Control; no idea how Van Horn is doing. He's got the hallway blocked with rubble, not sure where from. Rodgers and I are stuck on the other side, no way to get to him. I think he's got a radio."

A brief silence over the air followed. A wild impulse rushed into me, that mad glee that always seems to take me in situations like this. I'd faced demons and beasts beyond their imagining; a jail full of deputies with batons was really not a threat. It was the law enforcement on the outside, undoubtedly responding to the jail in force, that I was worried about. Time was of the essence now.

"The lady is quite correct," I said into the radio, doing my best Bond-villain impersonation. "I am certainly in possession of your radio. I have also, shall we say, disabled the good Deputy Van Horn. You all seem like nice people, but I think you know those batons of yours are worthless in this fight. I do not wish to run up a body count here; I am simply coming to right an injustice that's been done to innocent people. You would be well advised to simply let me pass." I knew that wouldn't work, but I had to give them the opportunity.

As I started up the stairs, the jail began to fill with noise. Clanging, banging, hooting, screaming noise. The prisoners were figuring out something was up, and had begun to celebrate the fight. I guess any kind of action broke the monotony of a long jail stay.

I barreled up the stairs two at a time, passing floors two and three. Allen had placed my fosties on the top floor; no reason to stop on the intervening levels. By the time I rounded my way toward four, I could hear the troops descending on me.

Direct or indirect? I wasn't worried about my ability to get there, just my ability to do so without inflicting damage. Indirect, then. I used the door to floor three as a makeshift barricade on the stairs. That let me simply duck through the doorframe onto floor three.

Another long, narrow, cement hallway greeted me. This one had two doors on the opposite side, painted bright orange. The one directly across the hall from me read "3E." Down the hall, the other door was labeled "3W." Third floor, east pod and west pod. From what Allen had told me, I needed to get into the east pod on the tenth floor. Logic dictated that the pod I was aiming for be directly above 3E, and seven stories up.

Right. First step, get into 3E. The door had three guards on the other side, batons at the ready. In an effort to avoid that kind of confrontation, I simply removed a portion of the wall into one of the cells instead.

"What the fuck!" The current occupant of the cell had been facing his door, but he turned to face me as I removed his back wall. He was wearing orange jail clothes and sandals, standard garb in here.

"Hey. Just passing through. Don't mind me." I kept my voice casual.

"Shit, man. You must be one of them reality terrorists. I don't want no shit with you, man. Just, like, don't fucking hurt me or whatever." A closer look revealed that he was pasty-faced, sweaty, and shaking.

"Like I said, just passing through. You OK?"

"Yeah. Just feeling a little sick, you know? Just got hauled in yesterday." Withdrawal was a bitch, but not my problem. I upped my Sense and felt around. We were close to the east wall of the jail, and I had plenty of open space to work with. I grabbed a section of the ceilings for the next three floors up and removed them, putting them outside the building and letting them fall toward the parking lot below. When they'd dropped toward the low end of my Sense, I stole their force and applied it underneath me, sending me flying upward.

Yes, that meant giant blocks of concrete falling to earth behind the jail. That side of the jail was all Dumpsters and open parking lot, though. I couldn't be *sure* it was safe, but the chance of hitting someone was pretty low.

Let's pause here for a second to discuss some basic physics. I should have paused *before* making this move, but instead I'd been doing the safety assessment of dropping the block in the first place. I'd pulled basically a square yard of concrete floor out of three different floors, and each floor was about a foot thick. That meant I was dealing with twenty-seven cubic feet of concrete, which weighed I don't know how much, but a hell of a lot more than me. I'd then let them fall for about sixty feet, from the top edge of the outside arc of my Sense toward the bottom. I'd then applied the force of that counterweight to myself, in an effort to elevate a much lighter object forty feet instead of sixty.

Force, of course, is equal to mass *times* velocity. The mass and the velocity of the concrete far exceeded what I needed, and I shot upward at a tremendous rate. I pulled the next chunk of ceiling away in front of me before I slammed into it, but sailed into the ceiling of the seventh floor. I managed to get myself bent ass-first and take the hit to my more padded areas, but as soon as I hit, I began to fall. There was a fat old man in the cell of floor seven, his paunch hanging out from under his too-small jail uniform, and he stared at me as I slammed into his ceiling before falling away from his view back down to floor six.

I managed to grab my falling energy and apply it to my side, sending me sprawling into a lady in a cell of the six-east pod.

"Uh, sorry?" I said, trying to disentangle myself from the woman beneath me. She was middle-aged, her skin slightly wrinkled but not entirely unattractive, until she opened her mouth.

"Get the fuck off me, psycho." Her mouth was a mess of crooked, blackened teeth, and her breath reeked of the rotting enamel. No wondering what she was in for.

"Sorry, sorry," I mumbled. The fat man from floor seven poked his head down around the edge of the hole.

"Everyone okay down there?" he asked.

"Uh, yeah. Totally fine."

"Looked like you got into a little bit of a pickle there."

"I'm fine. I just—I'm fine." The old man seemed nice, kind, and calm. I had a hard time picturing why he'd be in here, but I chose not to ask. Instead, I removed the wall between me and the hallway, and got out of meth-mouth's room before I had to smell that breath anymore.

She followed me.

"What are you doing?" I asked.

"Getting the fuck out of here. Aren't you?"

"Well, I'm headed upstairs, first. But that's eventually the idea. I'm not here to rescue you."

"Fuck rescue. I just need out. Can't stay in here no longer. I bet these county fucks put more effort into you than me."

I grabbed her by the scruff of her jail uniform. "Lady, you don't want to follow me where I'm going, and I don't want to break you out." I pushed against her, sending her staggering back into her cell. Then I replaced the wall, trapping her inside. "Stay put!" I shouted. Then I pulled the door away from the stairwell.

The clomping feet on the stairs were below me now. The chatter over my stolen radio was confused, with people estimating me on the third, seventh, sixth, fifth, and fourth floors. I was running up the steps past floor eight when I heard a low, hard voice on the radio say "Clear coms."

All the chatter stopped.

"Mr. Lorents, I assume you can hear me? Good. We have re-taken the control room, and can tell you are on the eighth floor, east stairwell. The Feds are responding to our location; you will not be able to leave. I appreciate very much the lack of bloodshed to this point, but if you continue to resist we will be forced to apply lethal pressure."

I found the nearest video camera with my Sense and thought about disabling it. If I did that, though, they'd be able to track my presence through the trail of disabled cameras just as well as by watching me. There was no help for it; they knew who I was, which meant they knew why I was here. I flipped the camera off. Unobserved, I ran up to the ninth, then the tenth floor.

I breached the doorway into the east pod of the tenth floor. I disarmed the guards immediately, and they took a nervous step back and away from me. The pod proper was a large room, lined with cells all facing a common area.

"Which?" I asked the guards. They stood, mutely, shaking their heads.

I picked the burliest of them, a large man, and dropped the floor out from under him. He plummeted down to the ninth, but it wasn't fatal.

"*Which?*" I yelled, my voice cracking at the end.

The youngest guard, a boy not that much older than me, pointed across the room at a cell. I stalked toward it, pulling the door off. My heart raced; my breathing quickened. I'd made it. I could get my fosties out of the cell, I could—

I could get distracted. Why do I *always* get distracted in my moment of triumph? I must have let my Sense slip, because I failed completely to notice the tranquilizer dart before it took me in the chest.

In the movies, a tranq dart takes the target out of commission in no more time than it takes to get out one last, pithy word. That's not how it really works; the drugs take a little time to kick in. I didn't pass out immediately. Instead, I stared at the dart for a second. *On the clock.*

I made a beeline for the fosties' cell. I brought my Sense back, struggling against the impending fogginess in my brain. I ripped the door off its hinges, then walked in to see—

Nothing. No one. The cell was empty.

"Mr. Lorents," said the low voice on the radio. "We don't store same-gendered prisoners together, ever. We certainly don't store married prisoners together. And we never, ever put summoners in the county jail. You came to the wrong place, Mr. Lorents. Fortunately, we knew you were coming." Mr. Voice sounded altogether too smug about this.

Allen.

I didn't think he'd actually do it. Stupid. I had walked into a trap. I'd put myself on the top floor of a building designed to keep people in, and I'd let myself get hit with this dart.

"You've been injected with a high dose of ketamine. Usually, it's used to tranquilize horses and bears, so I'm pretty sure it will work on you. It may, in fact, kill you. It was still our best possible option. Lie down, go to sleep, and we'll make sure you get medical treatment to live."

Fuck that. As soon as I let myself drop into a K-hole, I wouldn't get up. I sent a screaming plea across my bond to Rick. *Help.* Through the bond I felt him begin to tunnel upward. A foxtrot was playing, and Charlie was headed for the dance floor. I needed to get out of this building.

I made my way back into the pod and began a lurching shamble toward the east wall of the jail. My Sense stayed up, though I had to struggle with consciousness. Still, if I could simply make the wall, pulling momentum away from myself should, in theory, give me a safe fall to the ground.

Get me and go, I thought at Rick. I couldn't tell whether he got the message. Didn't matter. If I didn't get my body clear of the jail, the bloodbath when Rick hit the building would be tremendous. I didn't really have a particular fondness for meth-mouth or any of the other occupants here, but Rick would not have my delicate sensibilities when he came in.

I removed the wall and looked down at the pavement of the parking lot ten stories below. A wave of vertigo hit me, riding the drugs through my brain, dizzying me. I looked back at the guards in the pod; they were standing clear. A fourth guard had emerged from a separate cell, tranq gun in hand and pointed at me.

I jumped before he could fire.

My Sense slipped away, followed quickly by my consciousness. The last thing I remember is the rush of air as I headed for the pavement.

ANDREA

I DROVE toward the place in the Weave where my bracelet told me Robert should be and swore as I passed the "Entering Spokane" sign. Of course Robert would be attempting his rescue inside city limits. Silly me to hope he might pick a nice, out-of-the-way place to stage his intervention—somewhere hundreds of civilians wouldn't be waiting to report any suspected summoning activity to the authorities.

City driving in Spokane was a bit trickier for my rusty, half-remembered skills than the highway driving I'd been doing, but I managed to navigate the maze of one-way streets without turning down the wrong one or some other major mishap. I rubbed blood across the Mannaz-Wunjo-Ehwaz-Algiz charm and pinged Robert's location in the Weave again, wanting to make sure he hadn't moved too far since I'd last checked. I turned down a side road that looked to be a more direct route, not even paying attention to the street name. It led me to a large group of buildings. Pulling into one of the side streets, I brought the van up next to a large sign with a map proclaiming "You are here." Robert appeared to be in a building on the north side of the campus, which according to the map would be... the Spokane County Jail.

Piss and shit.

Of course it was.

Not sure what to do now, I drove down and into the parking lot across the street opposite the jail. It faced the side wall of the jail, so I parked in the front row, as close to the building as I could get. The jail itself was obviously built from reinforced concrete, with long slit windows. I tapped my fingers on the wheel, thinking.

I didn't want to barge in and alert them to Robert's presence if being there was part of his planned tactics. But on the other hand, I had no way of knowing if he was in trouble. Even if he was, I didn't have that many options available for breaking him out myself.

Sure, I'd made myself a bracelet of rune emblems that could be used in a multitude of ways depending on my will and intent when using my Sense. But I didn't know what kind of resources they'd have inside. The authorities here had a reputation for removing threats. My bracelet didn't mean I had a "get out of jail free" card.

If I charged in there now, there was every chance we'd both end up drugged and strapped to boards as in that hellhole I'd just visited. I wanted to keep Robert out of that detention facility if I could, but not at the price of my own freedom. Even if the captors were human this time.

I pricked a finger to summon light reflections to my eyes, magnifying and refining my focus like I'd done at the detention center.

Quickly, I scanned upward toward the roofline, looking for a way in. Mid-sweep, I froze when a section of wall about six floors up burst outward in a shower of debris. Robert's pallid, bruised, and grimy face appeared in the hole for a split second before he jumped, tumbling out of the opening. My mouth dropped open. Four more men wearing uniforms appeared at the hole, watching him fall. I watched for a fraction longer, expecting him to summon something to break or slow the fall, but nothing happened.

Swearing, I released my binocular summons and flailed for the correct charm on my bracelet. A few more drops of blood squeezed out of my abused fingertip slowed Robert's downward plunge as I stripped most of the kinetic energy away from him and redirected it at the gaping hole in the building. Next I took out several chunks of the flooring next to the hole, weakening its structure. The floor began to crumble, forcing the uniformed men back from the ledge, taking Robert's slowly falling form out of their line of fire.

More authorities started running out from a ground-floor door close to where Robert would land. I peeled more kinetic energy away from Robert's body. He slowed to cartoonishly slow-motion speed. Changing summons, I piled up two S.W.A.T. vans and several other transport vehicles, creating a blockade between Robert and the deputies. It would buy him a few more seconds to get out of there, but not much.

Robert settled to the ground like a sack of wet sand and lay sprawled motionless on the pavement. I willed him to get up and start moving, but he remained flat. I dropped my forehead to the wheel in frustration—if Robert didn't do something to save himself here, I wasn't about to get captured on his behalf.

Been there. Done that. Didn't ever want to do it again.

A tearing roar shook the ground and car earthquake-style, bringing my head back up in alarm. Robert still lay prone on the asphalt. It hadn't come from him.

I turned my head to the side and watched Rick rend his way up from under the street to my left. He rained dirt, asphalt, and concrete everywhere as his bright orange and red striped spines emerged from the road like some exotic and deadly form of demonic plant life. Utility lines and pipes hung speared from his quilled coat, dragging along. He freed himself from the hole he'd ripped open by launching himself upward with a resounding *whoomph*.

The broken, pierced pipes sprayed water around the hulking Cornuprocyon like some demented fountain with a giant, enraged, spiky raccoon/mud-monster as the centerpiece.

Another ten guards rounded the corner of the building as the first group ran out from behind my crude vehicle blockade, moving to surround Robert's limp body. Rick didn't like that. He unleashed a scream so high on the sound register that my ribcage shook. Then he launched himself at them with a vindictive set to his big, club-like tail. I was very glad he was headed *away* from where I sat in the van. No way did I want to get between that *thing* and its master. The deputies fired a few futile shots, trying to hold the line, but as Rick crash-landed among them, they scattered like ants, forced to avoid his snapping jaws and swinging tail. I sat back.

OK, Robert playing possum while Rick created a distraction made sense, but more and more guards were swarming out, which concerned me a bit. Rick was a powerful ally, though. Robert probably had a plan, right?

This obviously wouldn't be pretty, but at least I didn't have to expose myself to save this kid's reckless butt.

Or that's what I assumed for about the first thirty seconds, until Robert didn't get to his feet. My brow wrinkled as I considered the possibility that Robert *might be totally unconscious* and not controlling or directing the Cornuprocyon at all. None of the people I'd seen at the detention center had been conscious. No tell-tale bags of stuff appeared hooked up to Robert, but if they'd already put the whammy on him...

The personnel pouring out of the jail were starting to bring bigger guns and riot gear to the party with the Cornuprocyon. Rick launched himself into the air, landing unexpectedly in the midst of a line of deputies still trying to group around Robert, laying about him with vicious swipes of his chitinous tail and flinging several of them to the side.

The notion that the Cornuprocyon might be free to do anything it wanted scared the shit out of me. Right now, Robert was acting as a kind of focus. The demon would vent its anger and aggression on these deputies. In the best-case scenario, it would kill some deputies and jail personnel to get back to its master, then escape with Robert in tow.

If the deputies killed Robert in their attempt to stop the Cornuprocyon, this destruction would just look like the warm-up.

At that point, we'd be in *worst-case scenario* territory.

And with Robert dead, it would probably revert to its normal behavior of hunting down summoners as food sources. Of which I was the closest...

Deputies wearing riot gear and carrying some kind of large. shoulder-mounted weapon rounded the corner of the building and lined themselves up with Rick. The front two dropped to one knee, aimed at Rick, and simultaneously launched fiery, missile-shaped rockets. Rick roared, sending a wall of kinetic energy in front of him to meet the projectiles.

A third deputy dropped to his knee beside the other two and fired almost before his knee hit the ground. The rockets from the first two deputies exploded on impact with Rick's kinetic force shield. The third, lagging behind, headed straight for the demon's chest. It impacted on Rick's hide with a blossom of flame and smoke, leaving a singed spot. Rick roared in displeasure, but it didn't actually hurt him. Cornuprocyons are *tough* sons of bitches; that's why Cythymau liked them so much. That said, Cornuprocyons couldn't survive a direct headshot from those.

That rocket would have to hit him in just the right way, but these people *were* highly trained, as shown by their first volley already pinpointing the weakness in a Cornuprocyon's kinetic defenses.

The deputies with the rocket launchers scrambled to reload and adjust the aim on their next shot. The noise from helicopter blades started thumping in the distance, and I realized that more backup was a few seconds out at most. Vaguely I recalled Matt talking about the government moving more airborne summoner-response teams to some base outside of Spokane. It could have just been a news chopper, but I couldn't really take that chance. I only had a few seconds at most to decide what I was going to do. I didn't want to go up against the combined force of military-grade weapons, a summoner strike team, and the vanilla deputies while armed with only myself, one out-of-control Cornuprocyon, and the Amazing, Unconscious, Mr. Hero Complex.

The deputies with the rocket launchers finished reloading. Given how they had handled Rick so far, I didn't want to gamble that they couldn't take him out. They'd come prepared for the flaw in Rick's force generating abilities, so....

If I was going to do something, I had to do it. Now.

I blooded another charm and waited. The first two deputies fired, the third following with just that fraction of a second delay.

I released my summons, sweeping up excess energy from the impact between Rick's kinetic shield and the exploding rockets. That energy batted the third rocket off trajectory and sent it spiraling into the side of the jail, kissing the cinderblock with a blackened fireball of soot and flame.

The surrounding deputies turned toward Robert's limp form, looking for the source of the summons. Rick saw an opening.

He swept them with a blast of kinetic force, knocking them off their feet. Then he swung his tail through them like a giant wrecking ball before they could react and reset their stance. The whole group lay bloody and broken in less than a second. This was the type of behavior I had expected from a Cornuprocyon since the beginning. But it wouldn't help Robert in the long run, because Rick couldn't fight strategically. He wouldn't get to Robert before he took down all the remaining deputies, but he would try. And federal reinforcements for those deputies would be descending from the sky any second.

Red dots started blossoming on Robert's fallen body as multiple snipers set up on the roof across the walkway. I couldn't help Rick without the snipers shooting Robert, and I couldn't help Robert without exposing myself. One overgrown Cornyprocyon and a rune bracelet weren't going to get Robert out of this one.

If I wanted a chance at keeping these deputies from taking the kill-shot on Robert, I had to stop the Cornuprocyon before all the reinforcements got here. And I had to do it without alerting anyone else to my existence.

I closed my eyes in defeat. I only knew of one way to get the Cornuprocyon under control quickly. My better angels screamed at me that this would undo everything I wanted; turn me into the epitome of everything that I was trying to get away from. But unless I wanted to watch Robert and his pet Cornuprocyon die while I did absolutely nothing, I had no other options.

I took a breath and blooded the charm on my bracelet. It brought me the heavy, runed, stone dagger from Cythymau's cave. The blade weighed down my hand, but my heart even more.

A jet crested the skyline and fired what sounded like an immense Gatling gun into the Cornuprocyon. Rick deflected the first wave of bullets, but the second wave ripped open his flesh in a long tear, sending blood and quills in all directions. A helicopter swooped in from a different direction and hovered above Robert as a squad of heavily armored and armed soldiers rappelled down to surround his limp form.

No time left. I'd lost Robert already, but if I could get the Cornuprocyon under control, I might at least end the day with both of them still alive. I sliced my palm open with the dagger before I could change my mind. As my blood dripped down the blade, I sent my Sense and will through the archaic runes, forging a bond between me and the raging demon.

Rick's fear, pain, worry, and love for Robert hit me like a tidal wave. I had to struggle to keep myself from drowning in the overwhelming rush of emotions. I forced myself to breathe, to subdue the Cornuprocyon's feelings, pushing them down. Rick roared as he fought my manipulation of his emotions. I felt his horror, his hurt and betrayal, lash out at me, but I remained firm. I had to. Everything relied on my ability to salvage Rick from the disastrous wreck of Robert's rescue plan. I stomped down on my guilt and pushed my own feelings of horror aside, as I'd learned to do during all my time strapped to the slab.

Through the runes on the dagger, my Sense forged an unbreakable connection with the Cornuprocyon. Rick's mind bucked, trying to shake me off, but I gritted my teeth and slowly brought the great beast more and more under my control. His senses became part of mine, and one of us, or both of us, felt bone-deep sadness.

Rick's bond with Robert pulsed weakly, but I didn't try to break it. If I expected to find Robert wherever the Feds stashed him later, Robert's bond with Rick would become a homing beacon.

Through that bond, I could feel Robert's life force fluttering sluggishly. Alive, but drugged. As Rick felt me take my final, irrevocable hold on him, he roared and pushed futilely, trying to break free. I pushed back against his rage and confusion, throwing my concern and fear for Robert back at him, sending him the image of the snipers on the roofline and what they could do to Robert, if they thought Robert was controlling the Cornuprocyon's actions.

Rick's first impulse was to blast upward to take out all the snipers, but that wouldn't take care of the incoming soldiers or the increased air support. I harshly arrested the Cornuprocyon's leap and directed him to burrow instead. I needed him away before the jet came back for a second pass. Rick resisted, but I reinforced the command to retreat through the bond. He huffed an indignant, pained whimper, but plunged downward, tearing a new hole through asphalt, dirt, and buried pipes to make his exit. The tunnel collapsed behind him.

With the Cornuprocyon gone, the soldiers and unwounded personnel swept in like worker ants to secure Robert and pick up the wounded. As I watched, they drew sheets over several deputies' bodies. Rick had extracted a high price before I brought him under control. Ambulances, repair trucks, and emergency response vehicles started pouring in.

I worried what the death toll would mean for Robert in captivity. But he lived. I'd kept him alive by forcing another being to submit to my will. For its own good, and the good of others, but I had heard that line before.

My actions aren't evil. They're effective, yes? Cymthymau's murmured words ran around and around into my brain.

My actions had come from an intent to protect, to preserve life. But blood trickled down the stone blade, filling the runes and dripping to spatter against my jeans. I stared at the blade, still struggling to understand what I had done. The runes cut into the knife had helped me secure my bond to Rick. Those runes helped ensure his will would be subject to mine, making me stronger, the dominant one in our new kinship.

With this same blade, Cythymau had cut into my flesh eons ago, breaking my spirit and binding me to him for an eternity. With my own hands, I had cut my flesh open to bring that same captivity on another. Just like him. His shadow hovered over everything I had done since breaking free like a miasmic stench. I couldn't help feeling dirty, no matter how I tried to do the right thing.

Could there really be a "right thing" where Cythymau's methods were involved? I had promised myself I'd never pass on his knowledge and artifacts, but I propagated their use just by my continued existence.

From my seat in the van, I watched the authorities strap Robert down to a gurney and set up the bag of fluids over his head that dripped whatever cocktail of anti-summoner sedatives they'd put together. Too little. I hadn't saved him from sharing the same fate as me.

I looked down at the blood on my hands coating the stone dagger.

Hot tears flowed unexpectedly down my face. The salt burned fiercely where the tears fell into the still sluggishly bleeding cut. I hadn't gotten free to do this. I felt as though, even in his death, I was sinking further into Cythymau's web.

I didn't want this.

But I couldn't turn my face away from Robert, either. I *owed* him. I owed him for every breath of freedom and the free will that allowed me to act. Even if that meant I apparently followed in my enemy's footsteps. I hated it. I hated myself. But most of all I hated that I had traded others' captivity for my own freedom.

In this case, allowing man and beast to be restrained ensured they got to keep their lives. That had to mean something, right?

I had made the best choice I could, but I knew how empty life in a cage could be. It was really hard to convince myself I hadn't just headed down the same road as the monster I hated. I remembered how many nights I had lain as Cythymau's simulacrum, alive but wishing to die.

Taking a deep breath, I wrapped my hand in the edge of my t-shirt. If the authorities had Robert, I had to tell the others.

I was making a habit of going back to people and places I never wanted to see again. I prayed it was only a temporary madness.

ROBERT

"Hey, Robert, did you hear about that summoner they caught up at Rogers?" Jeanelle asked. It felt like forever since my high school paramour and I had made out in the Volvo. Her lithe body retreated from mine, and her blonde hair half-obscured her green eyes and perfectly chiseled face as she sank back into the passenger seat.

"What? No. A summoner? In Spokane?"

"Yeah. Well, at *Rogers*. You know how they are. Some stoner kid had, like, all these weird runes in his locker."

"Wow," I said. "Did anyone, uh, get hurt?" I was distracted from the conversation itself. Jeanelle's presence did that to me. Those long legs with a summer's worth of tan baked into smooth, taut flesh protruded from shorts that *earned* their name. Her delicate fingers traced intricate patterns on my arm, raising goosebumps down my back and across my thighs. Her lovely face, her round breasts, and her full, soft lips evoked the predictable erotic response. Along with the erection, though, came an intense feeling of nostalgia. I couldn't put my finger on why, couldn't grasp the thought, but I knew this moment rang with importance.

"Naw, they caught him with a random locker sweep. He didn't do anything. Still, trust Rogers High to literally manifest pure evil, right?"

I chuckled. Rogers sat in north-central Spokane and served a lower-income population. Jeanelle's prejudice against it stemmed from a longstanding tradition among Spokane-area schools wherein we looked down our nose at Rogers. I'd actually spent a part of my freshman year there, three sets of foster parents ago, but there was no *way* I would admit that to the leggy, blonde goddess in the passenger seat. For her, I too would hate my former classmates. When in Rome, right?

"Just like Rogers," I said. "You think he was actually a summoner, or just one of those weird kids who like to seem hardcore?" Rule One of teenagerdom: if there existed an antisocial behavior, there existed kids trying to emulate it. "Anyone could have runes in their locker. Doesn't make them a summoner. Just makes them desperate to seem more dangerous than they actually are. It's really no different than wearing leather, spiked dog collars or putting obscene amounts of metal through one's earlobe, nose, lip, et cetera."

"Et cetera. Eew. Anyone who puts metal into their et ceteras is a weirdo by any definition." Jeanelle rolled her eyes as she said this. Her snobby condemnation of those different from her stirred something, some memory of... but it slipped.

"No doubt, but weird doesn't mean dangerous. It just means weird," I said.

"The news is calling him a summoner, but I don't know if he actually used any blood magic. He had the paraphernalia, though, and that's a crime, too."

Jeanelle's voice rose in pitch, her need to condemn someone else in order to make herself feel better overriding the conversation track. If I was going to get back to the good part of the evening, it was time to find a way to reconcile.

"No doubt. I'm just trying to figure out if we're talking about a punk being a moron, or whether we're talking about a dangerous evil."

Summoners... dangerous evil. The words brought a faint taste of copper to my mouth as I said them, and I couldn't shake that feeling. I was *missing* something.

Girlfriend. Car. Focus.

Jeanelle entirely failed to notice my distraction. "Oh, well, I don't know," she said. "Probably just a poser, like you said. Still, you can never be too careful when it comes to the eternally evil, right?"

"Yeah. Scary, to think that summoners might be here in Spokane. After all, someone taught him all those runes, right?"

Jeanelle shuddered. I slipped my arm around her shoulders. This, of course, was the original *reason* for making a scary comment, and we both knew it. Still, best to have fiction. When it comes to teenage love, the forms must be obeyed.

Things progressed very quickly from there. Jeanelle and I never had sex, exactly—she maintained that she was "saving herself" for marriage. The lack of release simply increased the intensity of the kissing. Her hands moved across my torso, caressing my chest and sending a shiver through my spine. I rubbed her breasts, felt the weight of them in my hand, ran a finger over her nipple. She trembled, her eyes closed, and I raised my lips to hers once more.

In the midst of this hormonal fugue, she lifted her head away from me. "Are you OK?" she asked, concern in her voice, eyebrows raised.

"Wonderful," I said. It was a lie, of course; I didn't know why, but being with Jeanelle drove a bittersweet, nostalgic pain into my heart. "Why?"

"You're crying."

Teenage boys will never admit to crying. This is an ironclad rule. We don't cry. For her to even suggest that these were tears on my face was blasphemy. I absolutely was, of course, but I couldn't *admit* that to my gorgeous girlfriend. I wiped my sleeve across my face.

"Allergies." I leaned in to kiss her again. She recoiled.

"You've, um, got snot running down your..." Her words trailed off, but her finger pointed at my face. Right. That probably didn't look very kissable; I needed to fix that. I leaned across her lap, reaching for the glove compartment.

Jeanelle came in high from behind my head as I leaned down. She locked her lips around my right ear, sending a wave of goose bumps down my arm and leg. I shivered with the sensation as I fished through the glove box. Her breasts pressed hard into my back, and I rubbed her thigh with my right hand as I searched for the tissue with my left.

At last I came up with it, and honked my nose clear of the offending slime. Jeanelle leaned back in her chair and giggled at me. "Oh, yeah baby," she said in an exaggeratedly low and sultry voice. "You know how to keep the mood going for sure."

With my hands still holding the tissue to my nose, I laughed. I knew we were laughing *at* me and not *with*, but it was funny. The more I laughed, the more my beautiful girlfriend did. The more she laughed, the funnier I found the whole situation. Our senses of humor fed each other in a Möbius loop. Any feeling of eroticism was clearly shattered, but it was replaced by a moment of pure, serene joy.

The Lycaon chose that moment to break Jeanelle's window. It was a great wolf, nine feet at the shoulder, and its head went through the passenger window of the Volvo without flinching. I opened my mouth to scream, but no sound came out. I reached out to grab Jeanelle, but my hand passed through her body in a ghostly co-existence. The giant wolf's jaws closed over her head and sank their incisors into those perfectly-rounded breasts, then pulled her out the window. Her blood showered the inside of the car, coating me in gore. I crumpled against my door in fear, in sadness, in anger, and in longing.

That's when the pain started.

I COULDN'T GET to the source of the pain. The world was black, and the only sound in it was my screaming. It tore at me, and then just as suddenly disappeared.

"Ah, Mr. Lorents. You are awake. This is good."

Awake felt like a bit of a stretch. I saw nothing but the blurry melding of colors as my brain groggily struggled toward consciousness. I lay on my back on some sort of hardened metallic surface. It cooled my skin through my t-shirt. I turned my head, blinking, grasping for some better understanding of my location.

Well, I tried to turn my head. Someone had clamped it into a vise. I tried to raise my hand to feel it, but the arm was tied down too. Progressively, I tested all my limbs, my hips, my torso; all had been firmly strapped to this metal table.

"You are confused. That is normal. Do not struggle. Listen to me." The voice pitched these three-word lines to me in a soothing baritone, rising and falling with each set of three words as though I'd been tied down by a constantly-skipping Barry White record. After each set, he would pause and breathe. It was a steady, deep, hypnotic rhythm. I couldn't turn my head, couldn't see the man behind the voice, but I envisioned him as the funk legend himself. I even imagined his words with a backbeat. The image flashed in my head, made me chuckle over the pain.

Then, as my consciousness clawed itself up from the depths of my mind, I began to panic.

"You are remembering. You are captured. Accept this now."

Accept this? Barry here had made the boneheaded mistake of bringing me back to consciousness. He'd figured me for powerless without runes or blood— absolute mistake on his part. This was not going to be a problem. I let the panic subside, brought up my—

"*Aaaaaaaaaaaaaaaaaaaaaaaaaaaaaaaaaaaaaaaaaaaaaa!*"

My scream tore its way out of my lungs and into the air. It ran through the room, bouncing off hard cinder-block walls and back into my brain. I kept screaming, adding volume to bouncing reverberations. The pain that ripped through me caused every last muscle in my body to spasm, clenching. You ever had a Charlie-horse in the middle of the night, one that just won't go away? This felt like that, but *everywhere.*

"You tried Sensing. Learn the lesson. Brain is monitored. Sense shows itself. We prevent it." Barry's smooth, baritone voice stayed calm, as though my crippling pain was nothing more than noteworthy at best. He repeated each sentence in that soothing rhythm, and it drove the words home, forced my attention onto them.

I gasped for air, now truly in a panic. My muscles ached with the residual pain of their forced cramping. Once I finally had a lungful, I

162

decided to release my anger and break Barry's cant by the simple expedient of being a dick. "You know," I croaked in a half-whisper. My involuntary scream had torn its way across my vocal chords like a river over sand, leaving my voice fragile and broken. But it was still worth snarking him. "If you're trying the spoken word thing, I hear there's an open mic night down at the Blue Spark. Maybe check it out."

"I see fear. It is good. You understand now."

"Yeah. Though I can't match your talent for blank verse."

No, he wasn't talking in blank verse. But I never paid enough attention in English class, and it's what I could come up with on short notice.

"This is good. Drugs wear off. We can talk. You have information. Information is valuable."

This was an *interrogation?* They wanted me to rat on my friends?

"Go fuck yourself." I said it with the air of bravado, trying to mimic his three-word beats. After all, when a hero in the movies is getting tortured, he always tells the torturer to go fuck himself. It seemed like the thing to do.

Barry stayed out of my line of sight. I couldn't see his face, but his voice maintained that steady, slow, deep rhythm. "I tried, Robert. Conversation is pleasant. This is not."

Footsteps. Barry walking away? I couldn't be sure.

When the pain started again, I didn't care. They left it on for a while, left my muscles clenching and my mind in agony. I can't give you a time frame, because keeping track of time ceased to be a priority. *Everything* ceased to be a priority. The entire world condensed itself down to endless, clenching spasms as my body began to tear itself apart at my captor's command.

I want to tell you I kept tough, that I kept my lips shut. *I want,* so much, to tell you about how strong I was. I want, in short, to lie to you.

I am deeply ashamed of it, but I broke fast. I shouted the names of my friends to make the pain stop, shouted the address in Plummer, hoped desperately Matt had already moved on to a place I didn't know. I spouted forth everything to the empty room. It didn't stop the pain. Everything was black, in a world of clenched, spasming muscles and my humiliating treachery.

It hurt like hell until the drugs kicked back in.

I BREATHED in the timbered smell of Uncle Herman's cabin. The smoke from the wood oven mixed with the ancient logs of the cabin walls to produce an earthy, old smell. People had been comforted by that smell of combined shelter and warmth for hundreds of years, and the calming effect of it must be writ large on the human subconscious.

There was another smell, just as comforting, but sweeter. I opened my eyes to look down at the small wooden table and saw the result of all my efforts, steaming hot from the ovens at a nice restaurant down by Riverfront Park. The warm, cinnamon scent of Dutch apple pie filled the cabin.

"It's about damn time." Grace's demeaning, sarcastic tone belied the glowing smile on her face.

I cracked a grin at her. I had no idea how long the summoning had taken: forcing my Sense through the runes, finding the pie, bringing it back into the cabin. It wasn't my first summons using runes, but nothing I'd done had been quite at this level of complexity. Getting a specific flavor of pie from the midst of a pie shop may seem simple; let me assure you right now that it is not.

Grace produced a pair of plates and began to happily dish the pie. We sat in silence, eating, until finally I addressed the elephant in the room.

"You weren't here for this."

Grace looked up over her pie. "I know, kiddo. I wish I had been, but we both know that couldn't happen."

"I summoned the pie. I remember picking that because I could hear you setting the lesson out for me."

"You're not wrong. Forcing my apprentice to bring me delicious desserts seems like a stroke of pure brilliance."

I rolled my eyes at her. "But you weren't here. This was last summer, and you had already—"

"Died? Yeah. But you were thinking about me the whole time. I was here, in your head. And guess where we are right now?"

"Oh. Right."

"There it is. This is your drug-induced hallucination of me, you know. Not a hell of a lot you can do about it, though, so I say we sit here and enjoy the pie."

I sniffled. I'd wanted this so much. Grace went back to her pie, seemingly oblivious to the tear rolling down my cheek. I returned to mine as well. No sense in wasting the moment.

A brilliant flash filled the cabin. I looked at my mentor, who raised her head to stare into my eyes. "What was that?" I asked.

"That? That was worth it." Grace gave me her toothy grin, that devil-may-care smile that had carried me through so much fear and anger. She was perfect, sitting there in her chair in the old cabin, forkful of apple pie in her hand and a smile on her face.

Then the wall of the cabin blew in. Nothing touched me, though I felt the searing heat of the blast. There was no debris; the wall just incinerated, followed closely by everything inside the cabin that wasn't me and the chair upon which I was seated.

Including Grace.

In the end, I was left in my chair, on a burnt-bare mountaintop, weeping.

"Mr. Lorents! So good to see you. Welcome back to the world of the living." A new voice, pleasantly female, an alto-pitched voice with the confidence of adulthood but without the gravel of middle-age.

I croaked at her. My voice was hoarse, raw; I couldn't accomplish much else.

"Ow. That sounds like it hurts. Can I get you something? Maybe a glass of water?" I tried to nod but found myself simply jiggling my head inside the restraints.

"OK, I'm going to un-cuff your left hand. Understand that your brain is still hooked up to the EEG, so any attempt to summon will be met with, well, you know. Also, if you move to start disconnecting any of the electrodes, you might get some of them, but not enough before we flip a switch. You understand?"

Again with the quasi-nodding. I couldn't take any more of their pain. They'd already taken my secrets. They'd already taken my will. It's humiliating to admit this now, but I was in no position to challenge anyone.

"Good!" The woman was chipper, enthused. "Let me get you that water."

The promised beverage arrived in a plastic cup reminiscent of more than one kegger. The water was cool, refreshing on the lips. My parched, raw throat stung with the pain of it, but my body overrode my throat's protestations and demanded that I drink.

"There we go. Better?"

"Yeah. Thanks." Speaking still hurt, but this lady had been nice enough. I felt I should be polite. Now that she was standing in front of me, I could get a good look. She stood relatively tall, perhaps five-nine, maybe ten. She wasn't skinny, not in the classically-beautiful look that my college classmates went for. Still, the layer of padding around her waist paled in comparison to the breasts struggling to free themselves from the suit jacket wrapped around her torso. She wore narrow glasses, and her brown hair fell short to her shoulders.

"You're welcome. You know, I've got to say I'm pretty impressed by you. Not a lot of people hold up under that amount of pain. I've seen the scan results, so I know it wasn't your magic. You just took it. Even in that pain, you kept feeding us that line of hokum. Matt? Amy? We know of them, and on the off chance you were telling the truth about where they are, they'll be picked up in short order. Thad? He's one of the third-tier bigwigs; I doubt you've ever been near him. Andrea? Rick? I haven't even heard of them, and you couldn't come up with a family name so I'm guessing they were fake. Kudos on that whole performance, really. Mixing the truth and the lies always make them so much harder to pull apart."

She babbled, her voice moving at a mile a minute as she bustled about the room, checking first one monitor, then another. *Mixing truth and lies...* She was giving me far more credit than I'd earned. Or was this some sort of psychological trick, played for devious ends? My brain tried to sort it, but the aching pain in my muscles and the grogginess from the drugs barely allowed me to track her fast-paced chatter at all.

"Anyway, I just wanted to say—oop, are you done with that? Here let me take it. I need to get your arm secured again, too."

No choice in the matter. I gave her my arm, let her strap it back to the table.

"I just wanted to say, that was really impressive. You're one of the best at this. Top notch. But I can't help it. You and I both know it's Grace Moore we're after."

I spluttered at this, laughing.

"Grace? She's dead." Dead, dead, and all my fault. I'd just had a powerful hallucinatory reminder that I'd killed her.

"Oh, I know the party line. But we fell for that once, and what happened? Nuclear detonation! Your old high school gym now glows at night. Well, not really, but I've always liked that—never mind. Point is, last time we thought Ms. Moore dead, she set off a nuke. We're not making that mistake again."

"But... she really is dead this time."

"Fat chance. You know that she sent her demon raccoon thing to try to rescue you during your capture? Hadn't seen that beast for a year, but he killed some good men, banged more up pretty bad. Until we see a body, we know she's alive. Fool us once, and all that."

"You can't get the body. She was at the epicenter of that blast, and she set it off to protect *everyone*. Not just everyone in the city. Everyone. There's no body left."

"Oh, Robert. Bad lie. You expect us to believe Ms. Moore was a suicide bomber? No, no—it takes a different kind of fanaticism to go out that way. She's sneakier, and she's always shown a gift for self-preservation. No way she nukes herself. You'll have to pull the other one."

"I'm not *pulling!* There was an army of demons on the other side of the—"

"If there was an army of demons, I expect she would have been at the *head* of them. No, dear boy, those lies aren't going to help you here. I was hoping this would be pleasant. I didn't want to do this, because you seem like such a nice kid. I thought maybe we could get you into a rehab program, get this evil out of you. Maybe we still can, but not yet. We need to know where Grace is, and you're the one with the intel." She sighed and shook her head. Then she walked behind me.

I heard a distinct *click* echo through the room, and the pain started all over again.

I HELD MY BREATH, keeping my back straight and my head upright. Perfect posture was the key here. It made the difference between the neck of the painted cartoon alligator in the wooden cutout next to me and the ever-longed-for snout. It was the height of that snout that had tormented me for years, telling me I had to be "this tall" to go on the cool rides. Now I stood "this tall," and that alligator could eat his words.

"Looks like we got the measurement right after all," my father said. He'd been speculating, teasing me about "instrument calibration" being off, as though somehow the measuring tape he used at home wasn't calibrated for it. He was a tall, skinny man whose goofy smile covered his intelligence. His dirty-blonde hair was beginning to be speckled with white around the ears, but the almost perpetual smile on his face shone all the way to his eyes. To Dad, the whole world seemed like an ongoing joke made solely for his benefit. Since I was the center of the whole world, I tended to take offense at this.

"You *suuuure?*" Mom asked. "He may have been going up on tippy-toe. Maybe we should check again." Mom was a woman on the larger side, a dark-brown-haired woman whose mood could change in a flash. For now, though, she seemed content to go along with Dad's mockery. They'd planned this entire day for me, celebrating both my nine years of life and my achievement of the magical height: four feet, six inches.

As soon as my obnoxious parents stopped playing around, I wanted to get to the good part, and they were stalling! I shook my head at them and pronounced in my high-pitched, nine-year-old voice, "No! I'm tall enough. Let's go!" I grabbed my mother's wrist and pulled, trying to drag her deeper into the bowels of Silverwood Theme Park.

My parents laughed at me, a blow to my pride, but they began to move. Good enough.

The good rides, the big coasters all the kids at school talked about, were at the back of the park. To get to them, we passed any number of smaller rides. I'd been on these, the kiddy rides, and they held no interest for me this day. Dad knew that, of course, and took great delight in pausing before each one, asking me if this was the ride I wanted. You'd think that by my ever-increasing pitch as I said "No! The good ones are over theeeeeere!" that he'd get the point, but he kept up that ridiculous smile of his. Mom just chuckled.

Eventually we arrived before Tremors. This was the ride spoken about at school, the one for which Silverwood was known. The rest of the park existed merely as a trapping, decoration, to this one coaster. It traveled over several of the park's walkways, and many times I'd watched the smiling, screaming people having their fun as I simply walked beneath.

Not today. Today, I would slay that dragon. I would be one of those promised few, laughing as the rest of the park watched. It was My. Turn.

Or it would be as soon as I got to the front of this massive line. I stood in the queue, bitterly unhappy with my father. Mom had gone off and sat on the bench to watch. She had professed her dislike of roller coasters long ago. Dad and I stood in line, Dad with his stupid grin, me with my arms crossed in anger at him. Didn't he *realize* that the only reason these people in this stupid line had gotten in front of us was that he had stalled through the whole park? This was all his fault.

He probably *did* realize it. He had probably *planned* it. He was still smiling, still enjoying himself. He thought my frustration was funny. How dare he?

At last, we got into the promised cars. We managed to get the front car, which all my friends had assured me was the best. The safety harnesses fastened securely around my tall-enough shoulders, and we began our ascent up the coaster's first hill.

As we climbed, I began to look around. We were awfully high up—were they sure this was safe? There really wasn't much off to either side of us, and looking down was... *gulp*.

We got to the top of the coaster. Behind me, people started their screaming, their laughing, but I couldn't join in. This was suicide, not fun! They were about to send us straight *aaaaaaaaaaaaaaaaaaaaaaaaaaaaaaa*.

The ride went by in a blur. I wanted off. We were all going to die, I was sure of it. What kind of crazy man designed this sort of machine? My classmates had been pulling my leg, seeing if I would do it. Damn that alligator! Why couldn't he be taller!

The end of the ride came and I was still alive. This came as something of a surprise to me. We pulled up to the platform, and I prepared to get out of the death-trap.

"No," said Dad, the grin gone from his face. "We're going again."

Going again? How could he—wouldn't the ride people save me? But they didn't seem to notice us, and simply filled the cars behind. We remained strapped into the crazy death-machine.

I went for my ace-in-the-hole and started crying. "No! I want to get off! This is scary."

"I know," Dad said, his voice calm and soothing. "I knew you wouldn't like this ride. I knew this would scare you. But I had to let you learn for yourself."

"I learned! Let's go!"

"That was then. There's a new lesson to teach you now. Use the terror, Robert. You are my son, and you can do this. Pain, fear—you can't make them go away, but you can control them. It's just noise in the neurons, just a chemical response in your brain. It's all an illusion."

Right. I wasn't nine years old; I was twice that age. I could do this.

"Dad, I—"

"Not now, son. Someday, maybe. But not now. For now, you have to learn to do this."

The coaster began its plunge again, and the fear took hold. Even in the rushing wind, I heard Dad's voice plain and clear. "Stay centered. Don't pay attention to the illusion. Pay attention to you. You can stop all this in a heartbeat. You know how." His voice was stern, focused.

My father's hand rested on my shoulder, and he waited patiently for me. The coaster kept plunging, longer than it had before. I couldn't see an end to it. We were plummeting into blackness. Terror gripped me, but I listened to my father. Noise in the neurons. I tried to look past it, to grab my Sense despite my blinding terror.

Then it came to me. The Sense, the utter heart of calm that came with it, washed over me. It felt cleansing, like a cold shower. I used it to simply move the kinetic force from the coaster harmlessly into the air. We came to rest just on the other side of the fence from my mother. The other patrons on the coaster grumbled, but Dad and I just unfastened our straps and hopped the fence to sit next to Mom.

"Good job, Robert. Very, very good job," she said, her voice all warm milk and honey. I drank in the praise.

"I know you're not here, really," I said.

"You're wrong, Robert. We're here. We'll always be here when you need us. Don't forget."

A delivery van began careening through the crowd of people along the walkway.

"No," I said, looking at the van. "This is wrong. It didn't happen this way. It didn't happen today." Everyone in the park was dodging out of its way, scampering to get clear. My parents seemed unperturbed.

"No, but it's part of who we are, Robert. It's part of what we did to get here. But don't forget the good with the bad." Dad lifted me under my armpits, then placed me to the side. He sat down on the bench next to Mom and embraced her.

I brought my Sense up, tried to stop the van, but I couldn't Sense it. Mom looked at me. "It's okay, son. We'll still be here if you need us again."

Then the van slammed into the bench and left me on my own again.

ANDREA

I PULLED the van in next to the trailer and sat numbly in the driver's seat.

The front door slammed open, almost before I had the vehicle in park. Amy and Matt flew out. They closed the distance to the van in a matter of seconds before yanking open the van's sliding door.

Thad appeared in the doorway of the trailer and held the screen open, but didn't attempt to exit. His face still looked white and pinched with pain.

Amy scanned the interior of the van and demanded, "Where's Robert?"

I looked at everyone, my eyes scratchy and clogged with tears, anxiety, and guilt. "I didn't get there in time." The ground trembled as the Cornuprocyon below us rumbled his displeasure. "The Feds have him." Amy and Matt cursed in stereo.

"What about Rick? Is he murdercuting everyone again?" Amy struggled to hold back her fear, but her fair complexion had turned a pasty white.

"I have Rick. He's not real happy about that, though." I let my voice trail off, defeated.

"How'd you manage that?" Matt asked, his eyes a bit wild.

"I got lucky, I guess. Anyway, he's under control for now." Not exactly an untruth, but not the full answer either. Another Cythymau trick. Shit was distinctly *not* in control here.

I couldn't tell them what had gone down inside the jail before I got there, but I told them what I had witnessed, skimming uncomfortably over the part where I subdued Rick.

"Damn." Amy bit her lip. "I was hoping the news reports had gotten something wrong."

Matt directed his gaze at me, but whatever he saw was obviously inward. He thought so hard that I could Sense the heightened electrical activity in his brain, even if I couldn't interpret it.

"This location will be blown," he said after a moment. "If they have Robert, we have to assume they know where we are."

Amy threw Matt a shocked look. "You think Robert would blab about our location to the Feds?"

"You haven't seen the reports coming out of their facilities. I have. Summoners aren't considered humans anymore, so human rights don't apply. The interrogation methods have gotten real ugly." Matt's mouth thinned into a grim line. "I doubt he'll have a choice. Even if he manages to keep it under wraps, it's better for all of us to be safe rather than sorry."

"But what if he manages to break free?" Amy crossed her arms over her chest and thrust her chin out. "It's Robert. If anyone can do it, he can. He won't know where to find us."

That, at least, I had an answer for. "Rick still has his bond to Robert. If he gets out, we'll both know."

Director Nielsen finally spoke up from where he stood in the doorway of the trailer. "Then we'll be able to rendezvous with Robert no matter where we are. We should leave." Thad's voice lacked its usual crispness, sounding strained and tired. "Even if it weren't a moot point, staying here when we believe it may be compromised would amount to suicide. We've provided enough hospitality to the Feds at this point, I think. I don't want them to return the favor." He paused, "I shall need help dismounting from here, though. I'm still somewhat unsteady on my feet."

"I'll be right there, sir," Matt said. "We'll need the first-aid kit too, so I'll grab that and get everything settled. Then we need to be out of here."

"First-aid kit?" Amy called questioningly as Matt headed back to the trailer. "Director Nielsen should be OK for now, I think. We can always summon a new one later."

Matt slid past Thad and vanished into the trailer without answering. Either Amy's powers of observation were not the greatest, or the cab of the van was darker than I thought. I lifted my right fist with its bloody wad of t-shirt off the steering wheel and grimaced. I'd held my hand tightly closed for so long that my fingers had cramped. I turned my body to slide out of the driver's seat and give her a better look at it, the wound still bound tightly in the t-shirt.

"Oh, holy damn," she muttered. "Let's get you sitting in the back. I can drive while Matt helps you bandage that. You know what? You need to take better care of yourself. I'm so tired of people going off on their own and barely making it back. Or not making it back at all." She finished the last part under her breath as she levered her arm under my good hand to keep me steady.

Her concern embarrassed me, especially since my injury was self-inflicted. I relinquished the driver's seat happily. To be honest, I still wasn't very good at driving, but a sliced palm didn't make me an invalid.

"It's not really that bad. Don't worry about it. I just needed blood to summon, that's all." I hunched my shoulder in a shrug.

My attempt at nonchalance did not impress. Amy tilted her head to the side, put her hand on her hip, and huffed out a long-suffering sigh.

"Sure. I guess that explains why you're soaking your shirt with it. Just saving some for later, are we? My Sense isn't as developed as Robert's, and I'm not as fast as Grace was. But I'm not stupid, you know. If you needed blood to summon, you could have just pricked a finger. Summoning just doesn't require that much—" Her eye line fell to the wooden charm bracelet I wore on my left wrist. Quickly, I moved my sleeve down over it.

Not fast enough. I could see her taking in the archaic rune forms, but I wasn't going to offer any information. Amy's eyes widened and her chin sagged. I could almost see the cogs turning behind her eyes as she started putting two and two together.

No matter how much she speculated about what I'd done, though, she wouldn't get far if I refused to talk about it. I'd sent the dagger safely back to Cythymau's old storeroom before driving back.

In my Sense, I could feel her pulse speed up as she stared at me. I braced myself for the inevitable questions. Amy paused for several seconds as though struggling with which question to ask first, but no sound came out of her mouth. Finally, she cleared her throat and said simply, "Anyway, take better care of yourself."

I let out my trapped breath, relieved that she'd decided not to ask. She squeezed my shoulder and helped Matt maneuver Thad into the seat opposite me. Thad leaned his head tiredly against the glass of the window and turned his head to face me. His pose spoke of exhaustion, but I didn't doubt for a moment he watched me. I double-checked that my sleeve still covered the charm bracelet. Though I had finally decided I owed these guys my help, I didn't owe them *that* much.

Amy climbed into the driver's seat and started the engine without further comment, but I could feel her eyes watching me in the rearview mirror. She backed up and started rolling down the drive. Matt helped me unwind my hand from my blood-crusted shirt, then whistled as the cut came into view.

"That's a heck of a slash. I think we're going to need the butterfly bandages. Really, you should get stiches, but butterflies are what we've got. What the hell did you cut it on?"

He splashed iodine into my cut. I gritted my teeth against the pain instead of coming up with an evasive answer. Matt bent over my hand, totally absorbed in his task, and didn't seem to expect one anyway. He placed butterfly bandages across the slash like four little bridges, covered those with a pad, and wrapped the whole thing in clean gauze. "Try not to move it for a while."

Amy pulled out onto the winding gravel road in front of the trailer park as Matt stuffed everything back inside the first-aid kit and shoved it onto the floorboard. He moved up to the front passenger seat beside her.

"Which way are we headed?" She cocked an eyebrow at him. "I assume that wasn't your only backup safe house."

"Of course not." He grinned back. "Like any successful criminal mastermind, I have redundancies set up on my redundancies. We're going to head north on 95. I have another hidey hole arranged just north of Coeur d'Alene in Newport, Washington."

"Ugh, we're going back the way we just came." Amy groaned.

"And then some. I do want to keep us close to Robert's last known location. This one's not quite as good as the trailer on the reservation, but it should work to regroup and figure out what we want to do next. I have a new batch of IDs for everyone, too." As he said this, he passed a small card to me.

"Of course you do," Amy said.

I shuddered at my face staring awkwardly out at me from the card and shoved it into a pocket. I appreciated that his cards let us move freely about this Weave, but they made me uncomfortable. It wasn't like my face changed between cards. Only the tags associated with it.

"All these lovely paper trails, and it turns out the one thing I'm very good at is moving paper. They say love what you do and do what you love." Matt's voice had a smug tone. He settled back in his seat, lacing his hands behind his head.

"Uh huh. I just want a better name this time."

"Tell that to the people who originally gave that name to their child. I repurpose; I don't create. It's much cleaner that way. Harder to detect."

"Yeah, yeah, whatever. I'm just saying I better not be a Mildred or Eugenie." Amy shuddered dramatically.

"No promises."

"I swear you do it on purpose," Amy muttered.

"Nope." Matt leaned back in his seat, resting his head on his crossed arms. From the back, he looked perfectly calm, but I Sensed the corners of his mouth turn up slightly before he fell back into deep thought. Even if he didn't do it on purpose, he still enjoyed Amy's reaction.

How many safe houses had Matt set up around the Spokane area? That really wasn't something one did for fun or out of idle curiosity. I'd liked him first because he seemed not to care about "Grove business." Maybe he was a lot less disconnected than I'd originally thought.

In fact, with Thad injured and Robert gone, he'd basically taken de facto command of our little band. I tucked that information into the back of my mind as I stared down at my bandaged hand.

A spike of agony and fear shot through me. I fought to breathe as a cold sweat broke out on my skin. I felt the Cornuprocyon buck and writhe with pain as well, roaring in distress and anger through the bond. At first, I thought the Cornuprocyon must have been discovered and was under attack. The agony raged through us both, trying to consume everything around it. I lost track of time as it pulsed, filling me up to my pores, steeping me in a red haze. That pain surged through the bond connecting us both to... Robert.

Just as suddenly, it faded. As soon as the wave of pain passed, the Cornuprocyon tried to shake my control off, intent on reaching the faint tug that Robert exerted on both of us through the bond. I struggled with Rick, preventing him from barreling out of the ground and calling the Feds down on us like a beacon.

That had been *Robert's* pain. The Feds were doing something to him. But I hadn't Sensed him trying to fight back, or even reaching out to Rick through the bond.

Robert's presence settled into a faint tug that let me know he still lived, but not much else. I didn't know what I was going to do, but charging in after him wasn't the answer. I kept telling myself that as I tried to deal with the anger, fear, and distress one very unhappy Cornuprocyon sent me through the bond about our inaction.

I owed Robert my freedom. In return, I had allowed him to get captured and ripped away his greatest ally. He'd risked everything and paid a high price to free me; I would not forget. I just wasn't sure if I had the courage to do the same.

Amy's eyes met mine in the rearview mirror. "It looks like that hand is paining you a lot more than you'll admit," she said. "You should try to get some sleep while we drive. It's a good two hours until we reach the next safe house."

I fished the ID Matt had given me out of my pocket and tried to remember everything I could about this Weave that *should* have been my home. I had been born here. The centuries of captivity intervening didn't change that, it just made the memories harder to access. I *needed* to understand where I found myself now. If I couldn't be stronger than the Feds, I *needed* to be smarter.

MATT'S new hideout turned out to be a two-story red house with a gray gabled roof and a medium-sized shed with large, barn-like doors out back. It was a middle lot, with a bare field on one side and an elderly fenced-in storage shed on the other.

Matt stashed the van in the shed, then we all trooped into the house using the back door. From the front, you couldn't even tell someone new had arrived. Inside, the floors creaked under my feet and the sun shone through the old, wood-framed windows.

Just like the trailer, Matt had already seen to the furnishings. It came complete with an ugly green sofa, a worn-out dining set, cots, and those ubiquitous fake plants that seemed to be Matt's hallmark.

Thad sat down on the sofa with a groan. "We need to contact the Seattle Grove and let them know Robert's been captured. Amy, can I get your assistance with the summons? I don't think I'm strong enough to hold the connection." Amy nodded and pulled out a piece of paper, drawing a long sequence of runes. I frowned as I considered it.

The summons was perfectly functional, sure. But it seemed like an *awful* lot of extra work. I could have done the same thing with one rune emblem and a fraction of a second. Hers seemed to have a lot of needless fiddling and fine-tuning added to it that limited its scope and range to a very narrow window.

Amy triggered the summons. An image of the small birdlike woman from Seattle took form in front of Thad. He gave his report, but as it turned out, he needn't have worried about sustaining a prolonged summons. The woman shook her head through his recital, then responded with nothing more than a clipped, "We'll take care of Robert. He's no longer your concern. It may be best to vacate the Spokane Grove completely for the time being. Your remaining Grove members are advised to seek asylum in other Groves." The woman turned and walked out of range of the summons, effectively ending the conference. Amy sighed and released the summons.

"I don't like the sound of that," she said.

"It doesn't bode well for Lorents." Thad rubbed his good hand across his chin as he thought. "He does possess a great deal of knowledge about not only Spokane Grove affairs, but also other Groves. Whatever solution the Seattle Grove finds is likely to be... permanent." His words hung in the air for a moment, and I felt ice water slowly crawl down my veins and settle in my stomach.

I blinked. "Permanent solution? The Grove wouldn't kill another summoner while he's being held captive, would they? Any aid he's giving is against his will!" It's not like Robert had thought about *me* that way.

"Even if he's there against his will, the Feds having Lorents is a big security breach and potential danger. Seattle will remove the threat as quickly as possible. And since Lorents has a history of not taking direction, it's likely that they'll find ending him to be the most expedient solution."

"That's just bullshit. Robert's one of our own. We should do something ourselves. I just don't know what." Part of me couldn't believe what I was hearing. By this reasoning, I too should have been eliminated.

Matt sat down next to Thad and opened his laptop. "We don't necessarily have to go for a frontal assault," he said as the computer booted. "It's still a long shot, but we might be able to fake the paperwork to get him processed to a different facility and then sneak him out. It'll really take some—damn it." He swore suddenly, clicking on a flashing icon on his laptop screen.

The icon opened up into what appeared to be a grainy surveillance feed from several cameras.

I swallowed as I recognized the outside of the trailer in Plummer, and then the interior of the trailer from several different views.

Four black sedans and a S.W.A.T. vehicle surrounded it. As we watched, two teams in riot gear broke off, one to breach the front, another to circle around back and check for other exits.

The front door gave easily to the handheld battering ram. Armed figures flowed in, fanning out in a room where we'd been just hours before. They proceeded to toss the place, looking for any evidence of where we were or how many of us had been there.

Thad was still staring at the laptop screen. "You had the trailer wired for surveillance," he said finally.

"Yeah," Matt said. "Not much of a safe house if I don't have contingencies in place to tell me the Feds have found it."

"Those are highly trained law enforcement professionals," Amy said after a minute. "They check for stuff like that. Why didn't they find your cameras?"

"Because I don't use cameras. It's a light summons, like the one I used to get internet at the cabin. It's anchored to the potted plants."

"I always wondered about your fascination with artificial greenery," Amy said, her voice slow and distracted as she focused on the screen.

Over Matt's shoulder, we watched the Feds tear the trailer apart in surreal, frozen silence until the last of the officials shook their heads and left, leaving the trailer an absolute shambles in their wake.

"Well, I guess Robert broke," Matt said into the vacuum of sound. "Damn. I knew he didn't have much of a chance once they got hold of him. But... damn."

He got up, walked over to the doorframe, and punched it hard. More swearing ensued. This departure from his usual mild-mannered demeanor startled me so much my eyes just about fell out of my head.

I thought about the blinding flash of pain Rick and I had

experienced through the bond. "They tortured him for information?" Based on what I'd experienced, I already knew the answer. But I needed to hear it said. Cythymau had used torture whenever he found it convenient, but Cythymau was a demon. These authorities weren't demons. Not in the traditional sense anyway.

Matt's head jerked up, his lips compressed into an angry gash. I thought he was going to yell or refuse to answer. But finally he took a deep breath and flung himself down on the couch. "Yeah."

I chewed on that as Matt shifted with nervous energy, trying to find a comfortable way to sit.

He leaned forward and placed his elbow on the coffee table. His fist rapped repeatedly against his forehead. His eyes closed as he thought.

Amy caught his fist on the sixth or seventh rap. "Stop that," she said. "We'll think of something. Beating yourself up isn't going to help either. There was nothing you could do. You know how stubborn Robert is. I swear he and Grace were a pair of mules in a past life. We'll get him back."

"You don't know that. You don't even know what they're doing to him," Matt answered angrily, jerking at his hand.

"No, I don't. But I know we can't give up." Amy refused to let go of his fist. "We'll figure it out."

A rippling tide of pain tore through me once again. I groaned as cold sweat broke out across my forehead. My stomach spasmed with the intensity of the agony. I had to gasp in several large breaths to keep from losing its contents. Far below me, Rick bellowed with rage and fear. He began trying to claw his way to the surface. I soothed him with everything I could muster, holding him back, promising that I would make sure we got Robert out.

I didn't mean it as an idle vow, either. Rick would have felt the lie through the bond. Besides, I couldn't leave anyone prey to this kind of treatment. I had thought Cythymau the only being capable of delivering such a depth of pain. If I abandoned Robert to these captors to save myself, I would truly be no different than my most hated mentor.

The pain finally receded. I blew out a long breath. As I took stock of my surroundings, I recognized the ugly, green fabric of the couch and the grain of the polished wood flooring. I now lay stomach-down on the floor in front of the couch. As I lay there panting, my Sense finally took back over. Thad and Matt held down my legs while Amy sat on my back smack between my shoulder blades. My throat felt raw from screaming I didn't remember voicing, and my muscles spasmed with the sudden absence of pain.

Amy tentatively relieved the pressure she was exerting between my shoulders. "Are you OK?"

I shook my head, changed my mind mid-shake, and reversed it into a nod. Thad and Matt let go of my legs. Thad staggered, his legs trembling. "You should sit back down before you fall over. I'm fine," I told him.

He hesitated for a second, then moved to a chair. He sat, his hand braced on his knee as he waited for an explanation. I turned to Matt.

"I'm fine, but Robert's not. Whatever they're doing to him, it's so strong that I can feel it through the bond he has with Rick. If we're going to get him out of there, we need to do it now. But if Robert couldn't succeed with a frontal assault, then we can't either."

On top of everything else, this last conversation about the Seattle Grove had made it absolutely clear: without Robert, there never would have been cavalry coming to help me escape from Cythymau. The most likely thing the Groves would have sent was an assassin to take out Cythymau's power support. I owed Grace everything. The combat decision she'd made to save both Robert and me in Cythymau's Weave demanded my respect.

Still... I couldn't ignore the fact that Robert was the bullheaded catalyst who had made any rescue attempt possible in the first place.

I pulled out my wallet and fished for Matt's plastic ID card. I slapped it down on the coffee table in front of him. "What I need is clothes and a card like this so I can pretend to be like them."

"Um, Andrea," Matt said tentatively. "That card already does that."

"No, I need one of the cards that *tells* these 'Feds' people that I am supposed to be at that jail facility. I want them to think I can pick up Robert and take him somewhere else."

"Oh, honey," Amy said, apologetically. "It's not that easy."

"But it should be!" I took a deep breath, trying to calm my jangling nerves and adrenaline-pumped heart. "When I tried to go help Robert before, the uniformed people had one of these cards taped to their fronts, and they didn't attack each other. I want one of the uniforms and a card. To sneak in and take Robert without fighting."

"You're talking about an insanely high security clearance and extensive falsified paperwork to back that clearance up," Matt protested. "That kind of ID isn't like the ones I've been doing up until now. The ID you've got there holds up to some federal scrutiny because I based the IDs on the histories of deceased people. But what you're proposing means I have to create someone, *then* insert her into existing files, past federal-level security, without causing suspicion or raising any red flags. It will require precise, deliberate timing on placing both the digital and paper files. I might—just might—be able to do it if I'm lucky, but it won't be fast. It'd be like doing brain surgery over several thousand miles' distance. With a chainsaw."

"Do we have any other options?" I looked around the room, "Any other ideas?" No one volunteered anything. "You have to do it," I told Matt. He shook his head, but we were out of options. "How fast?" I asked him.

"I need at least two days. Even then, this is crazy. One wrong move and the ID won't be worth the paper it's printed on."

"Do it. I hope for Robert's sake it doesn't really take you that long. Between the torture and the Seattle Grove's 'solution,' Robert may not have two days."

"I'm not a miracle worker, but I'll try." Matt shook his head. "I'm heading up to the room. If any of you want a chance that this works, don't interrupt me until I come out."

All of my hope went into that room with Matt. With nothing to do while he worked, the waiting was torture on its own. The hours ticked by slowly as I paced, unable to sit still. Around midnight, I finally lay down on the couch and tried to rest, staring at the ceiling. Once we had a go-ahead from Matt, there wouldn't be time to eat or catch up on sleep. Might as well try to turn the high-stress boredom into something useful.

~

I WOKE UP DISORIENTED, my nerves sizzling with pain. No one else sat in the room with me. I grasped at the bond with Rick, restraining the Cornuprocyon on instinct as he made the ground around him shake and shiver. Robert was being tortured again. I clenched my jaw against the pain and the flood of helplessness that filled me. Bright sunlight slanted through the front windows of the old house, so I must have slept well into the morning. Soon, Matt would have the ID, and I'd go return the favor Robert had paid me when he'd braved Cythymau's lair against overwhelming force. I clung to that thought, fixing my mind and the Cornuprocyon's on it.

In the midst of all the pain, Robert's Sense suddenly flared, pummeling me with red-hot rage through our connection. I could feel him use his Sense to redirect his anger and lash out at the pain around him. His bloodthirsty, savage emotions flooded through me. I could taste the copper of violence in the back of my throat. Whatever actions Robert might be taking, his desire for freedom warred with his need for vengeance. Caught in the welter of pain and emotions, I couldn't tell which one was winning. Rick howled eerily, desperate to help his master. I could only hope any neighbors would mistake the noise for a coyote. Even if I loosed him now, we'd never make it in time to help Robert with whatever this was. Our new hideout in Newport was approximately an hour and a half away from Robert's location in the Weave. Either he'd make it on his own, or—

A savage joy crept into the anger flowing through the connection, followed by a grim satisfaction. My heart leapt into my throat and Rick whined hopefully even as all our muscles twitched with the pain flooding in from Robert's side of the link. I waited, scarcely daring to breathe. Robert's Sense stayed active, pulling at Rick and me through the Weave. Maybe he'd been able to free himself?

Horror and despair crashed through the bond from Robert. A fraction of a minute later, his Sense abruptly dropped, and my heart plummeted with it. Underground, Rick let out a grieving howl of protest. Very faintly, I could feel the tug of Robert's link with the bond, much weaker than before.

Fuck it. I ran up the stairs to where Matt sat typing on his laptop. He threw me an angry look.

"We're going with whatever you have ready," I said. "Robert needs help *now*."

"I'm not done!" He stared at me as though I'd suddenly grown two heads. Maybe I had. Just a few days ago I wouldn't even have offered to do this. Now, I demanded it. "You might be able to get in on what I've set up so far, but no way you get back out with Robert."

"Then keep working, but give me what you've got. Otherwise there may not be a Robert to save. I'm going now."

"Fuck. Stand still for at least five more minutes. Please." He drew a quick rune on his desktop and piffed a note to Amy, then continued to type, his fingers clicking rapidly on the keyboard. I tapped my foot nervously in counterpoint, already itchy to be gone.

A few minutes later, Amy ran into the room carrying some kind of small printer-like machine, a lanyard, and a sheaf of papers. "I summoned in the stuff you wanted," she said. "What's all this for?"

"I'm not letting Andrea go off with nothing, so this is the best we can do right now."

He took the machine, hooked it up to his laptop, and resumed his typing. After a few moments, it spat out a square piece of plastic with my picture on it.

Next he flipped through the sheaf of papers, muttering to himself, and typing something else into the laptop. Opening a folder, he stuffed everything in and turned to look at me. "This is everything I've got. Try not to get yourself killed. Or worse."

He threw the folder of papers and ID at me in his haste to turn back to the computer. I fumbled to catch it. For a moment, I thought he'd tossed them at me in frustration and anger. But as the furious typing resumed, I realized he'd taken up my challenge. He was going to keep hacking the Feds, trying to make sure my ID was in place by the time I needed it.

I quietly exited the room, going down the stairs thoughtfully with Amy trailing me, uncharacteristically silent. Whatever else you might say about this dysfunctional little Grove, I had to admit its humans were growing on me.

Thad waited for us at the bottom of the stairs.

"I'm going in," I announced. "Matt's still working on everything, but Robert can't wait any longer."

"I'm coming with you," Thad said immediately.

"No you aren't," Amy said just as fast. "You're injured. What the heck are you going to do while you have that hole in your shoulder?"

"I'm your director," Thad began pompously. "You have to—"

"Oh, stuff it." Amy's voice sharpened as she placed her hands on her hips in what I was beginning to recognize as a standard Amy pose. "I backed you last year when I thought Grace was going off the rails. I don't know if it was that or her own stupid bullheadedness that got her killed. Either way, this time, *I'm* going along on the rescue mission. If you want to be all heroic while you're wounded, stay here and guard Matt's back while he hacks the Feds. I'm with Andrea."

Amy grabbed my arm and dragged me out the door with her. She stomped down the driveway, the keys jingling in her hand, and opened the driver's door with a yank.

"No offense, but I'm driving. We'll get there faster." Amy tossed the comment over her shoulder. She climbed in; I followed, scrambling into the passenger seat.

The engine revved as Amy threw the van into motion. Then we were off.

Just like that.

So this was how heroes and martyrs were born. I wished I actually knew which one I'd be.

ROBERT

GROGGILY, I stirred awake once more in my cinder-block interrogation room. I had nothing more I could say, nothing to give, but we were apparently going to do this again.

"He is back."

The voice of Barry, my first interrogator, echoed in the room.

"Yes, well. I think between the psychotropics and the pain, he should be ready to talk to us. You *are* ready to talk to us, aren't you, Robert?" The woman. So both my torturers were here this time. Perfect.

"Go. Fuck. Yourself." It felt good to say it. All the pain in my body, all the pain of seeing Jeanelle, Grace, and my parents, I put into that spiteful phrase. They'd torture me regardless of what I said. I braced myself.

"I am *so* disappointed in you. No lies, no half-truths, no subtle dodges? I've come to expect *more*," that pleasant female voice simpered with an exaggerated pout.

"He is uncooperative. Needs more time."

"Yes, well. When the meat isn't done, I suppose we must let it cook a little more. I'm sorry, Robert. I want this to end, too, but it can't. It just can't until you tell us about Grace."

Click. Pain.

It ripped through me, completely. *Noise in the neurons.* I focused on my father's voice, but under the electrodes, my muscles turned and twisted. I couldn't think, couldn't focus.

Don't pay attention to the illusion. Pay attention to you. You can stop all this in a heartbeat. I pictured the roller coaster, plunging ever downward. Pain, fear, terror, all an illusion. *Noise in the neurons.* I tried to set it aside, to move the pain into one part of my mind and move past. I reached down through years of abuse and neglect from foster parents, through the deaths of the people I loved. I tapped into the anger, the rage. Pain might be an illusion, but my *response* to pain could be very, very real.

When the Sense finally came to me, it filled me with calm and relief for a moment. I felt my muscles twitching, felt the current running through the lines to them. I felt, on the other side of a mirrored glass panel behind me, two people in lab coats pointing at a screen with looks of consternation on their faces.

And then the anger came. The anger I'd used to reach past my pain boiled into my Sense. It fueled me, white-hot and blazing against these people. The Weave around me shuddered with the power radiating outward; my Sense sparked with the fabric of reality like a sweater that had spent too long in a dryer.

I tore the electrodes off my body in a blink. The machine they were hooked to was my next target; I scattered its component parts across the floor. I stumbled off the inclined bed, finding my feet for the first time in—however long it had been.

Didn't matter.

I took a breath, then faced my interrogators. The woman I recognized, but Barry standing next to her was smaller than I expected for such a deep baritone. He stood maybe five-six, tops, and couldn't have weighed more than a buck-forty.

The two of them looked surprised. I grinned at them.

There are a hundred things I *could* have done in that moment, at that time. I could have trapped them behind walls, under floors. I could have walked out of that facility with no casualties at all. I could have spared them. In the time since, I have replayed this scene in my head, counting the number of ways I could have made good my escape without blood.

But I didn't.

Instead, I gave my anger free rein. I let it carry me past my exhaustion, past the pain in my muscles. I needed power, and I found it in pure, boiling rage. Had I been better, had I been stronger—but there is no undoing the past. I let vengeance and bloodlust fuel me instead.

"Robert—" The woman began, extending an open hand toward me in a faux display of friendship. I cut the chatty bitch's words short through the simple expedient of removing her throat. I'm no student of anatomy, and I didn't know what the voice box felt like. I erred on the side of simply removing everything that had a hollow spot. Esophagus, trachea, spinal column...didn't really matter. I summoned it all into her outstretched hand, relishing the stunned look on her face in the split second before she collapsed with blood pouring out of her mouth.

The man turned toward the exit, trying to escape. That wasn't going to help him. He fumbled with the door, but I removed the mechanism inside the knob, effectively locking him in with me.

"So, Barry. This just got interesting for you," I said.

"Stop! Please! I have a family! I'm married, two kids. I'm just doing my job here."

"Speaking in more than three-word sentences now, I see. Lost a bit of that control, have we? No, Barry. *She* was the good cop," I snarled, pointing at the woman dying on the floor. I pulled Barry's left hand off at the wrist and let it drop down on his fallen comrade. He clutched at his stump, bleeding and screaming.

"Beg, Barry. Beg for death. You made me beg, and still didn't grant me relief. You *enjoyed* it. Payback's a bitch, eh, Barry? What's your real name, anyway?" The moron had a wallet. I summoned it, looked at the driver's license. "Joshua Dearborn. Huh. I always thought of you as a Barry. Hmmm... you're a local boy! 34212 South Achilles. That's upper South Hill, isn't it? Swanky. Being a torturer must pay well.

Looks like this thing was just issued, too. I'm guessing you recently moved in?"

He flailed wildly at the door. The techs approached from the other side.

"You're going to die now. I need for your last thought to be of your family, because when I get out of here I think I have a prior engagement at 34212 South Achilles. You're going to die, but you are also the reason for what's about to happen." My words spewed forth on a wave of hate, barely passing through my consciousness before echoing in the small room. Barry broke down sobbing.

Even in my rage, I knew I was bluffing. I wanted him to die in the same utter despair he'd made me feel, but I didn't have anything in particular against this man's wife other than her poor partner selection. I certainly wasn't going to do anything to his kids.

Except remove their father.

I pulled his brain out of his head. The panicked look on his face relaxed immediately into death. I could sense some electrical activity in the brain now lying on the floor, dimming quickly. Final thoughts? Still conscious? Really no way to know.

I faced the mirrored wall and shattered it. In a moment of dark inspiration, I filled the bodies of the two techs behind that pane with the shattered pieces of glass. These people had sat and watched as I screamed. They'd seen my brain flare with the pain of it. In return, they died screaming.

Then I picked a wall at random and opened it up.

By the time I was in the hallway on the other side of the wall, the alarms were blaring full bore. Sound is nothing more than kinetic energy. I could feel it pulsing its waves in the air, and I took it, forming it into a pinpoint ball. The first armed guard who came around the corner got a concentrated burst of sound energy leveled at his chest, instantly coating the wall behind him with his remains.

I could feel my muscles, sore from the electrodes. I could feel my mind, already at the edge of exhaustion, tiring further with the energy I expended. I didn't have the reserves for this, wasn't ready for a full battle.

I shook my head, took the pain, and let it fuel my rage. The fastest way out of here was a straight line; I simply pulled the wall in front of me away and stepped through.

Guards filled the hallway behind me, but didn't follow as I walked into a large room. People, strapped down on gurneys, IVs in their arms, lined the walls. I didn't recognize any of them. The door at the far end of the room burst open with another company of guards.

They opened fire.

I felt it all, the bullets on their trajectory. Not all the guards were within range of my Sense, but that was fine. I simply took each bullet and spun it around, sending it back in the general direction it came from with its own force. This wasn't terribly accurate; there were far too many bullets for that, so my aim was general at best. Even so, after the first burst of fire, five guards were on the ground and I stood tall. I also hit a couple of people on the gurneys, innocent bystanders.

They're better off, I rationalized to myself in my anger-fueled haze.

I moved toward the door on the far end at a slow, deliberate pace. As I did, I removed the needles and restraints on the people around me. Most wouldn't wake up in time, but it was worth the effort. Behind me, guards were yelling, commanding me to stop. I couldn't figure out why they thought that would work. The guards in front didn't open fire again, but they held their ground.

"Get on the floor!" they shouted, as though their weapons could do a damned thing to me. They couldn't, and by now these assholes knew it. When my stride brought me in Sense rage, I channeled the power from the electrical circuits in the walls into their clips, one at a time. Their weapons blew in their hands, mangling and injuring, but not getting through the armor on their chests.

A lance of pain ripped through my brain. I was running hot, using my anger to burn reserves I didn't actually have. It gave me a pause, let me look at the sheer destruction I was causing.

These bastards hadn't been *directly* involved in my torture, but they stood in my way. They wanted me to go back, and that was a mistake. Instead of expending more energy than I had to, I gave them a chance to fix that mistake. "Run. Now."

Some did. I counted to three, like my mother used to do when she was angry at me. "One." Slowly, forcefully. "Two." I took another step forward. More broke and ran, but seven of them continued their stand. They had no weapons, no defense, but they stood.

It was brave.

It was stupid.

I didn't, couldn't respect bravery. Not in that moment. They were in my way, which meant they valued my torture over their lives. "Three." I removed their brains, leaving them in a pile behind me for the guards who might think to follow me out.

None did.

I CUT my way through the corridors, offices, and the massive kitchen. The rooms had been cleared; my path was nothing if not predictable, and nobody else wanted to challenge me. Good. By the time I removed the wall of the kitchen and breathed in cool, clean night air, my rage had flagged and the pain in my muscles and head had begun to take over. I tried not to think about the things I'd just done, but the gruesome images I had created stuck with me.

I had another hundred yards or so to go before I'd be through the perimeter fence. I felt the bond to Rick go live, felt his excited glee, but something was holding him back. I couldn't tell what, but there was another presence in the bond.

Deal with that later. Spotlights swept across the prison yard, highlighting me, but no one came close. A helicopter flew overhead, and as I walked across the yard a small parcel attached to a parachute floated to the ground in front of me.

I considered the parcel with my Sense first, thinking it might be an explosive of some kind. Instead, it turned out to be a tablet computer with a note saying "Turn me on to see your foster parents" taped to it.

Francine? Donald? The thought of them drained away the last of my rage. As I let go of the anger, a wave of pain slammed into my brain, punishing me for the abuse I'd done to myself. My foster parents... I turned on the tablet.

A face appeared on the other side of the screen, a stern-looking man whose grey hair had been chopped short into the classic military crewcut.

"Hello, Mr. Lorents. My name is Warden Brown, and I run this prison. I need you to stop right now and get on your knees. We can tranquilize you from the helicopter and end this ugliness. You've killed some good men today. I want to simply take you out, but my orders are to try to keep you alive so we can have a grand trial before we execute you. Good fodder for the masses, political bullshit."

"You are no foster parent of mine. And I'm not stopping."

"If you do not, I will personally kill one of these people you so love." He changed the camera angle on his end to show me Donald and Francine, strapped to gurneys and unconscious. "Negotiations end now. Accept the dart, and you can go to sleep. We'll keep you alive for the trial, but you'll never see consciousness. It'll be easier that way."

I Sensed the dart coming in and reacted on instinct. I moved it away, let it sink harmlessly into the soil in front of me. It had been a reflex, not even a conscious thought.

He was ready for it.

"Wrong choice, Robert." He kept changing the camera angle, let me see him draw his sidearm.

"No!" I shouted, but it didn't affect him at all. He calmly placed the muzzle of his pistol next to Donald's sleeping head and pulled the trigger. The exit wound blew blood and other pieces of Donald over Francine's unconscious form.

"One down, one to go, Robert. I'm not screwing around here. I've got a strategic bomber on its way to sterilize the whole area if it has to, but I'm actually not sure whether that would kill you. It would certainly kill Francine and me. This is simpler. Now, are you going to behave, or do I need to repeat the process?"

They might kill Francine anyway, I told myself. She stood accused of being a summoner, or an accomplice at the least. She might not live through this regardless of what I did.

Didn't matter. Francine was the closest thing I had to a mother. My defiance faded from me. I'd lost. I collapsed to my knees and let the pain overtake me. My tank had run out, leaving me exhausted.

"Firing again, Robert. No tricks this time."

I dropped my Sense. I didn't feel the dart before it hit me. I knelt there and let the drug take effect. The last thing I saw before lapsing into sweet unconsciousness was the perimeter fence only a hundred yards ahead of me.

ANDREA

THE DRIVE from Newport to Airway Heights gave me plenty of time to study the dossier on my new identity. The more I read, the less it made sense to me. My present-day knowledge of this Weave was limited at best, and long government titles and security clearances might as well have been written in a foreign language.

I made sure to remember *my* name and title, Homeland Security Deputy Director of National Clandestine Services, Senior Adjunct and Field Commander Valerie Dunst. If anyone decided to pry more than that out of me, though, I was *so* screwed. No way could I remember enough of this information. I picked up the badge and the lanyard with its official identification card. My face and alias depicted on its shiny surface fascinated me. I let the rest of the dossier fall to my lap.

Calling off the plan wasn't an option. However, the possibility of another stint in captivity asserted more and more pressure. I had to stomp down on my panicky flight reflex.

"Even if Matt gets everything in place, I might not be able to pull this off," I admitted, closing my eyes and leaning back in my seat. "I don't understand what even half of this means."

I Sensed Amy nodding, appearing unfazed. "I expected that might be the case. I wasn't sure you'd admit it, though."

"If I'm going to do this, I'm going to give it everything I've got. And even then, I may need some kind of divine intervention." I laughed at myself wryly.

"It's not as bad as you think," Amy said. "Matt's essentially made you part of the anti-terrorist high command. The Deputy Director's personal aide."

"High command, deputy director's aide. I got the field commander part."

"That's the first thing you need to know. The second thing is that everyone else at this facility should be lower than you on the command food chain. There are only so many anti-summoning elites. *Most* of the personnel here are career law enforcement with a crash course in anti-summoner training. However, the Feds have sent in backup to fill out the roster and conduct the… interrogations. With any luck, you'll out-rank everyone there."

"In my experience, relying on luck gets you totally screwed."

She sighed and glanced over at me. "If you want to rescue Robert, it's what we've got. Your cover is still civilian, so you don't have to salute. Just act like you own the place; let the ID and papers do the talking for you. Be your usual taciturn, dour, and aloof self. That'll go a *long way* toward selling it. You've got acting cold down pat. Oh. Remember that you can't run away from anyone. That'll be a dead giveaway."

"Right. No running." Much easier said than done.

"That includes your usual evasive, squirrelly behavior. Be silent. Be certain. Be icy," Amy advised.

I could do silent. I preferred it, really. Icy wasn't going to be a problem. Hopefully, two out of three would see me through this. I wiped my sweaty palms on my running pants. Amy's mouth pulled down in a little grimace of disapproval.

"Those clothes won't work for your new ID at all. I summoned you something to wear last night, since I'm sure you don't own a business suit. You might as well get changed so you can get used to it."

I shrugged my way into the dark navy-blue suit, struggling a bit with the tan stockings. I'd missed many things from my previous existence during my long sojourn in Cythymau's Weave, but pantyhose was never one of them. I had a moment of dazed relief that the shoes were sensible navy-blue flats with practically no heel. After so many centuries without wearing shoes, I could do silent and intimidating, but keeping my balance on high heels? Not so much.

A mile from the detention center, Amy pulled the van over. "OK," she said, "this is as far as I go, but if you need me, just piff me a distress signal. And let me fix your hair to match that suit." She wound my fiery red hair into a tight bun held high on my head. When I checked my reflection in the rearview mirror, I did have to admit the style made me look older. The bun pulled my scalp up, highlighted my cheekbones, and gave my face an even more severe, rather unflatteringly pointy look. She clipped my ID to my lapel and stepped out of the car. I followed her out, circling over to the driver's side, expecting to take her seat in the van.

"Oh, no." Amy clicked her tongue. "You can't show up in that thing. That's completely out of character."

She stretched her arms out in front of her, cracking her fingers with an elaborate flair. Kneeling down, she drew runes in the dirt in front of the van. Next, she took a flask of blood out of her purse and winked at me. "Here goes nothing," she said as she splashed the blood across the runes.

She closed her eyes, focusing her Sense. I shifted awkwardly as the summons drew on for several minutes. Right when I was about to ask her if she was having trouble, a plain black SUV popped into existence beside the van, settling to the ground, its suspension creaking in protest.

"Whew!" Amy panted. "Grace always made that look so easy, but that sucker's heavy." She took a deep breath and blew it out. "Anyway, that's your ride. Or rather, 'Field Commander Valerie Dunst's' ride, I guess. It's got a double-reinforced cage in the back with room for Robert's gurney. They may send a deputy out with you and Robert as backup, but if it's just one or two extra guards, we should be able to handle that when the time comes."

She handed me the keys and flung herself on me unexpectedly in a hug. I tried (rather unsuccessfully) to hide the immediate stiffening of all my muscles. I swear, even my hair stood on end. I patted her back in an awkward gesture of reciprocation. She gave me one last squeeze and released me.

It surprised me to see her eyes glisten as she smiled.

"Good luck," she said. "You and Robert come back safe." She climbed back into the van. I slid into the shiny, new car-smelling interior of Valerie Dunst's SUV.

As I DROVE SLOWLY toward the guard station on the perimeter fence at the detention center, fear kept clawing its way up from my stomach and washing my throat with acid. I kept a death grip on my focus, consumed with keeping myself moving forward and Rick subdued. It took all I had to keep him from exploding upward from underground, ruining our covert plan.

Rick sensed my extreme unease. An image of him shredding the guards to pieces resonated in the bond, blinking out on a hopeful nudge. I appreciated the offer, but sent back a firm negative. The loop of conflicting emotions roiling through both us could have powered a small generator. One wrong thought sent to Rick and the whole plan could all fall to pieces in a blink.

The guards at the gate examined my ID, badge, and accompanying prisoner-transfer paperwork. They waved me through with instructions to park just behind the loading dock and check in with Warden Brown. I parked the vehicle and reminded myself to look assured and in control as I climbed out. A transport vehicle pulled into the dock; personnel began scurrying past to unload unconscious prisoners and rush them inside.

Biting down on the inside of my lip, I reminded myself that I was only here for one particular prisoner. But as the orderlies started whisking gurneys past me, I couldn't resist using my Sense to pull

IV needles free from veins to drip harmlessly into the prisoners' sheets.

The tape still held the needle firmly to the person's wrist, which should obscure what I'd done for a while. There was nothing to actually link the tampering back to me. When my guard escort came to collect me, I strolled purposefully behind him, but more slowly than was strictly necessary, unobtrusively dislodging as many IVs on my way to the warden's office as came in range of my Sense.

The guard signaled me to wait for a moment and strode to an inner door with a plaque labelled "WARDEN." I looked around the stained institutional hallway while he announced my arrival. I twisted my fingers in my skirt unobtrusively, trying not to fidget while I waited. The guard returned shortly and waved me in before leaving.

Outside Warden Brown's door, I took a deep breath, squared my shoulders, and walked briskly in, armed with just myself, Amy's advice, and a couple of meaningless symbols to back up my bluff.

Keeping my features tight, I stepped up to the warden's scarred metal desk and slapped my orders down on top of it. I couldn't help cataloguing the room with my Sense. Two windows behind the warden, both barred and locked. One door into the secretary's adjoining office and one into a back storage room. Amy had told me to be silent, but it felt like I should at least state my credentials.

"Valerie Dunst, Homeland Security, Adjunct to the NCS Deputy Director, and Anti-Terrorist Field Commander. I have jurisdiction over this prisoner." I crossed my arms over my chest and waited. Silent. Disapproving. Aloof. Not running screaming from this building and the rows of prisoners who served to remind me of my time in Cythymau's cave.

The warden looked from my ID to the transfer papers releasing enemy combatant X58793, aka Robert Lorents, into my custody. "This is a category one, high-threat prisoner," he said, looking up in surprise. "Why would they want to move him?"

I gave him a disdainful look, raising an eyebrow.

"He won't break out like that again," Warden Brown spluttered.

"We have him double-sedated. It's under control. This is an unnecessary risk."

I just looked pointedly at the papers and tapped my foot impatiently.

He sat down before trying again. "Look, I know that our previous interrogations on X58793 have yielded incomplete intelligence. Reviving him currently would most likely result in sub-optimal results, but solutions *are* in process. Moving him could have a negative effect on current efforts."

What the hell was he talking about? I grunted in response and left the interpretation up to him.

"X58793 may have displayed an anomalous reaction to current interrogation techniques; however, this presents a potential opportunity to refine future methods. An additional research period could be beneficial in this case."

This guy would not stop talking. I understood maybe one word in four. I had to stop him before he launched into another indecipherable speech and blew my cover wide open.

"Exactly how much time do you think I have?" I asked, looking down my nose at him and putting all of my disgust about this facility into my face. I stooped, banging my palm against the order on his desk for emphasis. I stayed bent, looming over him in his chair, and stared him down. "Are you refusing to comply with the transfer orders?"

"Of course not. But I'll need to verify them."

"So, why aren't you?" Even as I said the words, I sent a fervent prayer to whatever powers might be listening. Matt better have finished whatever he'd been doing. Otherwise, this was about to get ugly.

The man fumbled for the phone receiver and punched in a number. Keeping his eyes on my face, he transmitted my information and the papers' particulars to some unknown on the other side.

"Uh-huh, OK. Yeah, she's right here. Tall redhead with a mean stare. Ha ha, hmm. OK." I braced myself. "Yeah, sure, I'll hold." That might be good or bad. Right?

"Not like any of us are going anywhere," the warden continued. He looked over at me. "It'll be a few minutes. They're running your papers for approval." I hoped that meant through a computer and not to a human. Matt couldn't trick a human. I'd be hosed. After being bounced around a few times, the warden finally confirmed my order and apologized for the delay.

I firmed my face, not letting an ounce of my giddy relief show. In a flat voice, I uttered a cold, "Of course. If you are done obstructing my duties, I'd like to be on my way."

I headed deeper into the belly of the beast, two orderlies and a deputy by my side. No alarms blared, and no one threatened me with anything other than some bureaucratic posturing. I guessed Matt's cover ID must still be holding. I'd feel much better once I was headed out instead of farther in.

Once into the main hallway, I had to choke back my reaction. To each side were barred rooms lined with gurneys. Each room held at least six gurneys. The portion of hallway we passed contained at least forty such rooms. We weren't on a tour or anything, so this was just one small section of the detainment center. With the frequency of new detainees, I'd known there had to be many people being held here, but seeing it for myself was an entirely different matter. The cells were too deep for me to free any more IV needles, and it didn't sit well with me that I was walking past without doing something. I bit the inside of my lip, trying to keep myself focused on the task at hand.

"We're going to have to go down to containment, by interrogation," my deputy-guide told me. "Warden Brown might be sad to see that bastard go, but I'm not. You can have that sick fuck. He killed sixteen of our own before we got him under control the other day. If I had my way, he'd already be put down, not off to vacation in some other facility."

Not trusting myself to speak, I let an icy silence fill the air between us. The deputy shifted uncomfortably. "I know you're thinking someone must have mis-calibrated the dosage or intentionally left him untreated for a prisoner go berserk like that, but these summoners just aren't human. You turn your back for a second and they have no hesitation in killing or letting some demon eat you. I heard about a Fed in Spokane who had his heart ripped clean out of his body. If a demon didn't do that, I dunno what did." He shuddered.

I felt as if I'd just reached out and taken hold of a live electric wire. The jolt ran through me from head toe. I tried not to visibly jerk with shock.

There hadn't been any surviving witnesses, but I could still feel the weight of the federal agent's heart in my hand. To the guard next to me, my actions made me no better than a demon.

Our horror-house walk continued in silence, which I preferred. Row after row of comatose bodies continued to appear. I fought with my growing, incoherent fear, struggling to contain Rick's increasing exuberance as he Sensed me getting closer to Robert. Enough things battled for my attention without trying to listen to this guy.

Focus, Andrea. Get to Robert. Get out. Deal with everything else later.

"We've arrived, ma'am. Your prisoner's here," said the deputy. The hall ended in three separate doorways. One door labelled Interrogation had a slit window. Another room butted up against it, and one doorway led into a cell. The deputy pointed to a prone form on a lone gurney. I stepped closer to get a better look.

"The orderlies will go in first and make sure he's still sedated," the deputy cautioned. He stepped out of the way to let the orderlies enter.

On the left side of the room, I could see Robert's skinny form and tousled hair. He'd been trussed down to his gurney and appeared unconscious. The orderlies took his vitals and checked his IV cocktail of drugs. As soon as they finished, I gently pulled the IV needle out of his arm, leaving it taped to his wrist. They started wheeling him toward the door. I allowed myself to breathe an imperceptible sigh of relief.

As I stood there, waiting, so close to getting Robert to freedom, the door to the observation room opened. A broad-shouldered man in a dark suit stepped out. He had a military-type cut to his hair, and a weathered, lined face, leathery and tough.

"Deputy?" he intoned, throwing a questioning look our way.

"Afternoon, sir," the deputy replied. "We'll be out of your way soon. Homeland Security's Field Commander Dunst here has an order to take custody and transfer this prisoner personally."

"Field commander," he drawled. "Well, that's a high rank for escorting one prisoner, even one as troublesome as Lorents."

I met his challenging stare haughtily, as if my feet weren't sliding around in my suddenly sweaty shoes. "And who might be questioning my orders?"

"Special Agent Warner, of the reality terrorist interrogation unit. It was my understanding that this one *was not* to be moved."

"The situation has changed," I said firmly.

"Transfer papers check out," the deputy informed the man helpfully.

His voice trailed off as neither of us replied.

I let the silence stretch, then said, "As you can see, I am moving this prisoner. If you do not let me pass, I will have no choice but to report you for impeding the official duties of a field commander."

He stepped to the side, but continued to stare at me challengingly. "The papers check out, hmm?"

I met his gaze coolly. "Now if you'll excuse me, I do not want to take any chances with this one. Don't let me keep you from your duties." I turned to the deputy and orderlies. "I have a schedule to keep. We need to keep moving."

The agent nodded an assent. I walked briskly down the hallway with Robert and company in tow.

The deputy muttered apologies and hustled to take the lead once again. When I glanced back over my shoulder, Agent Warner stood to the side of the hallway with a cellphone pressed to his ear. He was too far away for me to Sense who he called, but I hoped Matt's cover identity would hold up a few minutes longer.

Not risking another look back—this man was trained in interrogation, after all—I marched straight down the hallway. My Sense is all that saved me. Without it, I would have totally missed the tranq dart aimed at my back. As it was, I diverted it with my Sense at the last minute, lodging it in the Kevlar shielding the deputy's back. I dropped into a crouch, using Robert's gurney as cover.

"What the heck?" the deputy spluttered, drawing his weapon and leveling it across Robert's prone body. Agent Warner ran toward us, firing another dart at my crouched form. I siphoned kinetic energy away from the dart with my Sense. It clattered harmlessly to the ground in front of the gurney. Should I assume my cover was blown? Even so, could I possibly still bluff my way out? Either way, I couldn't afford to let them render me unconscious.

"What's your problem?" I yelled down the hallway. "I'll be sure to write a report detailing this entire incident to the Deputy Director!"

"Don't listen to her. She's a summoner," Agent Warner yelled. "My superior at the D.C. office just confirmed that no one over there has heard of a Field Commander Dunst."

Well, damn. You might be able to alter digital and paper files with summoning, but one guy with a cell phone and a direct line to D.C. turned this into a whole different ballgame. No use trying to prevaricate with some other excuse now.

My Sense reached out in a twenty-foot sphere around me. Sadly, the agent was still about forty feet away. He reloaded and fired, closing the distance between us.

Agent Warner might have been outside of my sphere of influence, but the others weren't. Next to me, two orderlies and the deputy stared, unsure what to believe.

I'd better do something with them *before* they made up their minds.

First, I redirected the dart flying at me into the shoulder of the left-hand orderly. He flinched and looked from me to Warner before crumpling to the floor. The deputy swore, reaching for his tranq weapon. I stole it out of his hands with my Sense and fired it into the second orderly. The deputy had more tranq darts in a pouch on his waist. He reached for me, intending to grapple me. I stabbed a dart into his waist using my Sense, no gun needed. The deputy's arms closed over me, and then relaxed as the drug took hold. He slid to the ground.

I hurled the whole IV stand as far away from Robert as possible. The bag jarred loose and burst, its contents splashing harmlessly to the floor. Agent Warner skidded to a halt in his headlong rush to meet me, apparently wanting to wait for backup. I couldn't let that happen. But I had my own.

Sending my Sense through the bond, I released my chokehold on Rick's leash. The ground vibrated as Rick sent a surge of glee and relief through the bond. At least someone was happy to see some action. I *wished* I could share his joy.

Just because Warner wasn't in Sense range yet didn't make me unarmed. I reloaded the tranq pistol with my Sense. It couldn't be that hard to fire one of these things. I squeezed the trigger. The dart flew over the agent's head.

Warner ducked reflexively but kept coming. I reloaded, running down the hallway to close the space between us. I fired one last dart. He dodged behind a door, avoiding the projectile.

But he was in range of my Sense now. I could feel the pounding of blood through his muscles, the chemical impulses in his brain, the small electric charges that telegraphed which way his limbs were about to move. He dropped his tranq gun and pulled a pistol out of his shoulder holster.

"Damn reality terrorists," he snarled as he fired, obviously aiming for my center mass. I turned it aside easily. "I don't know how you and that other abomination are managing to practice your black arts without runes, but once I get a chance to run tests on the two of you, I'll—"

I removed four of his cervical vertebrae.

For a fraction of a second I just stood there holding them. His eyes slowly widened. Then his neck sagged under the weight of his skull, and his head skewed sideways, crushing his spine.

If he was going to offer me lethal force, I could offer it right back. I discarded the vertebrae and cleaned the blood off my fingers. I ran back to Robert's gurney, arriving just before the alarm started to blare.

The radio in the deputy's belt crackled with reports of backup en route and requests for status. I turned my attention to evaluating my current situation. Several people had exited the interrogation room at the end of the hallway by Robert's cell. At the other end, toward freedom, I still had about fifty feet to the main corridor that led out to the warden's office. And an unknown number of deputies beyond that.

Robert's fingers twitched like he might be waking up, but I couldn't risk leaving him alone. The last thing I wanted was to give the Feds an opportunity to use him as a hostage. If I failed that badly, death would be preferable. I already had several lifetimes of torture and captivity under my belt, thank you very much.

Outside, I could hear screams and gunshots as Rick started bullying his way inside, taking out several walls.

The people who had exited the interrogation room began advancing down the hallway toward us, slowly. One pulled out a radio and started to report.

Fine. I just needed to even the odds a little bit. I propelled Robert slowly down the hallway, tucking him up against the doorway to a cell to provide some cover. Robert groaned. I summoned all the restraints off him in case he woke up before I finished this.

A sour-faced female guard rounded the doorway, firing a tranq. I batted it aside with my Sense. It flew wild, striking a spark off the metal of the gurney. She fumbled with her waist pack for another syringe. Growling, I summoned the pack from her waist and tangled it around her feet. She went down swearing. I bound her with the restraints that I'd just removed from Robert. She cursed more, struggling to get free. I stuffed her shirt in her mouth so I didn't have to listen.

The two remaining men tried to lunge at me in tandem and grapple me to the ground. Inside my Sense range, they were at a severe disadvantage.

I dodged backward and took care of them both with a couple of quick tranquilizer darts. At the far end of the hall, backup was flowing in at a steady rate. If they stuck with projectiles, I'd be OK. If they tried to rush me all at once, staying non-lethal would be a problem. I could count at least twenty so far.

The ground rumbled and the walls rocked. Rick blasted out the far wall next to where the deputies were gathered, cutting them off with an impressive slide of rock and rebar.

Ah, yes. There was the cavalry.

ROBERT

CONSCIOUSNESS CAME over me with the speed of a glacier, and even then it managed to be a surprise.

My eyes remained closed, but I could hear noises just to the side of me. They came across fuzzy, and my mind groped futilely to process them. *I'm supposed to be dead,* I thought to myself. Tranq, trial with me unconscious, execute me—that had been the plan, right?

I blinked. The light pierced to the back of my skull. Hmm, bright, blinding light but no fire. If I was dead, could this be heaven? I reviewed the past couple of years of my life. If I'd made it to Heaven, large portions of the basic Judeo-Christian belief system had simply gotten it wrong. Probably not Heaven, then.

Then I heard one noise that made sense. The one noise that could confirm, absolutely, that I certainly hadn't made it to Heaven, though it didn't rule out other portions of the afterlife. The one noise that galvanized me from absolute motionlessness up to simple sluggishness. No other noise could provide that shot of adrenaline.

Whoomph.

I rolled to my side and promptly fell off my gurney. Sore muscles screamed protest. Not Heaven. Not Hell. Not even a good old reincarnation. I lived, still. And in the vicinity of a Cornuprocyon.

Given that, either Rick was here with backup or this whole still-living thing would be more in the nature of an encore than an enduring condition. I blinked my eyes blearily, fighting the pain. I reached for my Sense, but the drug-induced fog did a better job of blocking it than the pain ever could have.

In the blurriness, I saw a single female form standing in the hallway beside me. One person against, by the sounds of it, an army. One woman, serving as my guardian.

Grace? I knew it didn't make sense, but sometimes when you're coming out of a drug-induced coma you don't make sense. Had I summoned her again? Unconsciously? I didn't know how that could be possible, but there she was.

The tears welling up did little to improve my vision. Down the hall, I could hear the sounds of Rick getting into the fight: more *whoomphing* and some screaming. I blinked, rubbing my eyes. The light still pierced them, but it hurt somewhat less. Colors started to filter in: the gray of the room, the red of my protector's hair.

Wait... Red? Not Grace. I only knew one summoner with fiery red hair. Only one summoner with red hair who could, in theory, coordinate an attack with Rick. Only one summoner with red hair who hadn't decided my death was best for the Groves. Just the one.

Huh.

Time later to figure out the hows and the whys of the situation. I didn't know how much strength Andrea had, or had left. I didn't know how long this fight had been going on. Had they already killed Francine? No, couldn't be. They'd use that card on me, but it would have next to no effect on Andrea.

I grasped once again for my Sense, relaxing into it. It filled me, but even with my Sense I felt sluggish. I felt the bullets cascading toward Andrea, but I couldn't react fast enough to do anything about them. My mind simply didn't move quickly enough.

Andrea's did. The bullets neatly missed their target, every one. She didn't have my precision with Sense-based summoning, didn't turn the bullets back at their source, but she was quite able to keep us protected.

For now.

We needed to move. I felt quite sure that the United States armed forces had more bullets than Andrea had stamina. I struggled to my knees.

"You're up. Good. Can you move?" Andrea didn't bother to turn her head, didn't shout at me. She felt my Sense, knew I could feel the vibrations in the air, so she simply spoke in a soft whisper and let me pick up on it.

"Slowly," I replied in the same manner. "I'm still pretty groggy. Not sure I'm going to be a lot of help."

I felt Rick's exuberance burst through the bond. I could hear slamming in the hallway and envisioned his club of a tail breaking into first one wall and then another as he failed to contain his excitement.

It was good to have friends.

"What about Francine?" I asked. "Have you already gotten her out?"

"Francine? I just came in for you. Didn't even think about her." Of course not. So I was on breakout round two. If we didn't go for Francine, it would end the same way round one did, except this time I'd lose Andrea too.

"We've got to go for her. She's somewhere in here, but I'm not sure where."

"Won't that get us killed, too?"

"Not leaving without her. They already killed Donald; they've made their point."

"I don't think we're going to make it farther in. I'm worried about just making it out."

I could have been more tactful, but to be fair I felt scared, groggy, and angry all at once. So I responded with, "Guess where you'd be if I'd followed that advice the last time I heard it?"

It hit Andrea hard. She turned her face to look at me, her lips pressing hard against each other and her nostrils flaring. I'd played my trump card with her.

"Fine. Where is she?"

Now *that* was a good question. "Not sure. Cover me."

There was already a body on the ground at Andrea's feet, dressed in a uniform similar to my previous interrogators. I used my Sense to grab some blood from inside that body, pooling it before me. It sufficed to scribe the runes I needed on the wall. Andrea kept up her defense, covering me from incoming bullets.

The drugs were a handicap for Sense-based summoning, but with the slow speed of my thoughts, sliding my Sense into the runes actually became easier. That hiding-away from the barrage of incoming information became a refuge instead of a confinement. I reached out to Francine, locating her general direction in the Weave. I don't know how long it took me, but it felt much faster than my normal runework.

When I came back to myself, I looked up at Andrea. The strain of the constant defense showed in the concentration on her face and the beads of sweat rolling down her cheeks.

"This way," I said, pointing at an angle that went kitty-corner to the maze of halls, and *up*. To emphasize, I removed a section of wall from the direct path. I couldn't stop a bullet, but I could do the slower stuff.

As we backed into the hole, I caught a flash of Rick weathering a barrage of small arms fire. As we stepped into the hole, he *whoomphed* a wall of force out at his attackers, sending them hurtling about like bowling pins. He began to bound after us.

No boy, I thought through the bond. *Keep them busy here.*

Rick *excelled* at keeping law enforcement busy. The guards carried their standard-issue side arms for the most part. The government had undoubtedly dispatched bigger artillery, but for now Rick remained safe. In my head, I heard Grace's voice from the time *she'd* been trying to kill Rick, echoing through time. *So far, I've tried rocks, a treant, C4, a steel plate, and an RPG. So we can check those off the list.* The more guards poured their futile rounds into Rick, the fewer bullets came at us.

The next *whoomph* sent walls crashing down in a direction away from us. Rick scurried through his new tunnel, gleefully, drawing a tail of guards along with him.

Good boy, I thought.

Then I turned back to Andrea, and we went to find my foster mother.

WE CUT a direct path through the prison. Hallways are built for people who can't simply remove walls. We tore through dark rooms filled with alleged summoners, hallways, a medical facility of some kind, and what appeared to be an employees' lounge, complete with coffee urn and vending machines.

Every wall I put a hole in I left in place behind us to obstruct our tail, but that served only as a minor hindrance. Andrea kept her defense up, but tried nothing offensive. That seemed conservative and well-planned, two adjectives that until now I never would have applied to her.

As I moved, I began to shake off the effects of the drugs, my thoughts speeding up. They still weren't *fast*; bullet deflection remained beyond me, but creative architecture I could do. I began creating pit traps behind us. Our pursuers ran into walls of rubble followed by deep holes, obstacles far more difficult to overcome. The pursuit lessened, though other troops still presented themselves in our path occasionally.

These Andrea dealt with in an efficiently brutal fashion by simply continuing to walk in their direction. If any remained by the time they came within Andrea's sense range, she would remove non-lethal body parts. Trigger fingers, and occasionally whole hands, were simply separated from their owners.

It was actually a startling display of non-lethality from her, but the guards didn't see it as mercy so much as they did pain. Word got around, and after the second time, the men in front of us continued to back up. They laid down steady fire, but never let us catch up.

I couldn't run, so our pace remained a steady walk. We didn't flag. The guards stayed thirty, forty feet in front of us, well outside Andrea's Sense range.

Not out of mine.

I pulled the ground out from under them, a favorite trick. I then replaced it, remaining careful to restructure it, leaving room underneath. They'd live, assuming someone came to rescue them.

I didn't have the rage fueling me like before, just a grim determination. I'd killed so many during my attempted breakout last time, and I'd felt them die. When you're on fire with the hatred and the anger, you don't feel the guilt and the shame of stuff like that.

You do afterward.

These men didn't *need* killing. I did what I could to avoid it.

After a couple flights of stairs, we came to a hallway, and I scribed out another summons on the wall using a broken shard of concrete. Francine was close: one of these doors. I began opening them, looking for my foster mother.

I found her three doors down, strapped to a gurney, IV in place. The man from the Skype conference stood over her, pistol in hand. Andrea's Sense lashed out through mine to kill him, but I blocked it. *This* one needed killing, but I didn't want Andrea to do it. *This* one was mine.

Andrea shot me a surprised look. "Why?" she asked.

I didn't answer.

Instead, I removed the gun from his hand and put it in my own, pointed at him. I stepped into the room, leaving Andrea to block the doorway. "This isn't Skype, asshole. This is real life, and you are *far* too close for comfort."

He backed up, his hands raised in a defensive gesture. "Look, you think I like hurting people? You damned terrorists make it *necessary*. You're responsible for the deaths of piles of my guards, my agents. You did nothing but lie to us about the location of your master. You are nothing more than violent criminals, and I will take whatever steps are necessary. But I don't *enjoy* any of this. *You* are the ones who make me do it."

"Yeah. He's lying." Andrea said from the doorway, this time loud enough for the man to hear. "He enjoys this. Petty little king of a petty little kingdom, and he'll say what it takes to keep it. Should have heard him earlier."

His eyes widened at the sound of Andrea's voice, and his face paled. Whatever had transpired between the two of them, her words clearly hit home with the warden.

No sense prolonging this. My Sense could end this immediately, but I liked the poetry of ending him with the weapon he'd used to kill Donald. Guns had never been a thing with me, but the situation called for it. I pulled the trigger, jerking my hand up like you see in the cop movies to control the kick. The recoil in my hand caught me by surprise.

The warden was, at this point, maybe ten feet away from me, and I'd been aiming at his head. The bullet struck the wall about a foot and a half over his scalp, then followed the angle upward into the ceiling. He recoiled in terror, looking down in surprise at his still-living form as concrete chips and dust showered him from above.

Andrea raised an eyebrow at me, lifted her hands and clapped them softly in an exaggerated golf-clap of mocking congratulations. The corner of her mouth turned slightly upward in what I could have sworn was a smile, were it not on Andrea's face.

I flushed, then laughed at myself. The warden wasn't talking any more, no more defiance, no pleas for mercy. He simply stood, staring at me, breathing in choked sobs. *Not worth it.* I kept the gun on him with my left hand as I removed the IV from Francine with my right. I looped Francine's limp arm around my neck, then leaned back against her weight to pull her off her perch. "Get on the table," I said to the warden in my most menacing voice.

He did. I tossed the useless gun to the side and strapped him down. I used my Sense to stick the same IV in him that he had stuck in Francine. He didn't resist, and he didn't say anything. He got to live. I figured he should be happy with that.

"OK," I said to Andrea. "Let's get the hell out of here."

DRAGGING FRANCINE off the gurney had been one thing. Carrying her effectively through a combat zone was something else entirely. They make it look really easy in the movies, but the fact is, a limp human body is really tough to move. I tried walking with her arm over my neck, but that was awkward and felt like I might be doing some damage to her shoulder. I tried to pick her up in both arms like a man crossing the threshold of a new home with his wife, but that didn't work either.

I don't want to say that Francine was *fat*, because that wouldn't be a really accurate description. That said, she'd given up on being *skinny* years ago, and had a comfortable amount of cushion on her body. "Comfortable," of course, is a relative term, and when I finally gave up and carried her fireman-style over my shoulder I found myself wishing for twenty to thirty pounds less weight on my foster mother.

Nothing to do for it now, though.

OK, boy. Let's get out of here, I sent through the bond to Rick. As soon as I did, the entire building began to shake and rumble. Thirty seconds later, as we were moving down a hallway lined with gurneys, the ceiling blew down in front of us. I summoned chunks of concrete away from unconscious forms on gurneys, protecting the innocents from the shower of debris. Sunlight came in through the hole in the roof, followed quickly by the head of one oversized Cornuprocyon, his tongue lolling out.

"Hey, boy. Good call," I said. I climbed up the pile of rubble, holding my foster mother. Andrea covered my rear as we gained the roof. We jogged across it. Once we reached the edge, I jumped, pulling the force of my fall away from me. I fell gently downward, landing easily on my feet. Andrea followed, mimicking my technique. Rick also jumped, though his *whoomph* lacked the measured grace of our descent.

Once again, I found myself looking at the perimeter fence of the prison compound. Beyond it was a section of scrub pine forest, overgrown in bushes.

Once again, I heard the whirring blades of a helicopter overhead. Once again, a tablet computer came floating down on a parachute. I double-checked the unconscious form on my shoulder. It was definitely Francine. What threat were they going to come up with this time?

I thought about simply bypassing the tablet. Would they carry through with whatever threat they were going to make if I did? If I'd never picked it up the first time, would Donald still be alive? Or would Francine be dead as well? And what could they possibly be threatening me with? Did they have Matt, or Amy?

Too many questions, not enough answers. I picked up the tablet and turned it on.

"Robert, hello." This was a new face, a female face. It was older, with dark brown hair and crow's feet next to green eyes. She wore a drab beige uniform: Army, and there were two five-pointed stars on her collar.

"You are a very potent young man, and I have the record of your last conversation on one of these devices. I understand that Warden Brown is dead now, and not able to do this."

"Not dead. Just hooked to one of his own IVs. He'll be fine."

The lady general's eyebrows raised in surprise. "Well OK. Still not in the picture at the moment. I, on the other hand, am far enough away to not be threatened by you. We've tactically analyzed your performance. You are very potent, but not very long range."

She had me there.

"Anyway, since your last attempt, I have had the facility from which you are escaping equipped with self-destruct capabilities. No more nonsense." She displayed a small red button on top of a cylinder. It looked movie-like in its simplicity. "One push of this and everyone in there dies. The guards knew about this, signed up for it. Your fellow summoners, strapped to their gurneys? All of their deaths will be on your head."

"You know they're not summoners, right?" I said. "I mean, there never were that many summoners in Spokane. You're going to kill a bunch of innocents."

"A decent attempt, Robert. Obviously a lie, but worth a shot. Well done. No more chances, though. Either you die or they do. You might live through the blast. I'm not sure. But they won't. What's it going to be?"

There were hundreds of people strapped to gurneys in that building. I didn't know any of them, had no connection. What did it matter to me if the government killed them?

It mattered.

I looked at Francine, at Andrea. Andrea's face was torn; she stared at the scrub pines so close to us. A red dot appeared on her head, and I was sure that another one appeared on me. Rick bellowed, echoing our confusion.

I lowered my head. I couldn't do it; couldn't condemn hundreds for my selfish purposes. I didn't know if Andrea could, or would. I didn't know what choice she would make. *Run,* I told Rick. *Run away.*

Then I lowered my head and waited for the end. Andrea looked at me. It took her a moment before she nodded. "I'm sorry," I whispered to her.

I never got to hear the response. Instead, I heard a keening cry like that of a hawk, but a hundred times louder. It pierced the air, snapping me out of my pre-death reverie. Shortly after, the tablet had another voice on it.

"Ma'am? They're gone. All of them. They just—disappeared." The feed on the tablet cut short.

Then a massive hawk with metallic grey feathers hit the tail of the helicopter and broke it off, sending the chopper into a death spiral. At almost the same time, more massive birds slammed into the guard towers around the perimeter.

Out of the scrub pines, out of nowhere, stepped a crowd. They wore no uniforms, but were dressed as people from all walks of life.

The perimeter fence around the prison simply vanished. Andrea, Rick, and I began to move toward the crowd, our energy renewed by these unexpected reinforcements. At their head stood Annalisa Miller, the Seattle Grove historian.

As we reached her, she smiled at me. Her eyes maintained focus elsewhere, though. She had a runeboard strapped to her arm, a magnetic surface with runes and rune phrases stuck to it like refrigerator poetry. One of Grace's old tricks; it struck a chord of nostalgia in me.

I walked past Ms. Miller, nodding at her. I wanted to ask so many questions, but with this many summoners working in concert I knew that the government response on its way would turn the entirety of Airway Heights into a shitshow not seen in this country since the Civil War. She had things on her mind.

Once past her, however, I got my true surprise. A smaller man, hunched over, with blue, whorled, rune-like symbols tattooed on his body, stood cloaked in a robe in the rear of the Grove. His face broke into a crooked smile when he saw me. *No.* I thought. *You are dead. I saw you get nuked. You can't be here.*

"*Whuft!* You have, once again, become something of a bother, Mr. Lorents," said Cythymau. "We have business to discuss, yes?"

ANDREA

Something here smelled rotten.

I didn't know what, but this scale of effort rarely, if ever, came without cost. I lagged a few steps behind Robert, my feet slowing even further as I recognized the small birdlike woman Thad had spoken to just a few days ago. Her last promise to Thad had been to "take care of" Robert.

This was not the welcoming committee Thad had expected her to send.

The Grove had dispatched a sizable contingent, far more than would be needed to assassinate Robert, especially if drugged. I scanned the rows of busily summoning members, looking for the loophole. Movement in the sky grabbed my attention instead. Summoned avian creatures swarmed above us, crowding the airspace.

A giant hawk swooped down on a guard tower overlooking the facility. The guards in the tower opened up with all the weapons at their disposal. The summoned beast flew into a barrage of gunfire. Unharmed, the hawk screamed its challenge. It dispatched the tower personnel with brutal strikes from wings, talons and beak. One guard tried to retreat, climbing over the railing and hanging off the edge of the tower. The hawk swiped him up with a talon, twisting mid-air with the man still in its claws. The beast drew in its wings and tumbled toward the ground, releasing the man just before they both would have hit the earth. Red blood from the guard's broken body stained the grass.

The bird soared away unhurt, looking for new prey. A line of heavily armored deputies rushed to block the main entrance of the detention facility and form a perimeter. The mammoth bird wheeled, talons extended, calling to its brothers. They descended on the hapless deputies with a gleam of certain death in their eyes, but I couldn't look away. After a few minutes of firing failed to harm the summoned birds, or even slow down the gruesome rending of their victims, the deputies stopped sending reinforcements.

I didn't believe the authorities had run out of armed staff. They bided their time, planning their next tactic. The giant contingent of summoners removed the perimeter fence and other defenses to the facility with swift efficiency.

As the barriers around me disappeared, relief to be free again flowed through my whole body. I didn't want to spend one more minute in this hellhole. Death would be preferable to being taken captive, especially since these officials appeared to be interested in "examining" Robert's and my Sense ranges.

As the ranks of summoners shifted, I realized Robert had continued without me. He had his back to me, standing next to someone I couldn't see. I hastened toward him, weaving through rows of unknown summoners. Many of them had small boards strapped their arms, and they slid small, runed magnets into long, convoluted summons. The summoning technique they used struck me as unwieldy and long-winded, especially when compared to my emblems.

Beyond Robert's skinny frame I saw a flash of sun-bronzed skin with a hint of blue. My muscles seized.

I stuttered to a halt several feet from Robert, unable to keep moving. Electric, remembered pain sizzled through my nerve endings. The world flowed around me in snips and flashes like a child's flip book, but no matter how long I waited, the man next to Robert didn't transform into a harmless figment of my imagination.

My old master, my captor, my false savior, stood calmly talking with Robert. It didn't make sense. Cythymau wasn't of this Weave. He didn't exist here. Couldn't. Not anymore.

I'd already *finished* my self-destructive dance with this particular demon. I'd won. Hadn't I? If Cythymau still lived...

My mind clouded over in a blinding haze of rage and panic. I shook myself, trying to hear what the hallucination spoke. Even the cadence of his voice reminded me of Cythymau.

"—business to discuss, yes?" he asked Robert. Robert's features closed down into an icy mask as he glowered at the man suspiciously.

"Cythymau." Robert's breath hissed out between his teeth and his knuckles whitened where he was holding his foster mother. "I don't have anything to say to you."

I jerked into a run, closing the last few feet between Robert and me. "Wait," I spluttered, gasping for breath, groping for Robert's arm, my chest suddenly constricted. This had to be some kind of waking nightmare. Robert glanced at me, his face even grayer and more exhausted than just moments before. "You see him too?" I asked.

Robert's chin jerked down in one reluctant nod. Damn.

"You don't belong here. We killed you," I said to Cythymau, my voice echoing thick and stupid in my own ears. Even as I said it, there could be no denying Cythymau's distinctive craggy face with its deep-set brow, beaklike nose, and concave cheeks. The swirling blue tattoos inked into his face, peeking out from under his long-sleeved shirt over chest and arms, taunted me; I should have known his sinewy form anywhere.

"Tsk, tsk," the demon chided. "And here I convinced all of these people to join me in saving you both. Very generous of me, I'm sure you would agree. One might expect you to at least offer your thanks before you start bringing up past hurts and insults between us. All forgiven now, of course. Grudges have never been my habit."

No, but vindictiveness, deceit, and cruelty were. The words died on my tongue.

Bands of pain squeezed my chest, crushing my new-found equilibrium. I wasn't ready to go back. I couldn't return to how things were. My Sense headache quadrupled as all the rage, pain, and confusion came crashing back down on me.

I heard a guttural growl. Rick had started bristling, his spiky red-and-orange coat standing on end, his club of a tail twitching in agitation. Hate flowed in a vicious, never-ending loop between our trio in the bond, focused on the small man in front of us. Red obscured my vision as the blood pounded fiercely through my head. Whatever Cythymau wanted, for my own sanity, I couldn't let him have it. Desperation and fear clogged my mind, my temples reverberating like drums.

The weight of all my years of helpless futility, unable to act, finally drove me into action. I wouldn't stand by this time. Cythymau had to pay. I bit my thumb, drawing the summons for my rune bracelet on the spotless white shirt Amy had given me that morning. I sent my Sense into the rune emblems, focused on killing the demon even if I had to end myself in the process. The charm bracelet formed where I summoned it. Its charms dangled against my wrist. I brought the rune I needed to my bleeding thumb.

Just before I launched my attack, I heard a familiar *whoomph*. Rick beat me to the punch.

My killing intent had clearly communicated itself to him through the bond. If Cythymau had been declared fair game by his humans, Rick wanted the first crack at him. I snarled, frustrated, but not willing to call off the Cornuprocyon. More than anyone else, I knew just how badly Cythymau had treated all creatures under his so-called "care." Rick had his own grudge to settle. I collapsed a section of the detainment facility, hurtling toward Cythymau in a coordinated attack with Rick's leap. Cythymau deflected my speeding debris, but didn't move to counter Rick's impending onslaught.

Unexpectedly, unbelievably, one of the Seattle summoners stepped in front of Cythymau, reflecting Rick's force ball and fending off Rick's claws and tail.

Kill anyone who gets between you and Cythymau, I messaged Rick.

The Cornuprocyon rumbled in agreement and immediately devoured the summoner blocking his attack on the demon. Blood dripped down Rick's jaws and quills in a spray of grisly red.

Robert's dismayed shock hit me through the bond. He started trying to wrest control of Rick away from me. His concern and belief that we would be throwing away our lives picking a fight now battered at me through the bond. I didn't believe him, wasn't truly sure I cared, but the contest of wills slowed my headlong flight toward Cythymau. I had to pry away some of my focus to wrestle for control of the Cornuprocyon. The Seattle summoners formed a defensive ring around the demon-pretender, fending off Rick's kinetic bursts. I yelled with vexation.

Cythymau finally turned his head in my direction, but my victory was short-lived. My bond to Rick snapped like wet tissue. The Cornuprocyon bounded back to Robert, standing down.

My resentment erupted in a bellow that left my throat raw, my sight clogged with tears. I tried to throw myself forward to continue the fight alone, but something wrapped around my waist, stopping my advance. I couldn't get free, which only heightened my frustration and panic.

"Foolish *plentyn*," Cythymau's voice whispered in my mind. "You and I made a pact. Did you really think to be rid of me so effortlessly? *Whuft*, you've learned *nothing* in the time since we first met. Young and foolish still." My head jerked up, and I froze mid-struggle. He faced straight toward me, a knowing mockery in his stance.

I sagged, shaking my head in denial. Only then I realized that Robert had wrapped his arms around me from behind. I'd been so deep into my struggle for control over Rick and my determination to kill Cythymau that I hadn't even registered his physical presence until now.

"*Whuft!* You'd think the three of you weren't pleased by the assistance I brought," Cythymau chided mockingly from behind his line of Seattle Grove defenders.

"Oh, we're very happy for the help. We just don't trust any

assistance provided by you. It tends to have a steep price tag," Robert replied tersely, his arms tightening where he still held me.

"Ah, but this is—what delightful term did your mentor use last I saw her? Hmm, yes, yes—gate crashing. It has rewards of its own, although if you are offering to reimburse the Grove for its trouble I am sure we will not refuse. What would you have left that is worth such momentous remuneration, I wonder?"

Cythymau's attention centered on Robert as if I didn't exist. As if I, and my supposed freedom, held no significance to him. Robert, though... he still coveted Robert's Sense.

And yet even here, I knew Cythymau's words toyed with us. He *never* just had one goal, one potential reward in play. Never trust the face value of a devil's bargain.

Especially not with a demon of Cythymau's caliber. He wouldn't expose himself to the Feds and mobilize the Seattle Grove into an unprecedented attack without seeing some large-scale benefit. If he did manage to recapture me and gain Robert, well then, that would be a bonus. We weren't his goal here; we were just the excuse to show up.

"I'm fine," I muttered, my voice coming out hoarse and strained. "Let me go. I'll be fine." It was a lie; I could never be OK with that demon standing in front of me, but I was back in control of myself, at least. Robert dropped his arms and stepped back, but not by much.

The Seattle Grove remained poised around Cythymau, waiting to see if Rick would resume his attack. Annalisa Miller dropped to one knee, taking up a battle stance against us. Several more of the summoners followed suit, lining runes up on their magnetic boards. The battle between the prison officials and the summoned beasts still raged, but an eerie calm settled around us.

"Hold your summons. These three are not who we came to fight. Save your strength for the larger battle to come." Cythymau's voice rang out over the Seattle Grove summoners, confident of his absolute authority. My stomach heaved. I had to struggle to keep down the little I'd eaten today.

"They are rogue!" Annalisa's voice was low, vicious. "They dared to attack their fellow Grove member with a demon, the very summoners who came to assist them."

"And for that we will punish them," Cythymau assured her. "But not today. Today, we fight a much bigger enemy. Today, we assert our dominance against this oppressive regime, and signal an end to our acceptance of their tyranny." He laid his hand against her cheek and leaned in close. "Patience. We shall bring all our enemies to their knees in time, starting with this arrogant government of ignorant cattle."

This time I couldn't stop the heave of my stomach. I ran to the edge of the group, the summoners clearing a wide path for me, and dry-heaved. But Cythymau still spoke.

"Today, there are matters of more import than any of our personal grievances, however recent. And our reprieve from the fighting grows short. Do I have your pledge, Mr. Lorents, that you will join me in freeing these people from oppressive rule and keep your companions in line for the remainder of our assistance?"

"No—don't," I whispered, my voice gone.

I wiped the back of one hand across my sour mouth, turning toward where Robert now stood with Rick. Cythymau waited, surrounded by the members of the Seattle Grove and the horde of summoned fliers.

"You have my promise that I will help you fight against the Feds and clear this facility for today only." Robert's voice was grim.

I wanted to scream at him. Or maybe cry. You never, ever make a promise. Not with this demon. Not even once.

"Fabulous." Cythymau's face split into a wide grin. "Now that business is settled between us, let us welcome the airborne forces we've been waiting for, and continue to make sure to strike hard and true against the assets of this unjust magistracy."

Four missiles crested low on the horizon, obviously on trajectory for the detention facility. Not far behind them, three wings of attack jets flew. The military had mustered a full response to our incursion.

The forty or fifty summoners who had been combating the facility personnel shifted their group summons. The missiles abruptly turned back on their trajectory, targeting the four planes in the first wing of fighters.

The jets attempted evasive maneuvers, but the summoners with their boards of runes kept altering the trajectory and speed of the missiles to remain on target. The whole exchange took only a few seconds, and yet the fragment of time seemed to stretch on impossibly. Each missile eventually found its jet, and the sky erupted into fire and smoke. High above the destroyed jets, parachutes bloomed, only to be plucked out of sky by the giant hawks. That left two more wings of jets. On the horizon, black dots appeared, too far away for me to distinguish.

The next group of summoners pulled the fuel tanks out of the incoming jets. The remaining planes crashed, exploding before firing their weapons. More parachutes bloomed; the thick flock of summoned giant hawks screeched and swooped in, snatching them from the sky. Not one reached the ground.

Such a wanton and unnecessary waste of life and freedom on both sides of this conflict. But I knew that for Cythymau, it was just him getting warmed up.

The spots on the horizon resolved themselves into at least four squads of attack helicopters with giant guns hanging under their bellies. Only one group of summoners hadn't triggered a summons yet.

When they activated their runes, the helicopters exploded like firecrackers, one after another. The choppers hadn't even reached the scrub hills bordering the facility before being taken down. I looked at the blooded runes under the summoners' hands and realized they'd simply summoned fire into the helicopters' fuel tanks simultaneously. So simple, yet horribly devastating. The giant hawks landed on the hill where the flaming husks of the helicopters lay, combing the wrecks for survivors.

The people in the detention facility hadn't necessarily done anything to be captured, drugged, locked up, or tortured. But this. This wasn't right either. The military didn't stand a chance in front of the summoner army's combined strength. The stench of death surrounded me. A meaningless, pointless waste of lives that sickened my soul.

I'd been aware that Cythymau still lived for all of five or ten minutes, and already he had brought more death with him than I had seen since coming to this Weave.

More missiles crested the horizon. Cythymau knelt by one of the many pools of blood, before swiping a lazy, crimson-soaked hand across his tattoos. The missiles swung wide, redirected into the far side of the detainment building.

Annalisa Miller rearranged the runes on her board, throwing up a barrier of rock and kinetic force between the explosion and the rest of the Seattle Grove summoners, blatantly leaving Robert, Francine, Rick, and me unshielded.

Concentrating, I laid my bleeding thumb against my rune bracelet and protected us with an improvised blast-shield made from several of the detention facility's large, triple-reinforced steel doors. I couldn't trust that Robert's drugged Sense would be recovered sufficiently to absorb and redirect the blast enough to keep us from getting crushed by debris or worse. The upper story of the building was engulfed in a destructive fire ball that rained chunks of flaming debris and concrete down on the courtyard.

Cythymau hooted with gleeful laughter as the military sent more jets to follow the cruise missiles. His summoners were already preparing the summons that ensured these new jets' demise.

"Our diversion is wildly successful!" he crowed. "Keep them busy! Keep them coming. The more resources they throw at us here, the more quickly we can crush their unfounded self-importance. Wonderful work, my soldiers!"

My body felt drained and heavy. I stared at Robert's dark head as he clutched his foster mother to him. He knew what he wanted to protect. If I couldn't escape Cythymau in this Weave either, who did I expect to protect, and what was there to hope for?

ROBERT

THE WORD "BATTLE" implies, at the very least, an armed contest between two sides. As the day wore on, it became very apparent that what was happening was not a battle. "Massacre" would be the more appropriate term.

Until this point in American history, the Groves had stayed underground. Summoners tended to keep their heads down and go about their business. Overt confrontation with the authorities could (and, in fact, *had* in my case) get you a death sentence with the Grove. Cythymau had obviously changed up Grove policy.

The armed forces of the United States simply hadn't been ready for it.

One summoner is going to tire eventually. They're going to get distracted. Your average summoner doesn't have Andrea's Sense-range, let alone mine. That means they've got far less time to do things like, say, stop a bullet. Sense-based summoning works at the speed of thought, but most people can't think in the space of time it takes a bullet to cross only two to three feet. Forty is hard enough, believe me.

Unless, of course, you have someone else backing you up and

simply summoning all lead from within, say, a fifty-mile radius into a pile behind the group.

Now, that kind of summons is intricate. Try it solo, and it's all you'd be able to do. You'd have a fancy rune pattern, and your Sense would be woven in tight. Sure, you'd stop all the lead bullets from hitting you. And the first time someone in an attack chopper fired a rocket composed of steel and explosives, it'd bebop right through your anti-lead summons and light you up like a Christmas tree. Besides, keep that kind of continuous summons running hot for wave after wave, and you'll be face-down in the dirt from sheer exhaustion in no time.

In other words, a single summoner (or even a small group) couldn't rely on that sort of thing to protect them in an out-and-out firefight. Which, according to what I'd picked up from Grace, is why summoners hadn't engaged a modern, armed force prior to this moment in history.

But the Seattle Grove had not brought a *small* group of summoners.

They executed a battle doctrine reminiscent of the old Roman Empire. Five summoners would take the front line for roughly ten minutes, then rotate out. With thirty summoners alternating the duty, that meant any given person had fifty minutes of resting time for ten minutes of fighting. With twenty more sharing a similar rotation on the defensive summons, the front ranks became essentially immune to any incoming attack.

The result was, as I said, less a battle and more a massacre.

The attacks kept coming. Aircraft comprised the first waves; much later, a couple of ground force units made the attempt. They came in piecemeal, each responding from a different base. The method of attack changed between waves, but the results did not. As I watched, again and again, the government forces would try some new trick, a different angle. Slowly, the reality of the situation dawned on me.

A Grove is not a military organization. Oh, sure, the chain of command is very para-military, but that's the same as any organized crime organization. It's not like summoners have never seen a battlefield. That said, no part of my Grove training involved working in a coordinated army. It may have been that Grace and I simply hadn't hit that lesson, but I thought it more likely that this form of butchery had been introduced by Cythymau. Very, very recently.

My point here is this: *no one* expected that this would ever happen. Looking at the wreckage of the facility and the bodies littering the field in front of me, it became very clear that the United States of America had never really developed a doctrine for taking on an *army* of summoners. Summoners didn't form armies, so a plan to deal with an organized militia of them simply did not exist on their books.

Good, I thought. *Fuck 'em.* After all, these bastards had imprisoned me, *tortured* me. They'd killed Donald just to make a point, and they'd threatened Francine with the same. What in the hell did I care if the Seattle Grove went through them as though Death had replaced his sickle with a full-blown combine harvester? They had it coming, right?

Then I looked at Cythymau. For him, this certainly wasn't a rescue mission. We could have been clear of the field hours ago. There were long periods of time in between attacking waves of troops where everyone could have simply melted away. He was here to *kill,* not to save. My gut churned.

The refugees from the prison were, for the most part, slipping away as quietly as the scene would allow. A few of them sat on the hill, watching the grisly work, but most of our refugees had gotten while the getting was good. Francine hadn't. She wandered, uncharacteristically quiet, through the other refugees on the hill. I didn't know what she'd been through in there. I knew what they'd done to *me,* and the thought of my foster mother being tortured like that gnawed away on my guts.

I stayed because I'd given my word. Cythymau might be using this as more than a rescue mission, but I did owe them for that nonetheless. I'd promised my service until sundown, and I made good on my word. I joined the defensive teams, preventing death instead of dealing it, but that was a Band-Aid on my conscience and I knew it.

As the sun went down, only the occasional drone far overhead showed that the United States still knew we were here. We'd fought the law, and the law lost. Utterly, completely lost.

"*Whuft.* The sun sets, yes?" Cythymau said from behind me. I'd been watching the progress of that orb too, waiting for the day to end. "You fulfill your bargain. But what now for you, I wonder?"

Tricky. Andrea and Rick had been staying as far away from Cythymau as they could, which effectively left me with no backup at the moment. I knew I was powerful, but no way could I take on Cythymau *and* a small army of summoners to boot.

This is where the skills of a foster child come in handy. I'd lived for years in the homes of adults that I, quite frankly, despised. I had therefore mastered the ability to passive-aggressively ignore someone while in a direct conversation with them.

I turned to him, shrugged my shoulders. "How'd you even get here? Last I saw you, there was a nuke about to go off."

"Getting here is easy, for the right price. I had power, and wished to gift it to others. There are many who will take power in exchange, hmm? I see how your Thaddeus hounds your Andrea, how he lusts after what she knows of me. I have leverage, yes? Levers move many things."

Of course. Of course that would work. The Seattle Grove had been *dying* to learn about Andrea's rune system, Cythymau's rune system. The only reports they'd had on Cythymau were from Grace, now considered a traitor to the Grove because of... me.

"So again, I ask. What now for you? You, and my *plentyn*, and your Francine? What do you do?"

I shrugged again. "I don't see where that's any of your business."

The demon's face drew into an angry scowl, his voice becoming menacing. "Not my *business?* I have an ongoing contract with Andrea, and you think it not my business? You I have no claim on, for now. You have refused my generosity time and again, save today, and that agreement dies with the sunlight. Where Andrea goes, though. My business. Mine. The girl is mine."

Okay, the brush-off wasn't working. Plan B: lie. "Fine. We're getting the hell out of here. Grace had some family down in Kentucky, maybe we'll head there."

"*Whuft.* You bluff poorly, Mr. Lorents. I Sense it, in your heartbeat, in your pupils. I can feel your lie in your voice. Do not think me a simpleton. Come, do you truly still believe me this great evil? A boogey-man who hides under the bed of your summoner children, waiting to consume them?"

Images of Andrea strapped to his table flashed in my mind, along with images of a second table, this one empty and waiting.

"You enslaved Andrea."

"No! Not enslaved! Bargained for. She *chose* it. It was not, perhaps, a good choice on her part, no, but I did *nothing* she had not agreed to."

"Bullshit. You tricked her into agreement and you know it."

"Still, she gave her word. She would give *anything,* she said. She offered; I accepted. Contract sealed. Not enslavement. I offered the same to you. You turned it down, remember? Are you strapped on the board? No."

"Not that you didn't try. Even after I turned you down, you tried." He'd almost succeeded, too. I shouldn't have been picking a fight with this demon; the smart play would have been to keep my head down, get out of the conversation quickly, then de-ass this place with alacrity.

"Oh, if I had *tried,* Mr. Lorents, truly made an effort, you would not be here right now. I did not try. I did enough to frighten you, get you out of my life. This is all."

What would Grace do? The thought flashed through my mind, and my mouth began to turn into a smile. In this situation, under these pressures, Grace would not have made the cautious play. That realization gave me all the permission I needed to get a little reckless myself.

"I'm trying to figure out right now whether you are intentionally lying to me, or just batshit fucking crazy. Enough to frighten me away? Bullshit. You intentionally *provoked* me into coming back, remember? You *gave me your fucking address,* you idiot. In fact, you know what? You and I had something of a business arrangement after all, one *you* agreed to."

"I know of no covenant between us, save today."

"No? You handed me that runeset. At the funeral for my friends and classmates that *you killed.* Do you remember that, you crazy bastard? Do you remember telling me, in so many words, to come after Andrea?"

"Yes, I remember this. You were not in your best emotional state, maybe, but still you concluded no pact with me. I even renewed my offer."

"I turned you down, because *fuck you.* But then you offered me something else. You offered me a chance to take back Andrea. We traded risks, you and I. You risked Andrea, I risked myself. I see it as a legitimate wager, *yes?*" I emphasized that last, mocking his speech pattern deliberately.

Cythymau was silent for a moment, his gaze fixed on me. I shot him back a cocky grin. "No, Mr. Lorents," he said. "My claim on Andrea remains, I think."

"You think?" I said. "I think different. Think we should ask her for the tiebreaker vote?"

"Regardless, that is not for the here and now. Here and now we are allies, summoners fighting against your supposed sovereign." His voice grew keen and mocking on the last word.

"Here and now? Here and now the government seems to be gone. It's just us on this field."

"*Whuft.* Yes, but that is the nature of victory, is it not? We have the field, the enemy is vanquished. Though it is a greater battle we have won. Yes."

"Greater battle?"

"Did you think us here for you, Mr. Lorents? That we only wished to rescue you? That was not the reason, no. It helped that you had already started the fight. It made the location of our distraction easy to select. The larger battle happened much closer to your Attle of the Sea."

I looked at him, trying to parse this last phrase. Mockery seemed appropriate. "I don't think that's where Seattle comes from. Also, what larger battle?"

"We attack here, first. We lure your legionnaires away, put on a great show. Most of the Grove, though, attacks the larger fortification after we begin. Lewis, I think? Yes. Lewis, and McChord. Between here and there the enemy is divided, in transit. He seeks to defend both, instead defends neither."

Holy hell. They'd hit Joint Base Lewis-McChord, the biggest military installation in the state. If the Grove had taken out that base, there wasn't enough military power within several hundred miles to challenge Cythymau, now.

I decided to change tactics. Let him brag.

"Lewis-McChord? Why bother attacking the military?"

"Mr. Lorents, you do not understand. You have lived a life of weakness here, you summoners. You have been the prey, not the predator. You hide from those you could simply kill. You obscure when you *could* confront. You submit when you should *rule*. What is it that stops you?"

"Historically? The fact that we tend to lose in the long run, I think. We're kinda outnumbered."

"*Whuft.* Lose. We were outnumbered today, yes? Did we lose? Did we abandon even *a single life* on our side?"

Well, Rick had eaten one; Cythymau must not have counted that as a casualty of the battle. "So you think you can unite the summoners of the world for—what? A global crusade against all the normal people?"

"Not all. No. Only against those who do not know their rightful place. Subjects, yes? A lower breed from those with the Sense. All dogs should be obedient to their masters. They have pronounced summoners to be other than human. They even put it in their document, voted on it, ruled you out of their species, yes? Well, do you not agree? Is the summoner species not different? Are you not *more* than they are?" As he spoke, he gestured about him, putting on a show for the Grove around him.

"I have a little extra skill in one area, but that's it. Doesn't make me a part of some master race."

"One area? *No.* You do injustice to yourself, to us all. All areas. You Sense them. You know what things *feel* like that they barely know exist. We are summoners, Mr. Lorents. We are the power of the world itself, and we are *above* these people!" His voice grew in a crescendo, pounding the notes as he spoke. Around him, responding to the fervor in his words, summoners nodded, smiling.

Heil Cythymau, I thought. Nothing like a charismatic leader to send a people on the path to war.

I had no further response to this, no more lip I could give. Cythymau wanted me to give him an excuse in front of his crowd. I daren't strike. The tension in the air weighed down on me, my Sense awake and keen for his first move. It didn't come. Minutes went by, and we stood, face to face, not talking. We waited for the other to strike; neither of us did.

The crescent of the sun barely peeked above the horizon; the day was in its last death throes when he spoke again. His face wore that warm smile he'd used to charm me in the first place, his wise-but-quirky-ancient-master act. I knew better, but for a moment it felt like we'd been old chums this last year and a half, waxing nostalgic over the memories.

"So I ask again, what now for Mr. Lorents? Do you and I have our final battle, here and now, our great contest settled? Or do you follow your destiny at last and venture forth with the Groves?"

I hadn't thought that far ahead. He had a point; my choice appeared to be between the devil and the deep blue sea. Hobson would have been envious.

"Look, bud. I'm not going to attack you because there are about fifty summoners with you that have, quite frankly, tried to kill me all on their own. I attack first, I'm dead in less than a second." But a thought began to form in my head.

"*Whuft!* You speak wisdom at last. I think you correct in this, yes."

"But those same summoners are going to get *mighty* nervous about you if you attack me, aren't they? After all, I just fought with them. Many of them trusted me with their lives. I'm not going to attack you, and I'm not going to attack them." I lifted my voice, pitched so the others could hear. "I will quit this field and offer no violence. And I can only imagine what kind of demon would, after so fair a peace given, attack *one of his own.*" A corner of my mouth curled up as I gave this speech.

Cythymau's head twitched, a quick look toward his shoulder. He pulled it back, but I knew I had him. "You don't have them all strapped to tables, so I'm guessing you've convinced them to follow you, not forced them. You turn on me when that sun goes down, they're going to wonder about whether they're next."

Cythymau's expression of kindliness slipped for a moment, his demon's anger flashing through his concerned-mentor impersonation, cracking it with furled eyebrows and tensed lips, but he controlled himself.

I leaned in toward him, lowering my voice to just above a whisper. "And you knew that. Which is why we're having this conversation. You wanted to manipulate me into a further agreement before this one ended. No dice, asshole. I'm not going to fight you now, but I'm not going to sit back and watch you become God-King of Earth or whatever the hell you're going for. I fought with you today because this was for *my* benefit. From here on out we are not friends."

He responded in the same hushed tone. "Our alliance concludes soon, then. What happens when all these summoners travel for home, and only you and I are left here?"

Then Cythymau and I would be free to throw down in a fair fight. I remembered a conversation Jake had gotten into at a Halo party last winter. He'd been camping, hanging out by the enemy's spawn points and shooting them before they could do much at all. This was a faux pas in most gaming circles, but Jake didn't care. I remembered his answer when our host confronted him about his moves, telling him that it wasn't fair.

If you are in a fair fight, your tactics suck.

I shrugged and nodded to Cythymau before walking away. I made no attempt to answer his question. It was time for us to get the hell out of here.

∾

FRANCINE STUCK with the few refugees who had stayed to watch the slaughter. She walked among them, describing Donald to each, asking if they'd seen him.

This conversation couldn't go well. The last week had included torture, murder, and the resurrection of my most hated demonic enemy, but this was going to be the hardest part of it.

I walked up behind her in the middle of her conversation with one of the other refugees and placed my hand on her shoulder. She started, then turned to look into my eyes.

But I didn't have to say it. My head shook, face toward the ground, lip trembling and eyes wet, and that said it all. Thank whatever God there might be that I didn't have to say the words.

"No," she said, her voice ragged and desperate.

I reached out to try to embrace her, to comfort her. She backed away from me as though I held a viper. I used my long legs to outstride her, and wrapped my arms around her shoulders. She turned and buried her face in my neck, gasping on her sobs.

As I held my foster mother in her grief, I saw Andrea with Rick. She simply looked at me, her face relaxed into a blank expression.

"Mom," I said, knowing that there were few words I could use on Francine that were more powerful. "I know this hurts, but we need to go. Now. None of us are safe at the moment, and things are about to get a lot worse before they get better."

Francine looked up, stifling her sobs. She took a deep breath before speaking in a voice more level than I had expected. "Right. How do we leave?"

I gestured Andrea over; she had been resting for most of the fight, not participating actively in the battle, and I judged that she'd be fresher than me. "Can you get us a ride out of here?"

She nodded. We walked to the road together. Andrea smeared blood on one of those weird runes, and a rusted grey van appeared on the road in front of us, presumably after having been summoned directly from the 1970s. It had a car seat in the back along with a number of children's books and a garish bead cover on the driver's seat. Still, better than nothing.

I turned to Rick following us as softly as his big, lumbering form would allow. I scratched his muzzle. "OK, boy. Time to go underground again. We need to get clear of here. You know the drill."

After Rick had tunneled into the earth, Francine and Andrea climbed into the van. I followed. The sun vanished under the horizon as I pressed the pedal down, leaving behind a demon in control of an entire army.

ANDREA

My skin itched and my rib cage rasped. I forced myself to focus on Robert as he stood talking to Cythymau. If Cythymau moved to harm Robert, gave me an excuse, I would be on him in the space of a breath. I wanted revenge so badly I could feel it's sting in my eyes and on my tongue.

The effort to keep myself from descending on the demon in a howling fury devoured my whole attention. Part of me argued that if I could expend my rage on Cythymau now, even if I died, it would be worth it. On the other hand, letting Cythymau control everything up to and including the manner of my death would be too pathetic.

That indecision kept me frozen on the sidelines as wave after wave of carnage played out in front of my eyes like a nightmare. Truly, today, every time I thought I'd descended to my ultimate nightmare, it got worse.

I had just started to put myself back together into some semblance of a human again. But Cythymau's mocking whisper still wound insidiously through my brain, and pieces of the new me threatened to slough off, revealing my instinctual fear, hate and pain. I didn't want to go back there. I liked the Andrea that could think of the future, value a friend, or enjoy the vivid beauty of a sunset.

Robert passed into range of my Sense, his foster mother cradled protectively under one arm. I blinked. He should have still been talking to Cythymau. Instead, Cythymau stood talking to the small, birdlike woman as the Seattle Grove readied to leave. What the piss had just happened?

I'd lost time. Disoriented, I shivered.

The inside of my skull felt fractured.

In my Sense, I could tell Robert's breath labored through his lungs and his muscles trembled with exhaustion. His plump, middle-aged foster mom's presence in my Sense manifested as a storm of grief. I knew that those tears sliding down her cheeks, the electrical impulses firing in her brain, and the tremors running through her muscles equated to an immense, debilitating sorrow, even though she wept quietly.

One mourner recognizes another.

Robert must have hated me. Covering my ass so far had given him nothing but pain, loss and trouble. If he spoke to me again, no doubt it would only be to say something like, "I wish you the best with Cythymau and all that, but I've already done everything in my power and then some. Since we've obviously failed to best the demon *again*, I'll just bow out. Let the chips fall where they may. You're on your own. Kill him, end yourself, I don't care anymore."

I couldn't blame him, but it didn't make me feel any better. My servitude loomed. Again. Thoughts of captivity painted goosebumps on my skin with chill fingers. It would've been better to die in battle.

Robert waved at me. I jogged over on leaden feet.

"Can you get us a ride out of here?" he asked. Relief flooded through me. He wasn't throwing me back to Cythymau?

He wanted *us* to leave. Could I hope that meant he hadn't finished fighting yet? If Robert thought we had a chance to escape under our own power, I would have the faith to believe him. Cythymau still lived, but so did I.

I smeared blood across the Eihwaz-Raidho-Kenaz-Ehwaz charm, sending my Sense through the runes to find us a safe mode of transportation. A gray, seventies hippie van, complete with beaded seat covers, appeared. Its similarities to a hazy memory triggered a sudden flash of nostalgia for cool summer evenings at the drive-in theater with popcorn, hotdogs, and a van filled to the gills with laughing teenagers... friends. The van felt like home.

Once upon a time, millennia ago, I too had people I loved and who watched out for me. People I called friends.

I watched Robert help his mother to the van. Correction. I had people here, willing to be my friends again. If I could work up the courage to accept and trust their support, giving up a little of my cynical self-protective armor in return. I really wanted to try.

My lips curved up in spite of how shitty this day had been. I slipped behind the wheel of the van. Time to rendezvous with Amy, Matt and Thad to figure out our next move.

Robert slid into the seat beside his foster mom and held her hand. When he saw me getting behind the wheel, he raised an eyebrow.

"Are you sure you can drive this thing?" he asked skeptically, double-checking his seat belt.

"How do you think I got here?" I asked.

"Honestly, I figured one of the others drove you or you summoned something. I dunno. With being half-drugged and all, I didn't have time to think that hard about it, really."

"Amy did drive me, at least partway. But it turns out driving is just like riding a bike: once you learn, you never forget. After a few millennia of disuse, you just get really, really rusty. Lucky for you, I've already knocked most of the rust off."

In my Sense, I could tell when Robert's lips slowly curved up in acknowledgement of my attempt at a joke. Driving only counted as one small step, but the time had arrived to stop running away from Cythymau's shadow and start living. I *did* acknowledge the irony in promising myself to stop running as I quickly put more distance between us, Cythymau, and the Seattle Grove.

This time, I'm not running away, I told myself. *This only counts as a strategic retreat. We'll be back.* I wasn't giving up; I wasn't giving in, either.

"Robert," the foster mom quietly spoke up. "You haven't introduced me to your friend."

"Oh, um. It's kind of a longer story, but Mom, this is Andrea. Andrea, this is my mom, Francine."

"Pleased to meet you," I replied automatically, surprising myself when long-forgotten manners from my childhood kicked in, responding to the maternal vibe this woman embodied.

"Thank you for helping my son." Francine cleared her throat and looked uncomfortable. Her hand tightened on Robert's. I could see she was struggling with her next question, but she voiced it anyway.

"Are you a... well—" She paused. "A summoned creature or... a spirit?" There was no judgment in her voice, just a desperate curiosity, as though she had to know what kind of entity her son had chosen to ally himself with. I couldn't blame her. She might not realize it yet, but the help Robert had given me had led to her husband's death.

"Mo-om," Robert groaned in acute teenage embarrassment. "You can't ask her that. Andrea's just a person." I hadn't been offended; I was the one who'd just cracked a joke about not driving for millennia. Robert's discomfort, though? Absolutely priceless.

To be honest, even I wasn't sure of everything Cythymau had done to me while I was in his "care." Maybe I wasn't entirely human anymore. Certainly no other human I knew had lived for as long as I had.

"No, it's OK." I paused, unsure of what to say. I felt, if I really wanted to try to live for myself from now on, I needed to make some kind of honest response.

Finally, I said, "I was born here in this Weave—this world, but I've lived most of my life trapped in another one by a demon. Your son helped get me out and back to this one. I owe him, and his teacher, a great debt for everything they risked to release me. Today, I wanted to reciprocate the favor."

"You arranged for that armed response to the military?" her voice took on disapproving undertones.

"No." I shuddered. "No, the demon did that. I came by myself."

She sat back, still clasping Robert's hand, her knuckles white. I could see she was thinking about the ramifications of my statement. Her grip had to be painful, but he didn't say anything.

As much as I hated to admit it, while Cythymau's contingent of the Seattle Grove had taken the bloodbath and carnage to unnecessary extremes, without them, the three of us would be just as dead as Francine's husband right now. I knew it, she knew it, and Robert knew it.

It didn't mean I would ever feel grateful for anything that demon did. He always had his own reasons. I didn't know what his full game was, but today had only been the opening gambit.

"WHAT?" I sat down on the couch in the living room of the Newport safe house, feeling like my feet had been swept out from under me. Robert had taken Francine to lie down upstairs as soon as we'd arrived. When he came back downstairs, Thad pulled our small Grove together in the front room to lay the latest news-bomb in our laps.

"Groves across the western U.S. have staged coups against jails, detention facilities, and military installations today. Summoners hit detainment facilities in ten out of fifty states. They all started at different times, and targeted different types of government assets, so by the time the pattern was clear, the government had few resources left to throw at the escalated situation."

"How?" Robert asked. "What happened to staying under the radar? If they were going to get so pissed at Grace for drawing the attention of the public, why just turn around and do this?"

"The majority of the Grove leadership that was against a violent response to the current governmental policies has been removed from power, in some cases with the very violence they spoke out against. For the most part, they've been replaced with young fire-breathers, or political hotheads willing to toe the "Grove Superiority" line. With the government's recent crackdown, it's been easier than anyone ever expected for them to gain support among the rank-and-file summoners. They're riling the Groves into a fever with talk of retribution and taking back 'summoners' rightful place' in society. Obviously it reached a head yesterday, when Cythymau called for a synchronized action to strike a decisive blow and debilitate what many summoners have come to see as a genocidal government."

This coup had Cythymau's fingerprints all over it. My stomach rolled up into my throat before dropping down to my knees.

It was all happening so much faster than I expected. If this was the demon's opening gambit, it was one hell of a killer move. Cythymau was a step ahead of me again. Hell, I'd believed him dead and out of my life forever.

But he couldn't resist an audience. Hence the reveal to Robert and me at the detainment center. He *wanted* us to know he could manipulate us, even from afar.

Cythymau had been busy indeed. Whispering in ears, pulling strings behind the scenes, aiding in the meteoric rise of these extremists. No doubt he had provided resources and advice to those he found the most useful, and cut away those he found inconvenient.

"How did you find out about all of this?" Robert asked. "Is there anyone still trying to shut this thing down? An all-out war between non-summoners and the Groves will be gruesome. Not to mention giving credence to all the summoner-bogeyman stories. All those things that Grace taught me summoners don't actually do. Normal people won't even have a chance." His last few words were almost a plea, like he was asking someone to please put back together the world he was supposed to know. I wished I could, but mine had been broken long, long ago.

"I know about this because I had a visitor," Thad answered cryptically. "One who would like to apply for asylum with us, and is equally against the frenzy Cythymau has started."

"Ahem." A throat being cleared brought everyone's attention to a short, heavily rotund man with gingerish curly hair standing in the kitchen doorway. His clothes were travel-stained, his face creased with worry and strain.

"May I introduce the director of the Seattle Grove, Phineas Brandiole?"

"Former director, as of yesterday morning." The words came out dully, as though Phineas Brandiole still couldn't believe it himself. "Normally, I would say it's a pleasure to meet you all, but please forgive my lack of enthusiasm at the moment. It's been an exhausting day." His face drooped in a woeful expression that seemed to imply the whole world rested on his not-insubstantial shoulders.

Robert's face, still stained with sweat and dirt from the long battle, scrunched up in a disapproving scowl. "Asylum? For this guy? How did he even know where to find us?"

"What the Seattle Grove knows, I also know. Or knew up until yesterday, that is." Phineas hunched his shoulders in an exhausted shrug. My Sense told me Robert's muscles trembled with the effort to keep his legs under him, yet adrenaline shot through him with this news.

He turned to the former Seattle Grove director, his finger jabbing out accusingly. "And just why should we help you—because you're all lost puppy-dog eyes after your cronies kicked you out? Do you even *know* how many times Grace asked you for help and you turned her down? I'm still trying to figure out if I even want to put up with this guy," he gestured at Thad, "that you sent to *replace* Grace and fucking *assassinate me*. The only reason I haven't shoved him out on his ass is that Andrea here seems to like him. You are goddamn out of your mind if you think I would want to protect you from one of your own pig-headed decisions. Serves you right." He crossed his arms across his chest and glared at the man.

I looked back and forth between the two of them. I hadn't cared enough before to really pay attention to Grove politics other than trying to avoid Thad, so I hadn't realized that the ties between Robert and other Groves were so fractured. I didn't know this guy, but Robert *really* seemed to hate him. Matt and Amy appeared content to watch how this would play out rather than jumping to the man's defense. Thad's expression was, as always, hard to read.

Wait. If this guy knew to come here because the Seattle Grove knew about this place, that meant Cythymau could show up here?

"We should leave," I told Robert.

"OK, fine. Agreed," Robert said. "But not with this guy."

"Look, I know we haven't had the best history," Phineas began.

"Best history? Really? That's the line you're going to go with?" Robert's voice rose with incredulous scorn. "You and your Grove have been trying to put a fucking fork in me ever since Cythymau first showed up in Spokane. Before I even knew you guys existed, you were happy to put a target on my back. But now that the shit's flying *your direction,* you want me to protect you from the exact fucking demon that Grace has been trying to tell you about since day one." Robert's anger had found a full head of steam. His voice vibrated off the walls in his disgust. "You wouldn't lift one goddamn finger to help her because it might 'endanger' your precious political standing. That, FYI, you still lost. Yeah, I guess that is a bad fuckin' history. *For you.*"

"Robert!"

The voice cracked across Robert's tirade. Stunned, I turned toward the rumpled form of Francine at the bottom of the stairs. Her hair stood up at odd angles; Robert's shouting had obviously woken her mid-nap. "Watch your language, young man." She strode across the room with purpose and thumped him on the head.

"Ow!" Robert clapped a hand to his head and turned wounded eyes on his foster mom. "Why are you thumping *me?* He's the one that's out of line."

"The only person I see shouting and carrying on with horrible language in here is you. You're being so rude to everyone, making them listen to you throw a temper tantrum while they can't even get a word in edgewise. I don't know what's gone on in the past between the two of you, but surely you can discuss it like the civilized human being I know is in there somewhere. You are better than this." She kissed Robert on the cheek and patted his shoulder. "Apologize to everyone here for yelling."

"What should I have to apologize for? He started it." The words were still defiant, but Robert's tone had become subdued.

"By what? Showing up?" Francine guessed astutely. "If he is hiding out from the same horrors I saw at the detention center, you should at least listen to what the man has to say. It would seem to me that you can't afford to be turning away any potential allies. I admit I don't know much about the situation, but even to me it looks like you need all hands on deck."

Abashed, Robert looked down at his feet and muttered, "Sorry, everyone." The words obviously stuck in his throat, but he got them out. I tried to put myself in his shoes and couldn't even imagine it. If someone tried to make me say sorry to Cythymau, I'd probably be on the next bus out of town.

Francine crossed her arms over her chest and sat down next to me on the couch. "Well, I'm awake now, I guess you can explain to me what this whole argument is about."

This galvanized both Thad and Robert into action. "You don't have to stay—" Robert started to say at the same time Thad said, "I'm not sure that would be a good idea—"

"If either of you thinks I'm leaving, you're sorely mistaken," Francine said firmly. "Besides, it sounds as if you could use a fresh perspective and referee. I'm up to my eyeballs in this world now, whether or not I stay, so I might as well know what I'm dealing with."

"Thank you for your defense, ma'am," Phineas spoke up.

"Oh, it wasn't necessarily a defense," Francine said, her tone cool. "If it turns out you are here to harm and defame my son, I won't have any problem denying whatever your request might be. However, neither will I condone overt rudeness, especially in my son."

"Ahem, yes. Ah, well, to get to the meat of the issue, then." Phineas shifted his weight nervously. "As Nielsen here has been telling us, before the more obvious military strikes began, summoners across the U.S. staged a coup against the moderate leaders of their Groves and replaced them with the new militant voices in the "Grove Superiority" movement. Fortunately, a loyal friend caught wind of the impending coup early in the morning. He couldn't stop the strike from happening without revealing himself, but he managed to get word to me and a few other targets before the hit squad caught up with us."

"Who is this loyal friend?" Robert asked skeptically

"I am not at liberty to divulge his identity without putting his efforts at risk, especially to a group that has, so far, offered me the barest of hospitality. I have no illusion that if I was to set foot inside the Seattle Grove right now, my life would be forfeit. Cythymau has managed to turn my support of Grace into a weapon that proves how my flawed leadership has led the Grove system to this pass."

"Well, I have to agree your leadership was flawed," Robert drawled, leaning against the wall by the front door. "Seeing as you ruled me a threat instead of Cythymau and demoted the one person actually trying to cover your ass."

"Language," Francine interjected.

"The one person trying to cover your back," Robert corrected himself.

"I admit that I misjudged the situation." Phineas ran his fingers through his hair in a gesture of defeat. "But you also have to admit that Grace's actions put the Grove system in a much more untenable position with the authorities."

"Only because you wouldn't help the Grove in Spokane recruit the manpower to recover to any kind of a workable position. Grace, Amy, Matt and I were working our as—rear ends off trying to make sure that Cythymau didn't manage to get more demons through to terrorize the local population. In case you forget, we didn't always succeed. You remember what happened to my graduating class?"

"It wasn't my idea that Grace pick a fight with the Feds to protect her pet cops," Phineas countered. "That's what really bit you in the keister that night."

"Boys, rather than flinging back and forth past wrongs," Francine cut in, "let's stick to the present situation, shall we?" She turned to me. "Tell me if I have this right. This Cythymau is the demon that imprisoned you and led the attack on the detention center yesterday?" I nodded. "And he is continuing to attack and massacre across the U.S. so that summoners can take over with this 'Grove Superiority' movement?"

"Sort of. Cythymau will definitely destroy any military assets that try to take him on. But I think it's more likely that this Grove Superiority schtick is another ploy for him to eventually consolidate all power for himself. Cythymau is the ultimate control freak. And if he manages to gather enough power that he feels secure no one can dislodge him, he will make the destruction at the detention facility look like a warm-up." Just saying it out loud started a shudder running through me, jerking my muscles from my shoulders to my feet. Francine didn't miss it. She shocked me by reeling me into her ample side with a warm arm thrown over my shoulders. I froze awkwardly.

"You have a long history with this demon?" she asked gently. "You know what kinds of things make his mind work?"

I nodded.

"Well, that can only be to the good. That gives us insight into what his next moves are likely to be. Although I am very sorry you had to encounter someone as morally corrupt and power hungry as this demon so young,"

"I'm not as young as I look." I muttered the words into the floral folds of her blouse.

"But you must have been when you met him." She squeezed me tighter to her side in a quick hug. "I can see you are a lovely girl who protects her friends and tries to pay her debts, so whatever happened between you and this demon, I'm glad you're here now."

I'm glad you're here now. I hadn't known I'd been waiting for that. Embarrassingly, tears rose up in my throat. I relaxed into her embrace rather than humiliate myself by giving in to a sob.

"Well," Francine said briskly, as if she hadn't just punched through years of my self-protective plating with five simple words, "if this demon is trying to take over all the Groves, then the more people we can keep away from him the better. It only makes sense to keep as much away from him as we can." She looked pointedly at Robert. "Including people. I assume sir, since it sounds like you had a high position in this summoner organization, that you still have some political influence and contacts?"

"Yes, ma'am," Phineas answered. "Although they aren't as good as they used to be and a great many of my friends are also dead, missing, or on the run."

"It seems to me that you don't have much choice but to take him in," Francine said to Robert. "He at least has a chance of bringing you some more allies. Which you need." She got up, releasing me. I took a deep breath, feeling like this woman must have the uncanny ability to create a home wherever she went. I felt more at ease with her in the room than I had since I'd got back to this Weave.

Francine crossed the room and took Robert's face in her hands. "I am so proud of you. You know that, right? We'll figure out a way to make this work." She folded him into her embrace.

Matt cleared his throat. "We still have the problem that the Seattle Grove knows about this safe house. So we're going to have to leave ASAP. They actually know about all the safe houses I've set up." Matt growled with frustration. "I wanted them to have access in case of emergency, and I'm glad I did, or Phineas wouldn't have known where to find us. But that also means there's nothing keeping Cythymau from paying us a visit."

"There's still the safe house Grace set up," Robert said. "She didn't put that on any Grove registers, right?"

"No, but it's right in the Seattle Grove's backyard, since she set it up when she was there."

"So much the better," Thad said, cocking an eyebrow at Phineas. "Do you think they'll be expecting you to hide out on their back porch?"

Phineas's lips curled in a slow smile. "No, I think that's the last thing they'll expect us to do. And since I definitely have never heard of this safe house that Summoner Moore set up, the chances of them running across it by accident seem extremely unlikely."

"Grace to the rescue again. Somehow that doesn't surprise me, even though I know she's gone," Robert said somberly. "I guess we're headed to Shelton."

ROBERT

I'VE LIVED in the state of Washington my whole life, but up until summoning Grace I had never heard of Shelton.

It's not a large city, to be sure, but it's still a county seat. It's just that it hides in the shadow of Olympia, our state capitol, only twenty miles away. It sits on the Puget Sound, one of the strangest bodies of water known to man. It's not a shorefront, though; the area where the water meets the land is filled entirely by a massive lumber yard. The downtown, nestled between two hills, smells of the sea air passing over freshly debarked cedar and fir.

Grace's "safe house" turned out to be less a house and more a tiny, two-bedroom apartment. We figured it for temporary, but at the moment there were seven of us crammed in like sardines in a can. Matt assured us that he could get a larger area in a more secluded spot with time, and asked us to be patient while he worked out the details.

I couldn't look Francine in the eye, knowing I had been the death of Donald. There had been little love lost between Donald and me; the foster-parent thing had always been Francine's bag, not his. He'd tolerated me, barely. I felt little personal sense of loss with his passing, but I grieved for Francine's grief. I grieved at what I'd done to her. I couldn't stand being in her company or watching her struggling to appear strong in front of me. The pressure strangled both of us, leading to awkward silence in a small apartment.

Phineas and Thad were another matter. With them, I felt little guilt and abundant rage. The political machinations of these assholes had allowed Cythymau to throw us all in this shit stew. I knew, of course, that much of our current situation came from my own attempts to have Thad arrested, but that remained one of those pieces of guilty knowledge that I simply tried to avoid dealing with. Still, Francine was right; we needed all the firepower we could get. Plus it was nice for Francine to have someone her own age around. She and Phineas had taken to sharing tea on the porch together, talking about... whatever it was that middle-aged people talk about.

The *normality* of life in Shelton stunned me. The battles that had erupted across western America were not a secret. The attacks had made the news. The President had gone on television to deliver a rousing speech about how America would survive its darkest yada-yada. But the people here still went to work. The children still went to school. The stores and restaurants remained open, and cash circulated as though the backing of the United States of America still meant something to the value of currency. The police force still operated, but with a distinct lack of arrests for "reality terrorism."

Life, in short, went on, much to my surprise.

I spent more time in the Olympic National Forest than I did in the apartment. I tended to ignore the multiple warnings to *"Stay on the Trail"* in favor of getting as far away from hipsters with backpacks as I could.

Rick didn't understand the bigger issues. He could feel my sadness, but he didn't know the hows or the whys. He just wanted me to play and be happy. He took a simple joy in what amounted to the destruction of not-insignificant swaths of America's only rainforest, urging me all the while to play with him. The comfort he offered was simple, pure, and without condition.

It was in the midst of one such excursion that I Sensed Andrea moving through the woods like a ghost. I knew what it felt like to move with the Sense, knowing the placement of each step, feeling the location of each twig. Andrea was a master of it. She moved through the whole world that way, and the silence of her travel came as naturally to her as breathing. She could have taken me entirely unaware, but when in the woods with Rick it is best to keep one's Sense up. Thus, our Senses touched each other before our eyes did.

I turned my head and saw her walking through the woods toward me. The last time I'd seen Andrea in a forest, she had looked like one of the wild beasts within. Now she moved upright, with a graceful mastery of herself. I knew she still had issues, but the fires we had been through in the past couple of weeks had forged her into something more... human. Her eyes met mine and did not wander, and her face curled up into a smile I had seen, but rarely.

That smile, that ordinary expression of happiness, made my heart surprise me by skipping a beat. In that moment, surrounded by nature and carrying herself with a confidence that looked easy, but I knew to be crushingly hard, Andrea was beautiful.

I shook *that* thought off. She might have been pretty, but she was also just becoming comfortable with me. Anything more than my presence would scare her off again. Better to not think about her in any light other than comrade. I tucked the image of her smile into the recesses of my mind, to be cherished in the most appropriate manner. Privately.

Instead, I greeted her with a smile of my own.

"I couldn't take it inside either," she said as she drew near.

"Yeah," I said. "It can get kinda—"

Rick, feeling excluded from the conversation, took the moment to blast a massive ball of force at us. At forty feet, I grabbed it and began swirling it about myself to send back. That brought it within Andrea's Sense range, and I felt her remove half of it from my control, stripping it effortlessly from me before I had time to react. I might have had the longer Sense, but it was clear that Andrea had something to teach me in a Sense versus Sense situation.

Then she projected her half at me, her gentle smile turning mischievous for the first time in my memory. I quickly brought up the remaining half in defense, applying force to force and causing the whole thing to nullify.

Rick sat, looking expectantly at us. This was not how the game should be played, in his estimation. He'd done us the courtesy of flinging a massive, train-like ball of kinetic energy, and he expected one back in reply. The lack of response clearly confused him, and he bounced back and forth on his front paws, waiting for us to return the favor.

I pulled volcanic rock from under the loose covering of topsoil and set it falling from forty feet above me. Andrea started back, surprised at the sudden crater behind me, but the earth settled gently back into position when I stole the force of the falling rock to send back at Rick. It wasn't quite a freight-train, but it looked good enough in his estimation. He countered it with another force-ball, which absorbed my force and left a decent amount still heading toward me.

Unfazed, I took that remainder and simply redirected it toward Andrea, keeping my Sense on it and trying to lock it out of her control. She slipped her Sense through mine with the precision of a surgeon. At the last moment, the force ball simply disappeared.

Then reappeared a millimeter behind me, though dissipated to non-lethal levels. I didn't have the reaction time to deal with it. Instead, I ended up sprawling across the dirt, coming to rest bruised and battered, with Andrea giggling.

"Truce!" I shouted. "Truce!"

"You say 'truce,' " she said, "but all I hear is 'I surrender.' "

"Fine! I surrender!"

Rick sidled up to Andrea and nuzzled her, clearly impressed with her victory. Up until now, I had been the reigning king of force-ball tag, but I had been clearly dethroned in Rick's eyes. Andrea scratched his muzzle as I turned myself right-side up and got shakily back on my feet, dusting myself off. I'd been scratched up and bruised pretty good; tomorrow was going to hurt. Andrea played rough.

We didn't talk much. We didn't need that kind of filler. The woods were beautiful, Rick carried us in his childlike joy, and nobody was currently trying to kill us.

It was enough.

~

BACK AT THE TRAILHEAD, I did a quick survey of the vehicles in the parking lot. There were a couple, but the only one I recognized was the beat-up red Subaru Matt had found for me on the cheap. I looked at Andrea.

"How did you get here?"

She shrugged. "Francine drove me. She seemed to think you could use the company."

"She didn't stick around?"

"She said something about not really feeling too safe with Rick." Well, that was probably valid. Rick tended to assume that you could play at his level, and Francine wasn't exactly equipped to deal with that.

So Andrea and I piled into the Subaru instead. We began to trundle down the mountainside. I flipped the radio on to fill the silence. I'd long ago preset the station to the local pop-music scene, so I was surprised to hear a single voice with no musical accompaniment or background of any sort.

Half a second later, I recognized the voice. So did Andrea, and the silence in the car went from peaceful to tense as we both leaned forward to absorb every word that Cythymau said.

"—the people of this Weave, I offer greetings. Many words I have heard you use to describe one such as I: demon, beast, evil. None of these hold truth. I am here for the freedom of my people. I am here because your Weave has oppressed the summoners, has declared them outlaw, has made them not-people. A summoner is a person. Different than you, yes. But a person. Without us, your world crumbles. You will hereafter give proper respect to those who fight for you, who protect your world from invaders that only your nightmares could conjure."

I scoffed at this, the invader claiming to protect us. Andrea's face blanched white and froze into a rigid, emotionless mask. Cythymau's voice continued over the radio, heedless of our reaction. In an experiment, I tried changing the station, only to find out that his voice occupied *every wavelength*.

"I am making this announcement to the people, you. I make it through your technology: your television, your radio, your computer, your phones. I make it to tell you that I am a man of peace. I believe in tranquility, in stability, in accord. But your Weave cannot be trusted to treat its own protectors fairly, and so I have come to save you all. I make this offer to you now. Do not resist. Allow for a transition of power, smooth, clean, to those who protect you, and no violence need occur. No attacks, no bloodshed. But if you fight, I say *you* are the reality terrorists. I say *you* bring terrors to your reality by hunting the ones who would stop them. I say *you* are a traitor to your world and your people. No longer will the protectors of this Weave tolerate such treachery, and those who commit it shall be put to death unless they repent immediately."

The radio suddenly snapped back to its normal programming, a tweeny-bopping pop star nattering about the myriad uses for her secondary sexual characteristics. I pulled the car over to the side of the road.

We'd made it to a place of relative safety. We'd obtained new identities, we'd seen some peace. But our greatest enemy had just declared war on the entire world, and from what I'd seen in Airway Heights, he damn well might win.

I looked Andrea in the eye. She returned the look. Escape was a temporary solution and we both knew it. We couldn't hide while our world tore itself apart. I had no idea what we could do, or who we could support. All I knew was that Cythymau could not be allowed to rule the world, no matter how much he tried to tell us it was for our own good. It was time to do something crazy.

But neither of us would have to do it alone.

ABOUT THE AUTHORS

Frog and Esther Jones are a husband-and-wife writing team who live in the wilds of the Olympic rainforest in Washington State. They can usually be found pursuing one of several geeky pursuits, including board games, video games, anime, rpgs, or firing things out of Frog's catapult (a hand-built Roman onager).

You know, just the common things you might find yourself deciding to do after sitting around the garage on a Saturday. You can find out more about what they're up to, and forthcoming projects at www.jonestales.com or www.impulsivewalrusbooks.com.